THE LINWOODS;

OR,

"SIXTY YEARS SINCE" IN AMERICA.

BY THE

AUTHOR OF "HOPE LESLIE," "REDWOOD," &c.

The Eternal Power
Lodged in the will of man the hallowed names
Of freedom and of country.
MISS MITFORD.

IN TWO VOLUMES.

VOL. I.

Catharine Sedgwick

Catharine Maria Sedgwick was born on 28th December 1789 in Stockbridge, Massachusetts, United States.

Catharine's mother was of the New England Dwight family, daughter of General Joseph Dwight (1703–1765) and granddaughter of Ephraim Williams, founder of Williams College. Catharine's father was Theodore Sedgwick, a successful politician and lawyer, and in 1802 became the Speaker of the United States House of Representatives. In his role as a lawyer he successfully argued the case of a slave who became known as Elizabeth Freeman. Elizabeth went on to work for the family and to care for young Catharine.

Segdwick attended a finishing school in Boston where she completed her education and met Susan Anne Ridley Sedgwick (1788–1867), who would later become her sister-in-law and a published author. Upon leaving education, she took charge of a school in Lenox, Berkshire County.

Catharine converted from Calvinism to Unitarianism, a move which prompted her to produce a pamphlet that denounced religious intolerance and inspired her to write her first novel *A New England Tale* (1822). This began a successful career writing short stories for a variety of periodicals and leading her to produce several novels, such as *Hope Leslie* (1827), *The Linwoods* (1835), and *Home* (Boston, 1835).

Although she had success during her lifetime, by the end of the 19th century she had been relegated to near obscurity. Male critics of the time were keen to suppress works by women and the spirited heroines of her novels made her works undesirable. She only regained appreciation in the late 20th century when the feminist movement began to re-evaluate the place of women in American literature.

Catharine Maria Sedgwick died on 31st July 1867 and is buried in the family plot in Stockbridge, Massachusetts. Her family arranged to have Freeman buried in their family plot as well, and had a tombstone inscribed for her.

PREFACE.

THE title* of these volumes will render their readers liable to a disappointment, from which a few prefatory words may save them. It was chosen simply to mark the period of the story, and that period was selected as one to which an American always gratefully recurs, and as affording a picturesque light for domestic features. The writer has aimed to exhibit the feeling of the times, and to give her younger readers a true, if a slight, impression of the condition of their country at the most—the only

---

* It has been suggested, that the title might be deemed ambitious ; that it might indicate an expectation, that "this sixty years since in America" would take place with the "sixty years since" of the great Master. I have not yet forgotten the literature of my childhood—the fate of the ambitious frog. To those who know me, I need not plead "not guilty" to a charge of such insane vanity, and those who do not will believe me when I say, that the only moment when I could wish the benefactor of the universal reading public to be forgotten, is when my humble productions are under perusal.

suffering period of its existence, and by means of this impression to deepen their gratitude to their patriot-fathers; a sentiment that will tend to increase their fidelity to the free institutions transmitted to them. Historic events and war details have been avoided ; the writer happily being aware that no effort at

> " A swashing and a martial outside"

would conceal the weak and unskilled woman.

A very few of our " immortal names" have been introduced, with what propriety the reader must determine. It may be permitted to say, in extenuation of what may seem presumption, that whenever the writer has mentioned Washington, she has felt a sentiment resembling the awe of the pious Israelite when he approached the ark of the Lord.

For the rest, the author of these volumes is most happy in trusting to the indulgent disposition which our American public constantly manifest towards native literature.

THE LINWOODS.

CHAPTER I.

"Un notable exemple de la forcenée curiosité de notre natu: e, s'amusant se préoccuper des choses futures, comme si elle n'avoit pas assez à faire à désirer les présentes."—MONTAIGNE.

SOME two or three years before our revolutionary war, just at the close of day, two girls were seen entering Broadway through a wicket garden-gate, in the rear of a stately mansion which fronted on Broad-street, that being then the court-end of the city—the residence of unquestioned aristocracy—(sic transit gloria mundi!) whence royal favour and European fashions were diffused through the province of New-York.

The eldest of the two girls had entered on her teens. She was robust and tall for her years, with the complexion of a Hebe, very dark hair, an eye (albeit belonging to one of the weaker sex) that looked as if she were born to empire—it might be over hearts and eyes—and the step of a young Juno. The younger could be likened neither to goddess, queen, nor any thing that assumed or loved command. She was of earth's gentlest and finest

2

mould—framed for all tender humanities, with the destiny of woman written on her meek brow. "Thou art born to love, to suffer, to obey,—to minister, and not to be ministered to." Well did she fulfil her mission! The girls were followed by a black servant in livery. The elder pressed forward as if impelled by some powerful motive, while her companion lagged behind,—sometimes chasing a young bird, then smelling the roses that peeped through the garden-paling; now stopping to pat a good-natured mastiff, or caress a chubby child : many a one attracted her with its broad shining face and *linsey-woolsey* short-gown and petticoat, seated with the family group on the freshly-scoured stoops of the Dutch habitations that occurred at intervals on their way. "Come, do come along, Bessie, you are stopping for every thing," said her companion, impatiently. Poor Bessie, with the keenest sensibility, had, what rarely accompanies it, a general susceptibility to external impressions,—one might have fancied she had an extra set of nerves. When the girls had nearly reached St. Paul's church, their attendant remonstrated,—"Miss Isabella, you are getting quite out to the fields—missis said you were only going a turn up the Broadway."

"So I am, Jupe."

"A pretty long turn," muttered Jupiter; and after proceeding a few paces further, he added, in a raised voice, "the sun is going down, Miss Isabella."

" That was news at 12 o'clock, Jupiter."

" But it really is nearly set now, Isabella," interposed her companion Bessie.

" Well, what if it is, Bessie ?—it is just the right
time—Effie is always surest between sundown and
dark."

" Mercy, Isabella ! you are not going to Effie's.
It is horrid to go there after sundown—please Isabella, don't." Isabella only replied by a " pshaw,
child !" and a laugh.

Bessie mustered her moral courage (it required
it all to oppose Isabella), and stopping short, said,
" I am not sure it is right to go there at all."

" There is no right nor wrong in the matter,
Bessie,—you are always splitting hairs." Notwithstanding her bold profession, Isabella paused,
and with a tremulousness of voice that indicated
she was not indifferent to the cardinal points in her
path of morality, she added,—" why do you think
it is not right, Bessie ?"

" Because the Bible says, that sorcery, and div-
ination, and every thing of that kind, is wicked."

" Nonsense, child ! that was in old times, you
know."

Isabella's evasion might have quieted a rational-
ist of the present day, but not Bessie, who had
been bred in the strict school of New-England orthodoxy ; and she replied, " What was right and wrong
in old times, is right and wrong now, Isabella."

" Don't preach, Bessie—I will venture all the

harm of going to Effie's; and you may lay the sin at my door;" and with her usual independent, fear-naught air, she turned into a shady lane that led by a cross-cut to "Aunt Katy's garden",—a favourite re-sort of the citizens for rural recreations. The Chat-ham-street theatre has since occupied the same spot —that theatre is now a church. Isabella quicken-ed her pace. Bessie followed most unwillingly. "Miss Belle," cried out Jupiter, "I must detest, in your ma's name, against your succeeding farther."

"The tiresome old fool!" With this exclama-tion on her lips, Isabella turned round, and draw-ing her person up to the height of womanhood, she added, "I shall go just as far as I please, Jupe—fol-low me; if anybody is scolded it shall be me, not you. I wish mamma," she continued, pursuing her way, "would not send Jupe after us,—just as if we were two babies in leading-strings."

"I would not go a step farther for the world, if he were not with us," said Bessie.

"And pray, what good would he do us if there were danger—such a desperate coward as he is?"

"He is a man, Isabella."

"He has the form of one—Jupe," she called out (the spirit of mischief playing about her arch mouth), pointing to a slight elevation, called Gal-lows hill, where a gibbet was standing, "Jupe, is not that the place where they hung the poor crea-tures who were concerned in the negro-plot?"

"Yes, miss, sure it is the awful place:" and he

mended his pace, to be as near as might be to the young ladies.

"Did not some of your relations suffer there, Jupiter?"

"Yes, miss, two of my poster'ty—my grand-mother and aunt Venus."

Isabella repressed a smile, and said, with un-affected seriousness, "it was a shocking business, Bessie—a hundred and fifty poor wretches sacri-ficed, I have heard papa say. Is it true, Jupe, that their ghosts walk about here, and have been seen many a time when it was so dark you could not see your hand before your face?"

"I dare say, Miss Belle. Them that's hung on-justly always travels."

"But how could they be seen in such darkness?"

"'Case, miss, you know ghosts have a light in their anterior, just like lanterns."

"Ah, have they? I never understood it before—what a horrid cracking that gibbet makes! Bless us! and there is very little wind."

"That makes no distinctions, miss; it begins as the sun goes down, and keeps it up all night. Miss Belle, stop one minute—don't go across the hill —that is right in the ghost-track!"

"Oh don't, for pity's sake, Isabella," said Bessie, imploringly.

"Hush, Bessie, it is the shortest way, and" (in a whisper) "I want to scare Jupe. Jupe, it seems to me there is an odd hot feel in the ground here."

2*

"There sarten is, miss, a very onhealthy feel·ing."

"And, my goodness! Jupiter, don't you feel a very, *very* slight kind of a trembling—a shake—or a roll, as if something were walking in the earth, under our feet?"

"I do, and it gets worser and worser, every step."

"It feels like children playing under the bed, and hitting the sacking with their heads."

"Oh, Lord, miss—yes—it goes bump, bump, against my feet."

By this time they had passed to the further side of the hill, so as to place the gibbet between them and the western sky, lighted up with one of those brilliant and transient radiations that sometimes immediately succeed the sun's setting, diffusing a crimson glow, and outlining the objects relieved against the sky with light red. Our young heroine, like all geniuses, knew how to seize a circumstance. "Oh, Jupe," she exclaimed, "look, what a line of blood is drawn round the gibbet!"

"The Lord have marcy on us, miss!"

"And, dear me! I think I see a faint shadow of a man with a rope round his neck, and his head on one side—do you see, Jupe?"

Poor Jupe did not reply. He could bear it no longer. His fear of his young mistress—his fear of a scolding at home, all were merged in the terror Isabella had conjured up by the aid of the traditionary superstitions with which his mind was previously filled; and without attempting an answer, he fairly ran off the ground, leaving Isabella laughing, and Bessie expostulating, and confessing that she did not in the least wonder that poor Jupe was scared. Once more she ventured to entreat Isabella to give up the expedition to Effie's, for this time at least, when she was interrupted and reassured by the appearance of two friends, in the persons of Isabella's brother and Jasper Meredith, returning, with their dogs and guns, from a day's sport.

"What wild-goose chase are you on, Belle, at this time of day?" asked her brother. "I am sure Bessie Lee has not come to Gallows hill with her own good will."

"I have made game of my goose, at any rate, and given Bessie Lee a good lesson, on what our old schoolmaster would call the potentiality of mankind—but come," she added, for though rather ashamed to confess her purpose when she knew ridicule must be braved, courage was easier to Isabella than subterfuge, "Come along with us to Effie's, and I will tell you the joke I played off on Jupe." Isabella's joke seemed to her auditors a capital one, for they were at that happy age when laughter does not ask a reason to break forth from the full fountain of youthful spirits. Isabella spun out her story till they reached Effie's door, which admitted them, not to any dark laboratory of magic, but to a snug little Dutch parlour, with a nicely-sanded floor—a

fireplace gay with the flowers of the season, pio-
nies and Guelder-roses, and ornamented with storied
tiles, that, if not as classic, were, as we can vouch,
far more entertaining than the sculptured marble of
our own luxurious days.

The pythoness Effie turned her art to good account, producing substantial comforts by her mysterious science; and playing her cards well for this
world, whatever bad dealings she might have with
another. Even Bessie felt her horror of witch-
craft diminished before this plump personage, with
a round, good-humoured face, looking far more
like the good vrow of a Dutch picture than like the
gaunt skinny hag who has personated the professors
of the bad art from the Witch of Endor downwards.
Effie's physiognomy, save an ominous contraction
of her eyelids, and the keen and somewhat sinister
glances that shot between them, betrayed nothing
of her calling.

There were, as on all similar occasions, some
initiatory ceremonies to be observed before the fortunes were told. Herbert, boylike, was penniless;
and he offered a fine brace of snipe to propitiate
the oracle. They were accepted with a smile that
augured well for the official response he should receive. Jasper's purse, too, was empty: and after
ransacking his pockets in vain, he slipped out a
gold sleeve-button, and told Effie he would redeem
it the next time he came her way. Meanwhile
there was a little by-talk between Isabella and Bes

sie; Isabella insisting on paying the fee for her friend, and Bessie insisting that "she would have no fortune told,—that she did not believe Effie could tell it, and if she could, she would not for all the world let her." In vain Isabella ridiculed and reasoned by turns. Bessie, blushing and trembling, persisted. Effie at the same moment was shuffling a pack of cards, as black as if they had been sent up from Pluto's realms; and while she was muttering over some incomprehensible phrases, and apparently absorbed in the manipulations of her art, she heard and saw all that passed, and determined that if poor little Bessie would not acknowl edge, she should feel her power.

Herbert, the most incredulous, and therefore the boldest, first came forward to confront his destiny. ".A great deal of rising in the world, and but little sinking for you, Master Herbert Linwood—you are to go over the salt water, and ride foremost in royal hunting-grounds."

"Good!—good!—go on, Effie."

"Oh what beauties of horses—a pack of hounds —High! how the steeds go—how they leap—the buck is at bay—there are you!"

"Capital, Effie!—I strike him down?"

"You are too fast, young master—I can tell no more than I see—the sport is past—the place is changed—there is a battle-field, drums, trumpets, and flags flying—Ah, there is a sign of danger—a pit yawns at your feet."   .

"Shocking!" cried Bessie; "pray, don't listen any more, Herbert."

"Pshaw, Bessie! I shall clear the pit. Effie loves snipe too well to leave me the wrong side of that."

Effie was either offended at Herbert's intimation that her favours might be bought, or perhaps she saw his lack of faith in his laughing eye, and, determined to punish him, she declared that all was dark and misty beyond the pit; there might be a leap over it, and a smooth road beyond—she could not tell—she could only tell what she saw.

"You are a croaking raven, Effie!" exclaimed Herbert; "I'll shuffle my own fortune;" and seizing the cards, he handled them as knowingly as the sibyl herself, and ran over a jargon quite as unintelligible; and then holding them fast, quite out of Effie's reach, he ran on—"Ah, ha—I see the mist going off like the whiff from a Dutchman's pipe; and here's a grand castle, and parks, and pleasure-grounds; and here am I, with a fair blue-eyed lady, within it." Then dashing down the cards, he turned and kissed Bessie's reddening cheek, saying, "Let others wait on fortune, Effie, I'll carve my own."

Isabella was nettled at Herbert's open contempt of Effie's seership. She would not confess nor examine the amount of her faith, nor did she choose to be made to feel on how tottering a base it rested. She was exactly at that point of credulity where much depends on the sympathy of others. It is said to be essential to the success of animal magnetism, that not only the operator and the subject, but the spectators, should believe. Isabella felt she was on disenchanted ground, while Herbert, with his quizzical smile, stood charged, and aiming at her a volley of ridicule ; and she proposed that those who had yet their fortunes to hear should, one after another, retire with Effie to a little inner room. But Herbert cried out, " Fair play, fair play ! Dame Effie has read the riddle of my destiny to you all, and now it is but fair I should hear yours."

Bessie saw Isabella's reluctance, and she again interposed, reminding her of " mamma—the coming night," &c. ; and poor Isabella was fain to give up the contest for the secret conference, and hush Bessie, by telling Effie to proceed.

" Shall I tell your *fortin* and that young gentleman's together ?" asked Effie, pointing to Jasper. Her manner was careless ; but she cast a keen glance at Isabella, to ascertain how far she might blend their destinies.

" Oh, no, no—no partnership for me," cried Isabella, while the fire which flashed from her eye evinced that the thought of a partnership with Jasper, if disagreeable, was not indifferent to her.

" Nor for me, either, mother Effie," said Jasper ; " or if there be a partnership, let it be with the pretty blue-eyed mistress of Herbert's mansion."

"Nay, master, that pretty miss does not choose her fortune told—and she's right—poor thing!" she added, with an ominous shake of the head. Bessie's heart quailed, for she both believed and feared.

"Now, shame on you, Effie," cried Herbert; "she cannot know any thing about you, Bessie; she has not even looked at your fortune yet."

"Did I say I *knew*, Master Herbert? Time must show whether I know or not."

Bessie still looked apprehensively. "Nonsense," said Herbert; "what can she know?—she never saw you before."

"True, I never saw her; but I tell you, young lad, there is such a thing as seeing the shadow of things far distant and past, and never seeing the realities, though they it be that cast the shadows." Bessie shuddered—Effie shuffled the cards. "Now just for a trial," said she; "I will tell you something about her—not of the future; for I'd be loath to overcast her sky before the time comes—but of the past."

"Pray, do not," interposed Bessie; "I don't wish you to say any thing about me, past, present, or to come."

"Oh, Bessie," whispered Isabella, "let her try —there can be no harm if you do not ask her— the past is past, you know—now we have a chance to know if she really is wiser than others." Bessie again resolutely shook her head.

" Let her go on," whispered Herbert, " and see what a fool she will make of herself."

" Let her go on, dear Bessie," said Jasper, " or she will think she has made a fool of you."

Bessie feared that her timidity was folly in Jasper's eyes ; and she said, " she may go on if you all wish, but I will not hear her ;" and she covered her ears with her hands.

" Shall I ?" asked Effie, looking at Isabella , Isabella nodded assent, and she proceeded. " She has come from a great distance—her people are well to do in the world, but not such quality as yours, Miss Isabella Linwood—she has found some things here pleasanter than she expected— some not so pleasant—the house she was born in stands on the sunny side of a hill." At each pause that Effie made, Isabella gave a nod of acquiescence to what she said ; and this, or some stray words, which might easily have found their way through Bessie's little hands, excited her curiosity, and by degrees they slid down so as to oppose a very slight obstruction to Effie's voice. " Before the house," she continued, " and not so far distant but she may hear its roaring, when a storm uplifts it, is the wide sea—that sea has cost the poor child dear." Bessie's heart throbbed audibly. " Since she came here she has both won love and lost it."

" There, there you are out," cried Herbert, glad of an opportunity to stop the current that was becoming too strong for poor Bessie

" She can best tell herself whether I am right," said Effie, coolly.

"She is right—right in all," said Bessie, retreating to conceal the tears that were starting from her eyes.

Isabella neither saw nor heard this—she was only struck with what Effie delivered as a proof of her preternatural skill; and more than ever eager to inquire into her own destiny, she took the place Bessie had vacated.

Effie saw her faith, and was determined to reward it. "Miss Isabella Linwood, you are born to walk in no common track,"—she might have read this prediction, written with an unerring hand on the girl's lofty brow, and in her eloquent eye. "You will be both served and honoured— those that have stood in kings' palaces will bow down to you—but the sun does not always shine on the luckiest—you will have a dark day—trouble when you least expect it—joy when you are not looking for it." This last was one of Effie's staple prophecies, and was sure to be verified in the varied web of every individual's experience. "You have had some trouble lately, but it will soon pass away, and for ever." A safe prediction in regard to any girl of twelve years. "You'll have plenty of friends, and lots of suiters—the right one will be—"

"Oh, never mind—don't say who, Effie," cried Isabella, gaspingly.

"I was only going to say the right one will be tall and elegant, with beautiful large eyes—I can't say whether blue or black—but black, I think; for his hair is both dark and curling."

"Bravo, bravissimo, *brother* Jasper!" exclaimed Herbert; "it is your curly pate Effie sees in those black cards, beyond a doubt."

"I bow to destiny," replied Jasper, with an arch smile, that caught Isabella's eye.

"I do not," she retorted—"look again, Effie—it must not be curling hair—I despise it."

"I see but once, miss, and then clearly; but there's curling hair on more heads than one."

"I never—never should like any one with curling hair," persisted Isabella.

"It would be no difficult task for *you* to pull it straight, Miss Isabella," said the provoking Jasper. Isabella only replied by her heightened colour; and bending over the table, she begged Effie to proceed.

"There's not much more shown me, miss—you will have some tangled ways—besetments, wonderments, and disappointments."

"Effie's version of the ' course of true love never does run smooth,' " interposed Jasper.

"But all will end well," she concluded; "your husband will be the man of your heart—he will be beautiful, and rich, and great; and take you home to spend your days in merry England."

"Thank you—thank you, Effie," said Isabella,

languidly. The "beauty, riches, and days spent in England" were well enough, for beauty and riches are elements in a maiden's *beau-ideal ;* and England was then the earthly paradise of the patrician colonists. But she was not just now in a humour to acquiesce in the local habitation and the name which the "dark curling hair" had given to the ideal personage. Jasper Meredith had not even a shadow of faith in Effie; but next to being fortune's favourite, he liked to appear so; and contriving, unperceived by his companions, to slip his remaining sleeve-button into Effie's hand, he said, " Keep them both ;" and added aloud, " Now for my luck, Dame Effie, and be it weal or be it wo, deliver it truly."

Effie was propitiated, and would gladly have imparted the golden tinge of Jasper's bribe to his future destiny; but the opportunity was too tempting to be resisted, to prove to him that she was mastered by a higher power : and looking very solemn, and shaking her head, she said, "There are too many dark spots here. Ah, Mr. Jasper Meredith—disappointment ! disappointment !—the arrow just misses the mark—the cup is filled to the brim—the hand is raised—the lips parted to receive it—then comes the slip !" She hesitated, she seemed alarmed ; perhaps she was so, for it is impossible to say how far a weak mind may become the dupe of its own impostures—" Do not ask me any farther," she added. The young

people now all gathered round her. Bessie rested her elbows on the table, and her burning cheeks
on her hands, and riveted her eyes on Effie, which,
from their natural blue, were deepened almost to
black, and absolutely glowing with the intensity of
her interest.

" Go on, Effie," cried Jasper; " if fortune is
cross, I'll give her wheel a turn."

" Ah, the wheel turns but too fast—a happy
youth is uppermost."

" So far, so good."

" An early marriage."

" That may be weal, or may be wo," said
Jasper; " weal it is," he added, in mock heroic;
" but for the dread of something *after*."

" An early death !"

" For me, Effie ? Heaven forefend !"

" No, not for you; for here you are again a
leader on a battle-field—the dead and dying in
heaps—pools of blood—there's the end on't," she
concluded, shuddering, and throwing down the
cards.

" What, leave me there, Effie ! Oh, no—death
or victory !"

" It may be death, it may be victory; it is not
given to me to see which."

Jasper, quite undaunted, was on the point of pro-
testing against a destiny so uncertain, when a deep-
drawn sigh from Bessie attracted the eyes of the
group, and they perceived the colour was gone

from her cheeks, and that she was on the point of fainting. The windows were thrown open—Effie produced a cordial, and she was soon restored to a sense of her condition, which she attempted to explain, by saying she was apt to faint even at the thought of blood !

They were now all ready, and quite willing to bid adieu to the oracle, whose responses not having been entirely satisfactory to any one of them, they all acquiesced in Bessie's remark, that "if it were ever so right, she did not think there was much comfort in going to a fortune-teller."

Each seemed in a more thoughtful humour than usual, and they walked on in silence till they reached the space, now the park, then a favourite play-ground for children, shaded by a few locusts, and here and there an elm or stinted oak. Leaning against one of these was the fine erect figure of a man, who seemed just declining from the meridian of life, past its first ripeness and perfection, but still far from the decay of age. "Ah, you runaways !" he exclaimed, on seeing the young people advancing. "Belle, your mother has been in the fidgets about you for the last hour."

"Jupiter might have told her, papa, that we were quite safe."

"Jupe truly ! he came home with a rigmarole that we could make nothing of. I assured her there was no danger, but that assurance never quieted any woman. Herbert, can you tell me what these boys are about? they seem rather to be at work than play."

"What are you about, Ned?" cried Herbert to a young acquaintance.

"Throwing up a redoubt to protect our fort," and he pointed as he spoke to a rude structure of poles, bricks, and broken planks on an eminence, at the extremity of the unfenced ground.

"And what is your fort for, my lad?" asked Mr Linwood.

"To keep off the British, sir."

"The British! and who are you?"

"Americans, sir!"

A loud huzzaing was heard from the fort.— "What does that mean?" asked Mr. Linwood.

"The whigs are hanging a tory, sir."

"The little rebel rascals!—Herbert!—you throwing up your hat and huzzaing too!"

"Certainly, sir—I am a regular whig."

"A regular fool!—put on your hat—and use it like a gentleman. This matter shall be looked into —here are the seeds of rebellion springing up in their young hot bloods—this may come to something, if it is not seen to in time. Jasper, do you hear any thing of this jargon in your schools?"

"Lord bless me! yes, sir; the boys are regularly divided into whigs and tories—they have their badges and their pass-words, and I am sorry to say that the whigs are three to one."

"You are loyal then, my dear boy?"

"Certainly, sir, I owe allegiance to the country in which I was born."

"And you, my hopeful Mr. Herbert, with your huzzas, what say you for yourself?"

"I say ditto to Jasper, sir—I owe allegiance to the country in which I was born."

"Don't be a fool, Herbert—don't be a fool, even in jest—I hate a whig as I do a toad, and if my son should prove a traitor to his king and country, by George, I would cut him off for ever!"

"But, sir," said the imperturbable Herbert, "if he should choose between his king and country—"

"There is no such thing—they are the same—so no more of that."

"I am glad Herbert has his warning in time," whispered Isabella to Bessie.

"But it seems to me he is right for all," replied Bessie.

So arbitrarily do circumstances mould opinions. Isabella seemed like one who might have been born a rebel chieftainess, Bessie as if her destiny were passive obedience.

———

WE have thus introduced some of the dramatis personæ of the following volumes to our readers. It may seem that in their visit to Effie, they prematurely exhibited the sentiments of riper years—but what are boys and girls but the prototypes of men and women—time and art may tinge and polish the wood, but the texture remains as nature formed it.

Bessie Lee was an exotic in New-York. The history of her being there was simply this. New-England has, from the first been a favourite school for the youth from the middle and southern states. Mr. Linwood sent Herbert (who had given him some trouble by early manifesting that love of self-direction which might have been the germe of his whiggism) to a Latin school in a country town near Boston. While there, he boarded in the family of a Colonel Lee—a most respectable farmer, who had acquired his title and some military fame in the campaign of forty-five against the French. Herbert remained a year with the Lees, and he returned the kindness he received there with a hearty and lasting affection. Here was his first experience of country life, and every one knows how delightful to childhood are its freedom, exercises, and pleasures, in harmony (felt, long before understood) with all the laws of our nature. When Herbert returned he was cloquent in his praises of Bessie —her beauty, gayety (*then* the excitability of her disposition sometimes appeared in extravagant spirits), her sweetness and manageableness; a feminine quality that he admired the more from having had to contend with a contrary disposition in his sister Isabella, who, in all their childish competitions, had manifested what our Shaker friends would call

a *leading gift.* Isabella's curiosity being excited
to see this *rara avis* of Herbert (with her the
immediate consequence of an inclination was to
find the means of its gratification), she asked her
parents to send for Bessie to come to New-York,
and go to school with her. Mrs. Linwood, a model
of conjugal nonentity, gave her usual reply, "just
as your papa says, dear." Her father seldom said
her nay, and Isabella thought her point gained, till
he referred the decision of the matter to her aunt
Archer.

"Oh dear! now I shall have to argue the matter
an hour; but never mind, I can always persuade
aunt at last." Mrs. Archer, as Isabella had fore-
boded, was opposed to the arrangement—she
thought there would be positive unkindness in
transplanting a little girl from her own plain, frugal
family, to a luxurious establishment in town, where
all the refinements and elegances then known in
the colony were in daily use. "It is the work of
a lifetime, my dear Belle," she said, "to acquire
habits of exertion and self-dependance—such habits
are essential to this little country-girl—she does
not know their worth, but she would be miserable
without them—how will she return to her home,
where they have a single servant of all-work, after
being accustomed to the twelve slaves in your
house?"

"Twelve plagues, aunt! I am sure I should be

happier with one, if that one were our own dear good Rose."

" I believe you would, Belle, happier and better too ; for the energy which sometimes finds wrong channels now, would then be well employed."

" Do you see no other objection, aunt, to Bessie's coming ?" asked Isabella, somewhat impatient at the episode, though she was the subject of it.

" I see none, my dear, but what relates to Bessie herself. If her happiness would on the whole be diminished by her coming, you, my dear generous Belle, would not wish it."

" No, aunt—certainly not—but then I am sure it would not be—she will go to all the schools I go to —that I shall make papa promise me—and she will make a great many friends and—and—I want to have her come so much. Now don't, please don't tell papa you disapprove of it—just let me have my own way this time."

" Ah, Belle, when will that time come that you do not have your own way ?"

Isabella perceived her aunt would no longer oppose her wishes The invitation was sent to Bessie, and accepted by her parents ; and the child's singular beauty and loveliness secured her friends, one of the goods Isabella had predicted. She did not suffer precisely the evil consequences Mrs. Archer rationally anticipated from her residence in New-York, yet that, conspiring with events, gave the hue (bright or sad ?) to her after life. Physically and

morally, she was one of those delicate structures
that require a hardening process—she resembled
the exquisite instrument that responds music to the
gentle touches of the elements, but is broken by
the first rude gust that sweeps over it. But we
are anticipating.

> " There is a history in all men's lives,
>   Figuring the nature of the times deceased;
>   The which observed, a man may prophesy,
>   With a near aim, of the main chance of things,
>   As yet not come to life."

CHAPTER II.

"This life, sae far's I understand,
    Is a' enchanted fairy-land,
    Where pleasure is the magic wand,
        That, wielded right,
    Makes hours like minutes, hand in hand,
        Dance by fu' light."—BURNS.

As soon as Mr. Linwood became aware of his son's whig tendencies, he determined, as far as possible, to counteract them; and instead of sending him, as he had purposed, to Harvard University, into a district which he considered infected with the worst of plagues, he determined to retain him under his own vigilant eye, at the loyal literary institution in his own city. This was a bitter disappointment to Herbert.

" It is deused hard," he said to Jasper Meredith, who was just setting out for Cambridge to finish his collegiate career there, "that you, who have such a contempt for the Yankees, should go to live among them; when I, who love and honour them from the bottom of my heart, must stay here, play the good boy, and quietly submit to this most un- reasonable paternal fiat."

" No more of my contempt for the Yankees, Hal,
4

an' thou lovest me," replied Jasper; " you remember Æsop's advice to Crœsus at the Persian court?"

"No, I am sure I do not. You have the most provoking way of resting the lever by which you bring out your own knowledge on your friend's ignorance."

"Pardon me, Herbert; I was only going to remind you of the Phrygian sage's counsel to Crœsus, to speak flattery at court, or hold his tongue. I assure you, that as long as I live among these *soi-disant* sovereigns, I shall conceal my spleen, if I do not get rid of it."

"Oh, you'll get rid of it. They need only to be seen at their homes to be admired and loved."

" Loved !"

"Yes, *loved;* to tell you the truth, Jasper," Herbert's honest face reddened as he spoke, " it was something of this matter of loving that I have been trying for the last week to make up my mind to speak to you. You may think me fool, dunce, or what you please ; but, mark me, I am serious— you remember Bessie Lee ?"

" Perfectly ! I understand you—excellent !"—

" Hear me out, and then laugh as much as you like. Eliot, Bessie's brother, will be your classmate—you will naturally be friends—for he is a first-rate—and you will naturally—"

" Fall in love with his pretty sister ?"

" If not forewarned, you certainly would ; for there is nothing like her this side heaven. But remember, Jasper, as you are my friend, remember, I look upon her as mine. ' I spoke first,' as the children say; I have loved Bessie ever since I lived at Westbrook."

" Upon my soul, Herbert, you have woven a pretty bit of romance. This is the very youngest dream of love I ever heard of. Pray, how old were you when you went to live at farmer Lee's ?"

" Eleven—Bessie was six—I stayed there two years; and last year, as you know, Bessie spent with us."

" And she is now fairly entered upon her teens; you have nothing to fear from me, Herbert, depend on't. I never was particularly fond of *children*— there is not the slightest probability of my falling into an intimacy with your yeoman friend, or ever, in any stage of my existence, getting up a serious passion for a peasant girl. I have no affinities for birds of the *basse cour*. My flight is more aspiring —' birds of a feather flock together,' my dear fellow, and the lady of my love must be such a one as my lady aunts in England and my eagle-eyed mother will not look down upon. So a truce to your fears, dear Herbert. Give me the letter you promised to your farmer, scholar, friend; and rest assured, he never shall find out that I do not think him equal in blood and breeding to the King of England, as all these Yankees fancy themselves to be."

Herbert gave the letter, but not with the best grace. He did not like Jasper's tone towards his

New-England friends. He half wished he had not written the letter, and quite, that he had been more frugal of his praise of Jasper. With the letter, he gave to Jasper various love-tokens from Isabella and himself for Bessie. The young men were saying their last parting words, when Herbert suddenly exclaimed, " Oh, I forgot! Isabella sent you a keepsake," and he gave Jasper a silk purse, with a dove and olive-branch prettily wrought on it.

" Oh, you savage !" exclaimed Jasper, " had you forgotten this !" He pressed it to his lips. " Dear, dear Belle ! I kiss your olive-branch—we have had many a falling-out, but thus will they always end." Then slipping a ring from his finger, on which was engraven a heart, transfixed by an arrow—" Beg Isabella," he said, " to wear this for my sake. It is a pretty bauble, but she'll not value it for that, nor because it has been worn by all our Capulets since the days of good Queen Bess, as my aunt, Lady Mary, assured me ; but perhaps she will care for it for—pshaw." He dashed off an honest tear—a servant announced that his uncle was awaiting him, and cordially embracing Herbert, they parted.

As Herbert had expected, Eliot Lee and Meredith were classmates, but not, as he predicted, or at least not immediately, did they become friends. Their circumstances, and those habits which grow out of circumstances, were discordant. Meredith had been bred in a luxurious establishment, and was taught to regard its artificial and elaborate arrangement as essential to the production of a gentleman. He was a citizen " of no mean city," though we now look back upon New-York at that period, with its some eighteen or twenty thousand inhabitants, as little more than a village. There was then, resulting from the condition of America far more disparity between the facilities and refinements of town and country than there now is ; and even now there are young citizens (and some citizens in certain illusions remain young all their lives) who look with the most self-complacent disdain on country breeding. Prior to our revolution, the distinctions of rank in the colonies were in accordance with the institutions of the old world. The coaches of the gentry were emblazoned with their family arms, and their plate with the family crest. If peers and baronets were *raræ aves*, there were among the youths of Harvard " nephews of my lord," and "sons of Sir George and Sir Harry." These were, naturally, Meredith's first associates. He was himself of the privileged order and, connected with many a noble family in the mother country, he felt his aristocratic blood tingle in every vein. A large property, which had devolved to him on the death of his father, was chiefly vested in real estate in America, and his guardians, with the consent of his mother, who herself remained in England, had judiciously decided to **educate**

4*

him where it would be most advantageous for him finally to fix his residence.

The external circumstances—the appliances and means of the two young men, were certainly widely different. Eliot Lee's parentage would not be deemed illustrious, according to any artificial code; but graduated by nature's aristocracy (nature alone sets a seal to her patents of universal authority), he should rank with the noble of every land. And he might claim what is now considered as the peculiar, the purest, the enduring, and in truth the *only* aristocracy of our own. He was a lineal descendant from one of the renowned *pilgrim fathers*, whose nobility, stamped in the principles that are regenerating mankind, will be transmitted by their sons on the Missouri and the Oregon, when the stars and garters of Europe have perished and are forgotten.

Colonel Lee, Eliot's father, was a laborious New-England farmer, of sterling sense and integrity—in the phrase of his people, " an independent, fore-handed man ;" a phrase that implies a property of four or five thousand dollars over and above a good farm, unencumbered with debts, and producing rather more than its proprietor, in his frugal mode of life, has occasion to spend. Eliot's mother was a woman of sound mind, and of that quick and delicate perception of the beautiful in nature and action, that is the attribute of sensibility and the proof of its existence, though the possessor, like Eliot's mother, may, from diffidence or personal awkwardness, never be able to imbody it in graceful expression. She had a keen relish of English literature, and rich acquisitions in it; such as many of our ladies, who have been taught by a dozen masters, and instructed in half as many tongues, might well envy. With all this, she was an actual operator in the arduous labours that fall to the female department of a farming establishment—plain farmer Lee's plain wife. This is not an uncommon combination of character and condition in New-England. We paint from life, if not to the life : our fault is not extravagance of colouring.

It is unnecessary to enter into the details of Eliot Lee's education. Circumstances combined to pro duce the happiest results—to develop his physical, intellectual, and moral powers ; in short, to make him a favourable specimen of the highest order of New-England character. He had just entered on his academic studies, when his father (as our friend Effie intimated in her dark soothsaying) was lost while crossing Massachusetts Bay during a violent thunder-storm. Fortunately, the good colonel's forecast had so well provided for his heirs, that his widow was able to maintain the respectable position of his family without recalling her son from college. There, as many of our distinguished men have done, he made his acquisitions available for his support by teaching.

Meredith and Eliot Lee were soon acknowledged to be the gifted young men of their class. Though nearly equals in capacity, Eliot, being by far the most patient and assiduous, bore off the college honours. Meredith did not lack industry—certainly not ambition ; but he had not the hardihood and self-discipline that it requires to forego an attractive pursuit for a dry study : and while Eliot, denying his natural tastes, toiled by the midnight lamp over the roughest academic course, he gracefully ran through the light and beaten path of belles-lettres.

They were both social—Meredith rather gay in his disposition. Both had admirable tempers ; Meredith's was partly the result of early training in the goodly seemings of the world, Eliot's the gift of Heaven, and therefore the more perfect. Eliot could not exist without self-respect. The applause of society was essential to Meredith. He certainly preferred a real to a merely apparent elevation ; but experience could alone decide whether he were willing to pay its price—sustained effort, and generous sacrifice. Both were endowed with personal graces. Neither man nor woman, that ever we could learn, is indifferent to these.

Before the young men had proceeded far in their collegiate career they were friends, if that holy relation may be predicated of those who are united by accidental circumstances. That they were on a confidential footing will be seen by the following conversation. Meredith was in his room, when, on hearing a tap at his door, he answered it by saying, " Come in, Eliot, my dear fellow. My good, or your evil genius, has brought you to me at the very moment when I am steeped to the lips in trouble."

" You in trouble ! why—what is the matter ?"

" Diable ! matter enough for song or sermon. ' Not a trouble abroad but it lights o' my shoulders' —First, here is a note from our reverend *Præses*. ' Mr. Jasper Meredith, junior class—you are fined, by the proper authority, one pound ten, for going into Boston last Thursday night, to an assembly or ball, contrary to college laws—as this is the first offence of the kind reported against you, we have, though you have been guilty of a gross violation of known duty, been lenient in fixing the amount of your fine.'—Lenient, good Præses !—Take instead one pound ten ounces of my flesh. My purse is far leaner than my person, though that be rather of the Cassius order.—Now, Eliot, is not this a pretty bill for one night's sorry amusement— one pound ten, besides the price of two ball tickets, and sundry confections."

" How, two ball tickets, Meredith ?"

" Why, I gave one to the tailor's pretty sister, Sally Dunn."

" Sally Dunn !—Bravo, Meredith. Plebeian as you think my notions, I should hardly have escorted Sally Dunn to a ball."

"My service to you, Eliot!—do not fancy I have been enacting a scene fit for Hogarth's idle apprentice. Were I so absurd, do you fancy these Boston patricians would admit a tailor's sister within their *taboed* circle?—No—no, little Sally went with company of her own cloth, and trimmings to match (in her brother's slang)—rosy milliners and journeyman tailors, to a ball got up by her compeers. I sent in to them lots of raisins and almonds, which served as a love-token for Sally and *munching* for her companions."

"You have, indeed, paid dear for your whistle, Meredith."

"Dear! you have not heard half yet. Sir knight of the shears assailed me with a whining complaint of my 'paying attention,' as he called it, to his sister Sally, and I could only get off by the gravest assurances of my profound respect for the whole Dunn concern, followed up by an order for a new vest, that being the article the youth would least mar in the making, and here is his bill—two pounds two. This is to be added to my ball expenses, fine, &c., and all, as our learned professor would say, traced to the primum mobile, must be charged to pretty Sally Dunn. Oh woman! woman!—ever the cause of man's folly, perplexity, misery, and destruction!"

"You are getting pathetic, Meredith."

"My dear friend, there is nothing affects a man's sensibilities like an empty purse—unless it be an empty stomach. You have not heard half my sorrows yet. Here is a bill, a yard long, from the livery-stable, and here another from Monsieur Paté et Confiture !"

" And your term-bills ?"

" Oh ! my term-bills I have forwarded, with the dignity of a Sir Charles Grandison, to my uncle. Now, Eliot," he continued, disbursing a few half crowns and shillings on the table, and holding up his empty purse, and throwing into his face an expression of mock misery, " Now, Eliot, let us resolve ourselves into a committee of ways and means, and tell me by what financial legerdemain I can get affixed to these scrawls that happiest combination of words in the English language—that honeyed phrase, ' *received payment in full*'—' oh, gentle shepherd, tell me where ?' "

" Where deficits should always find supplies, Meredith, in a friend's purse. I have just settled the account of my pedagogue labours for the last term, and as I have no extra bills to pay, I have extra means quite at your service."

Meredith protested, and with truth, that nothing was farther from his intentions than drawing on his friend ; and when Eliot persisted and counted out the amount which Meredith said would relieve his little embarrassments, he felt, and magnanimously expressed his admiration of those ' working-day world virtues' (so he called them), industry and frugality, which secured to Eliot the tranquillity

of independence, and the power of liberality. It
is possible that, at another time, and in another
humour, he might have led the laugh against the
sort of barter trade—the selling one kind or degree
of knowledge to procure another, by which a
Yankee youth, who is willing to live like an anchor-
ite or a philosopher in the midst of untasted pleasures, works his passage through college.

Subsequent instances occurred of similar but
temporary obligations on the part of Meredith.
Temporary of course, for Meredith was too thoroughly imbued with the sentiments of a gentleman
to extend a pecuniary obligation beyond the term
of his necessity.

CHAPTER III.

" Hear me profess sincerely—had I a dozen sons, each in my
love alike, I had rather had eleven die nobly for their country
than one voluptuously surfeit out of action."—SHAKSPEARE.

THE following extracts are from a letter from
Bessie Lee to her friend Isabella Linwood.

" DEAREST ISABELLA,
" You must love me, or you could not endure my
stupid letters—you that can write so delightfully
about nothing, and have so much to write about,
while I can tell nothing but what I see, and I see
so little ! The outward world does not much interest me. It is what I *feel* that I think of and
ponder over; but I know how you detest what you
call sentimental letters, so I try to avoid all such
subjects. Compared with you I am a child—two
years at our age makes a great difference—I am
really very childish for a girl almost fourteen, and
yet, and yet, Isabella, I sometimes seem to myself
to have gone so far beyond childhood, that I have
almost forgotten that careless, light-hearted feeling
I used to have. I do not think I ever was so light-
hearted as some children, and yet I was not
serious—at least, not in the right way. Many a

time, before I was ten years old, I have sat up in
my own little room till twelve o'clock Saturday
night, reading, and then slept for an hour and a
half through the whole sermon the next morning.
I do believe it is the natural depravity of my
heart.   I never read over twice a piece of heathen
poetry that moves me but I can repeat it—and
yet, I never could get past 'what is effectual calling ?' in the Westminster Catechism; and I always
was in disgrace on Saturday, when parson Wilson
came to the school to hear us recite it:—oh dear,
the sight of his wig and three-cornered hat pet-
rified me !"

———

" Jasper Meredith is here, passing the vacation
with Eliot.   I was frightened to death when Eliot
wrote us he was coming—we live in such a
homely way—only one servant, and I remember
well how he used to laugh at every thing he called
à la bourgeoise.   I felt this to be a foolish, *vulgar*
pride, and did my best to suppress it; and since I
have found there was no occasion for it, for J   per
seemed (I do not mean *seemed*, I think he is much
more sincere than he used to be) to miss nothing,
and to be delighted with being here.   I do not
think he realizes that I am now three years older
than I was in New-York, for he treats me with
that sort of partiality—devotion you might almost
call it—that he used to there, especially when you

and he had had a falling out. He has been giving me some lessons in Italian. He says I have a wonderful talent for learning languages, but it is not so: you know what hobbling work I made with the French when you and I went to poor old Mademoiselle Amand—Jasper is quite a different teacher, and I never fancied French. He has been teaching me to ride, too—we have a nice little pony, and he has a beautiful horse—so that we have the most delightful gallops over the country every day. It is very odd, though I am such a desperate coward, I never feel the least timid when I am riding with Jasper—indeed, I do not think of it. Eliot rarely finds time to go with us—when he is at home from college he has so much to do for mother—dear Eliot, he is husband, father, brother, every thing to us."

———

" I had not time, while Jasper and Eliot stayed, to finish my letter, and since they went away I have been so dull !—The house seems like a tomb. I go from room to room, but the spirit is not here. Master Hale, the schoolmaster, boards with us, and gives me lessons in some branches that Eliot thinks me deficient in ; but ah me ! where are the talents for acquisition that Jasper commended? Did you ever know, dear Isabella, what it was to have every thing affected by the departure of friends, as nature is by the absence of light—all

fade into one dull uniform hue. When Eliot and
Jasper were here, all was bright and interesting
from the rising of the sun to the going down there-
of—now!—ah me!

"I am shocked to find how much I have written
about myself. My best respects to your father
and mother, and love to Herbert. Burn this worth-
less scrawl without fail, dear Isabella, and believe
me ever most affectionately

                              "Yours,
                                   "Bessie Lee."

Jasper Meredith to Herbert Linwood.

"Dear Linwood,

"I have been enjoying a very pretty little episode in my college life, passing the vacation at
Westbrook, with your old friends the Lees. A
month in a dull little country town would once
have seemed to me penance enough for my worst
sin, but now it is heaven to get anywhere beyond
the sound of college bells—beyond the reach of
automaton tutors—periodical recitations—chapel
prayers, and college rules.

"I went to the Lees with the pious intention of
quizzing your rustics to the top o' my bent; but
Herbert, my dear fellow, I'll tell you a secret; when
people respect themselves, and value things according to their real intrinsic worth, it gives a shock to
our artificial and worldly estimates, and makes us
feel as if we stood upon a wonderful uncertain

foundation. These Lees are so strong in their sim-plicity—they would so disdain aping and imitating those that we (not they, be sure!) think above them —they are so sincere in all their ways—no awk-ward consciousness—no shame-facedness what-ever about the homely details of their family affairs. By heavens, Herbert, I could not find a folly—a meanness—or even a ludicrous rusticity at which to aim my ridicule.

"I begin to think—no, no, no, I do not—but, if there were many such families as these Lees in the world, an equality, independent of all extrane-ous circumstances (such as the politicians of this country are now ranting about), might subsist on the foundation of intellect and virtue.

"After all, I see it is a mere illusion. Mrs. Lee's rank, though in Westbrook she appears equal to any Roman matron, is purely local. Hallowed as she is in your boyish memory, Herbert, you must confess she would cut a sorry figure in a New-York drawing-room.

"Eliot might pass current anywhere ; but then he has had the advantage of Boston society, and an intimacy with—pardon my coxcombry—your humble servant. Bessie—sweet Bessie Lee, is a gem fit to be set in a coronet. Don't be alarmed, Herbert, you are welcome to have the setting of her. There is metal, *as you know*, more attractive to me. Bessie is not much grown since she was in New-York—she is still low in stature, and so

childish in her person, that I was sometimes in
danger of treating her like a child—of forgetting
that she had come within the charmed circle of
proprieties.   But, if she has still the freshness and
immaturity of the unfolding rose-bud—the mysti-
cal charm of woman—the divinity stirring within
her beams through her exquisite features.   Such
features ! Phidias would have copied them in his
immortal marble.   How in the world should such
a creature, all sentiment, refinement, imagination,
spring up in practical, prosaic New-England !
She is a wanderer from some other star.   I am
writing like a lover, and not as I should to a lover.
But, on my honour, Herbert, I am no lover—of
little Bessie I mean.   I should as soon think of being enamoured of a rose, a lily, or a violet, an exquisite sonnet, or an abstraction.

    " It is an eternity since Isabella has written me
a postscript—why is this ?   Farewell, Linwood.
                              " Yours, &c.

    " P. S.—One word on politics—a subject I de-
test, and meddle with as little as possible.   There
must be an outbreak—there is no avoiding it.   But
there can be no doubt which party will finally prevail.   The mother country has soldiers, money,
every thing ; ' 'tis odds beyond arithmetic.'   As one
of my friends said at a dinner in Boston the other
day, ' the growling curs may bark for a while, but
they will be whipped into submission, and wear
their collars patiently for ever after.'   I trust, Her

bert, you are already cured of what my uncle used to call the ' boy-fever'—but if not, take my advice—be quiet, prudent, *neutral*. As long as we are called boys, we are not expected to be patriots, apostles, or martyrs. At this crisis your filial and *fraternal* duties require that you should suppress, if not renounce, the opinions you used to be so fond of blurting out on all occasions. I am no preacher —I have done—a *word* to the wise.

" M——."

We resume the extracts from Bessie's letters.

" Dear Isabella,—Never say another word to me of what you hinted in your last letter : indeed, I am too young ; and besides, I never should feel easy or happy again with Jasper, if I admitted such a thought. I have had but one opinion since our visit to Effie ; not that I believed in her—at least, not much ; but I have always known who was first in his thoughts—heart—opinion ; and besides, it would be folly in me, knowing his opinions about rank, &c. Mother thinks him very proud, and somewhat vain ; and she begins not to be pleased with his frequent visits to Westbrook. She thinks—no, fears, or rather she imagines, that Jasper and I—no, that Jasper *or* I—no, that I— it is quite too foolish to write, Isabella—mother does not realize what a wide world there is between us. I might possibly, sometimes, think he loved (this last word was carefully effaced, and cared substituted) cared for me, if he did not know you.

"How could Jasper tell you of Eliot's prejudice against you? Jasper himself infused it, unwittingly, I am sure, by telling him that when with you, I lived but to do 'your best pleasure,—were it to fly, to swim, or dive into the fire.' Eliot fancies that you are proud and overbearing —I insist, dear Isabella, that such as you are born to rule such weak spirits as mine; but Eliot says he does not like absolutism in any form, and especially in woman's. Ah, how differently he would feel if he were to see you—I am sure you would like him—I am not sure, even, that you would not have preferred him to Jasper, had he been born and bred in Jasper's circumstances. He has more of some qualities that you particularly like, frankness and independence—and mother says (but then mother is not at all partial to Jasper) he has a thousand times more real sensibility—he does, perhaps, feel more for others. I should like to know which you would think the handsomest. Eliot is at least three inches the tallest; and, as Jasper once said, 'cast in the heroic mould, with just enough, and not an ounce too much of mortality'—but then Jasper has such grace and symmetry—just what I fancy to be the beau-ideal of the arts. Jasper's eyes are almost too black—too piercing; and yet they are softened by his long lashes, and his olive complexion, so expressive—

like that fine old portrait in your drawing-room. His mouth, too, is beautiful—it has such a defined, chiselled look—but then do you not think that his teeth being so delicately formed, and so very, very white, is rather a defect? I don't know how to de-scribe it, but there is rather an uncertain expression about his mouth. Eliot's, particularly when he smiles, is truth and kindness itself—and his deep, deep blue eye, expresses every thing by turns—I mean every thing that should come from a pure and lofty spirit—now tender and pitiful enough for me, and now superb and fiery enough for you—but what a silly, girlish letter I am writing—' Out of the abundance of the heart,' you know! I see nobody but Jasper and Eliot, and I think only of them."

We continue the extracts from Bessie's letters They were strictly feminine, even to their being dateless—we cannot, therefore, ascertain the precise period at which they were written, except by their occasional allusions to contemporaneous events.

" Thanks, dear Isabella, for your delightful letter by Jasper—no longer Jasper, I assure you to his face, but Mr. Meredith—oh, I often wish the time back when I was a child, and might call him Jas-per, and feel the freedom of a child. I wonder if I should dare to call you Belle now, or even Isa-bella? Jasper, since his last visit at home, tells me so much of your being ' the mirror of fashion—the observed of all observers' (these are his own

c 3

words—drawing-room terms that were never heard in Westbrook but from his lips), that I feel a sort of fearful shrinking. It is not envy—I am too happy now to envy anybody in the wide world. Eliot is at home, and Jasper is passing a week here. Is it not strange they should be so intimate, when they differ so widely on political topics? I suppose it is because Jasper does not care much about the matter; but this indifference sometimes provokes Eliot. Jasper is very intimate with Pitcairn and Lord Percy; and Eliot thinks they have more influence with him than the honour and interest of his country. Oh, they talk it over for hours and hours, and end, as men always do with their arguments, just where they began. Jasper insists that as long as the quarrel can be made up it is much wisest to stand aloof, and not, 'like mad boys, to rush foremost into the first fray;' besides, he says he is tied by a promise to his uncle that he will have nothing to do with these agitating disputes till his education is finished. Mother says (she does not always judge Jasper kindly) that it is very easy and *prudent* to bind your hands with a promise when you do not choose to lift them.

"Ah, there is a terrible storm gathering! Those who have grown up together, lovingly interlacing their tender branches, must be torn asunder—some swept away by the current, others dispersed by the winds."

" DEAR ISABELLA,—The world seems turned
upside down since I began this letter—war (*war*,
what an appalling sound) has begun—blood has
been spilt, and our dear, dear Eliot—but I must
tell you first how it all was. Eliot and Jasper were
out shooting some miles from Cambridge, when, on
coming to the road, they perceived an unusual com-
motion—old men and young, and even boys, all
armed, in wagons, on horseback, and on foot, were
coming from all points, and all hurrying onward in
one direction. On inquiring into the hurly-burly,
they were told that Colonel Smith had marched to
Concord to destroy the military stores there; and
that our people were gathering from all quarters to
oppose his return. Eliot immediately joined them,
Jasper did not; but, dear Isabella, I that know
you so well, know, whatever others may think, that
tories may be true and noble. There was a fight
at Lexington. Our brave men had the best of it.
Eliot was the first to bring us the news. With
a severe wound in his arm, he came ten miles that
we need not be alarmed by any reports, knowing,
as he told mother, that she was no Spartan mother,
to be indifferent whether her son came home with
his shield or on his shield.

" Jasper has not been to Westbrook since the
battle. My mind has been in such a state of alarm
since, I cannot return to my ordinary pursuits. I
was reading history with the children, and the Eng
lish poets with mother, but I am quite broken up.

"I do not think this horrid war should separate those who have been friends; thank God, my dear Isabella, we of womankind are exempts—not called upon to take sides—our mission is to heal wounds, not to make them; to keep alive and tend with vestal fidelity the fires of charity and love. My kindest remembrance to Herbert. I hope he has renounced his whiggism; for if it must come to that, he had better fight on the wrong side (ignorantly) than break the third commandment. Write soon, dear Isabella, and let me know if this hurly-burly extends to New-York—dear, quiet New-York! In war and in peace, in all the chances and changes of this mortal life, your own
                                          BESSIE LEE."

Miss Linwood to Bessie Lee.

"Exempts! my little spirit of peace—your vocation it may be, my pretty dove, to sit on your perch with an olive-branch in your bill, but not mine. Oh for the glorious days of the Clorindas, when a woman might put down her womanish thoughts, and with helmet and lance in rest do battle with the bravest! Why was the loyal spirit of my race my exclusive patrimony? Can his blood, who at his own cost raised a troop of horse for our martyr king, flow in Herbert's veins? or his who followed the fortunes of the unhappy James? Is my father's son a renegado—a rebel? Yes. Bessie—my blood burns in my cheeks while

I write it. Herbert, the only male scion of the Linwoods—my brother—our pride—our hope has declared himself of the rebel party—' Ichabod, Ichabod, the glory is departed, is written on our door-posts.'

" But to come down from my heroics ; we are in a desperate condition—such a scene as I have just passed through ! Judge Ellis was dining with us, Jasper Meredith was spoken of. ' In the name of Heaven, Ellis,' said my father, ' why do you suffer your nephew to remain among the rebel crew in that infected region ?'

" ' I do not find,' replied the judge, glancing at Herbert, ' that any region is free from infection.'

" ' True, true,' said my father ; ' but the air of the Yankee states is saturated with it. I would not let an infant breathe it, lest rebellion should break out when he came to man's estate.' I am sorry to say it, dear Bessie ; but my father traces Herbert's delinquency to his sojourn at Westbrook. I saw a tempest was brewing, and thinking to make for a quiet harbour, I put in my oar, and repeated the story you told me in your last letter of our non-combatant, Mr. Jasper. The judge was charmed. ' Ah, he's a prudent fellow !' he said ; ' he'll not commit himself !'

" ' Not commit himself !' exclaimed my father ; ' by Jupiter, if he belonged to me, he should commit himself. I would rather he should jump the wrong way than sit squat like a toad under a hedge,

6

till he was sure which side it was most *prudent* to jump.' You see, Bessie, my father's words implied something like a commendation of Herbert. I ventured to look up—their eyes met—I saw a beam of pleasure flashing from them, and passing like an electric spark from one heart to another. Oh, why should this unholy quarrel tear asunder such true hearts !

" The judge's pride was touched—he is a mean wretch. ' Ah, my dear sir,' he said, ' it is very well for you, who can do it with impunity, to disregard prudential considerations; for instance, you remain true to the king, the royal power is maintained, and your property is protected. Your son —I suppose a case—your son joins the rebels, the country is revolutionized, and your property is secured as the reward of Mr. Herbert's patriotism.'

" My father hardly heard him out. ' Now, by the Lord that made me !' he exclaimed, setting down the decanter with a force that broke it in a thousand pieces, ' I would die of starvation before I would taste a crumb of bread that was the reward of rebellion.'

" It was a frightful moment; but my father's passion, you know, is like a whirlwind; one gust, and it is over; and mamma is like those short-stemmed flowers that lie on the earth ; no wind moves her. So, though the judge was almost as much disconcerted as the decanter, it seemed all to have blown over, while mamma, as in case of any ordi nary accident, was directing Jupe to remove the fragments, change the cloth, etc. But alas ! the evil genius of our house triumphed; for even a bottle of our oldest Madeira, which is usually to my father like oil to the waves, failed to preserve tranquillity. The glasses werę filled, and my father, according to his usual custom, gave ' the king—God bless him.'

"Now you must know, though he would not confess he made any sacrifice to prudence, he has for some weeks omitted to drink wine at all, on some pretext or other, such as he had a head-ache, or he had dined out the day before, or ex-pected to the day after; and thus Herbert has escaped the test. But now the toast was given, and Herbert's glass remained untouched, while he sat, not biting, but literally devouring his nails. I saw the judge cast a sinister look at him, and then a glance at my father. The storm was gathering on my father's brow. ' Herbert, my son,' said mamma, ' you will be too late for youɪ appointment.' Herbert moved his chair to rise, when my father called out, ' Stop, sir—no slink-ing away under your mother's shield—hear me— no man who refuses to drink that toast at my table shall eat of my bread or drink of my wine.'

" ' Then God forgive me—for I never will drink it—so help me Heaven !'

" Herbert left the room by one door—my fatheɪ bʸ another—mamma stayed calmly talking to that fixture of a judge, and I ran to my room, where, as soon as I had got through with a comfortable fit of crying, I sat down to write you (who are on the enemy's side) an account of the matter. What will come of it, Heaven only knows !

" But, my dear little gentle Bessie, I never think of you as having any thing to do with these turbulent matters ; you are in the midst of fiery rebel spirits, but you are too pure, too good to enter into their counsels, and far too just for any self-originating prejudices, such as this horrible one that pervades the country, and fires New-England against the legitimate rights of the mother country over her wayward, ungrateful child. Don't trouble your head about these squabbles, but cling to Master Hale, your poetry, and history: by-the-way, I laughed heartily that you, who have done *duty—reading* so virtuously all your life, should now come to the conclusion ' that history is dry.' I met with a note in Herodotus, the most picturesque of historians, the other day that charmed me. The writer of the note says there is no mention whatever of Cyrus in the Persian history. If history then is mere fiction, why may we not read romances of our own choosing ? My instincts have not misguided me, after all.

" So, Miss Bessie, Jasper Meredith is in high favour with you, and the friend of your nonpareil brother. Jasper could always be irresistible when he chose, and he seems to have been ' i' the vein' at Westbrook. With all our impressions (are they prejudices, Bessie?) against your Yankee land, we thought him excessively improved by his residence among you. Indeed, I think if he were never to get another letter from his worldly icicle mother, to live away from his time-serving uncle, and never receive another importation of London coxcombries, he would be what nature intended him—a paragon.

"I love your sisterly enthusiasm. As to my estimation of your brother being affected by the accidents of birth and fortune, indeed, you were not true to your friend when you intimated that. Certainly, the views you tell me he takes of my character are not particularly flattering, or even conciliating. However, I have my revenge—you paint him *en beau*—the portrait is too beautiful to be very like any man born and reared within the disenchanted limits of New-England. I am writing boldly, but no offence, dear Bessie; I do not know your brother, and I have—yes, out with it, with the exception of your precious little self —I have an *antipathy* to the New-Englanders—a disloyal race, and conceited, fancying themselves more knowing in all matters, high and low, especially government and religion, than the rest of the world—' all-sufficient, self-sufficient, and *insufficient.*'

"Pardon me, gentle Bessie—I am just now at fever heat, and I could not like Gabriel if he were whig and rebel. Ah, Herbert !—but I loved him before I ever heard these detestable words ; and once truly loving, especially if our hearts be knit together by nature, I think the faults of the subject do not diminish our affection, though they turn it from its natural sweet uses to suffering."

"DEAR BESSIE,—A week—a stormy, miserable week has passed since I wrote the above, and it has ended in Herbert's leaving us, and dishonouring his father's name by taking a commission in the rebel service. Papa has of course had a horrible fit of the gout. He says he has for ever cast Herbert out of his affections. Ah! I am not skilled in metaphysics, but I *know* that we have no power whatever over our affections. Mamma takes it all patiently, and chiefly sorroweth for that Herbert has lost caste by joining the insurgents, whom she thinks little better than so many Jack Cades.

"For myself, I would have poured out my blood —every drop of it, to have kept him true to his king and country ; but in my secret heart I glory in him that he has honestly and boldly clung to his opinions, to his own certain and infinite loss. I have no heart to write more.

"Yours truly,

"ISABELLA LINWOOD.

"P. S. —You may show the last paragraph (confidentially) to Jasper ; but don't let him know that I wished him to see it.		I. L."

CHAPTER IV.

"An' forward, though I canna *see*,
I *guess* an' *fear*."—BURNS.

THREE years passed over without any marked change in the external condition of our young friends. Herbert Linwood endured the hardships of an American officer during that most suffering period of the war, and remained true to the cause he had adopted, without any of those opportunities of distinction which are necessary to keep alive the fire of ordinary patriotism.

It has been seen that Eliot Lee, with most of the young men of the country (as might be expected from the insurgent and generous spirit of youth), espoused the popular side. It ought not to have been expected, that when the young country came to the muscle and vigour of manhood, it should continue to wear the leading-strings of its childhood, or remain in the bondage and apprenticeship of its youth. It has been justly said, that the seeds of our revolution and future independence were sown by the Pilgrims. The political institutions of a people may be inferred from their religion. Absolutism, as a mirror, reflects the Roman Catholic faith. Whatever varieties of names were attached

to the religious sects of America, they were, with
the exception of a few Papists, all Protestants—
all, as Burke said of them, " agreed (if agreeing
in nothing else) in the communion of the spirit of
liberty—theirs was the Protestantism of the Prot-
estant religion—the dissidence of dissent." It was
morally certain, that as soon as they came to man's
estate, their government would accord with this
spirit of liberty; would harmonize with the independent and republican spirit of the religion of
Christ, the only authority they admitted. The
fires of our republic were not then kindled by a
coal from the old altars of Greece and Rome, whose
freest government exalted the few, and retained
the many in grovelling ignorance and servitude:
ours came forth invincible in the declaration of
liberty to all, and equality of rights.

Such minds as Eliot Lee's, reasoning and religious, were not so much moved by the sudden
impulses of enthusiasm as incited by the convic-
tions of duty. His heart was devoted to his country, his thoughts absorbed in her struggle; but he
quenched, or rather smothered his intense desire
to go forth with her champions, and remained pursuing his legal studies, near enough to his home
to perform his paramount but obscure duty to his
widowed mother and her young family.

Jasper Meredith's political preferences, if not
proclaimed, were easily guessed. It was obvious
that his tastes were aristocratic and feudal—his

sympathies with the monarch, not with the people.
New-York was the headquarters of the British
army, and Judge Ellis, his uncle, on the pretext
of keeping his nephew out of the way of the seduc-
tions of a very gay society, advised him to pursue
the study of the law in New-England, and thus for
a while he avoided pledging himself. He resided
in Boston or its vicinity, never far from Westbrook.
He had a certain *eclat* in the drawing-rooms of
Boston, but he was no favourite there. A pro-
fessed neutrality was, if not suspicious, most offensive in the eyes of neck-or-nothing patriots.
But Meredith did not escape the whisper that his
neutrality was a mere mask. His accent, which
was ambitiously English, was criticised, and his
elaborate dress, manufactured by London *artists*,
was particularly displeasing to the sons of the
Puritans, who, absorbed in great objects, were then
more impatient even than usual of extra sacrifices
to the graces.

The transition from Boston to Westbrook was delightful to Meredith. There was no censure of any
sort, but balm for the rankling wounds of vanity;
and it must be confessed that he not only appeared
better, but was better at Westbrook than elsewhere:
the best parts of his nature were called forth ; he
was (if we may desecrate a technical expression)
in the exercise of grace. There is a certain moral
atmosphere, as propitious to moral wellbeing as a
genial temperature is to health. Vanity has a sort
of thermometer, which enables the possessor to

graduate and adapt himself to the dispositions, the vanities (is there any gold in nature without this alloy?) of others. Meredith, when he wished to be so, was eminently agreeable. Those always stand in a most fortunate light who vary the monotony of a village existence, and he broke like a sunbeam through the dull atmosphere that hung over West-brook. He brought the freshest news, he studied good Mrs. Lee's partialities and prejudices, and (without her being aware of their existence) ac-commodated himself to them. He supplied to Eliot what all social beings hanker after, com-panionship with one of his own age, pursuits, and associations. The magnet that drew him to West-brook was never the acknowledged attraction. Meredith was not in love with Bessie Lee. She was too spiritual a creature for one of earth's mould; but his self-love, his ruling passion, was flattered by her. He saw and enjoyed (what, alas! no one else then saw) his power over her. He saw it in the mutations of her cheek, in the kindling of her eye, in the changes of her voice. It was as if an angel had left his sphere to incense him. Meredith must be acquitted of a deliberate attempt to insnare her affections. He thought not and cared not for the future. He cared only for a present self-gratification. A ride at twilight or a walk by moonlight with this creature, all beauty, refine-ment, and tenderness, was a poetic passage to him —to her it was fraught with life or death.

Poor Bessie! she should have been hardened
for the changing climate of this rough world; but
by a fatal, but very common error, she had been
cherished like a tropical bird, or an exotic plant.
" She has such delicate health! she is so different
from my other children!" said the mother.—" She
is so gentle and sensitive," said the brother. And
thus, with all their sound judgment, instead of sub-
mitting her to a hardening process, it seemed an
instinct with them, by every elaborate contrivance,
to fence her from the ordinary trials and evils of
life. Only when she was happy did they let her
alone; with Meredith she seemed happy, and
they were satisfied. Bessie shared this unfounded
tranquillity, arising with them partly from confidence in Meredith, and partly from the belief that
she was in no danger of suffering from an unrequited
love; but Bessie's arose from the most childlike
ignorance of that study puzzling to the wisest and
craftiest—the human heart. She was the most
modest and unexacting of human creatures—her
gentle spirit urged no rights—asked nothing, expected nothing beyond the present moment. The
worshipper was satisfied with the presence of the
idol. Her residence in New-York had impressed a
conviction that a disparity of birth and condition
was an impassable gulf. It was natural enough
that she should have imbibed this opinion; for,
being a child, the aristocratic opinions of the society she was in were expressed, unmitigated by

courtesy ; they sunk deep in her susceptible mind, a mind too humble to aspire above any barrier that nature or society had set up.

There was another foundation of her fancied security. This was shaken by the following conversation :—Meredith was looking over an old pocketbook, when a card dropped from it on the floor at Bessie's feet : she handed it to him—he smiled as he looked at it, and held it up before her. She glanced her eye over it, and saw it was a note of the date of their visit to the soothsayer Effie, and of Effie's prediction in relation to the " dark curling hair."

" I had totally forgotten this," said he, carelessly.

"Forgotten it!" echoed Bessie, in a tone that indicated but too truly her feelings.

" Certainly I had—and why not, pray ?"

" Oh, because—" she hesitated.

" Because what, Bessie ?"

Bessie was ashamed of her embarrassment, and faltering the more the more she tried to shake it off, she said, " I did not suppose you could forget any thing that concerned Isabella."

" Upon my honour, you are very much mistaken ; I have scarcely thought of Effie and her trumpery prediction since we were there."

" Why have you preserved the card, then, Jasper ?" asked Bessie, in all simplicity.

Jasper's complexion was not of the blushing order, or he would have blushed as he replied, at

the same time replacing the card—" Oh, Lord, I
don't know! accident—the card got in here among
these old memoranda and receipts, ' trivial fond
records' all !"

" There preserve it," said Bessie, " and we will
look at it one of these days."

" When ?"

" When—as it surely will be, the prediction is
verified."

" If not till then," he said, " it will never again
see the light—this is the oddest fancy of yours,"
he added.

" Not fancy, but faith."

" Faith most unfounded—why, Bessie, Isabella
and I were always quarrelling."

" And always making up. Do you ever quarrel
now, Jasper ?"

" Oh, she is still of an April temper; but I"—he
looked most tenderly at Bessie—" have lived too
much of late in a serene atmosphere to bear well
her fitful changes."

A long time had passed since Bessie had mentioned Isabella to Meredith. She knew not why,
but she had felt a growing reluctance to advert to
her friend even in thought; and she was now
conscious of a thrilling sensation at the careless,
cold manner in which Jasper spoke of her. It
seemed as if a load had fallen off her heart. She
felt like a mariner who has at length caught a
glimpse of what seems distant land, and is bewil-

..dered with new sensations, and uncertain whether
it be land or not. She was conscious Jasper's eye
was on hers, though her own was downcast. She
longed to escape from that burning glance, and
was relieved by a bustle in the next room, and her
two little sisters running in, one holding up a long
curling tress of her own beautiful hair, and crying
out—" Did not you give this to me, Bessie ?"

" Is not it mine ?" said the competitor.

" No, it is mine !" exclaimed Jasper, snatching
it, and holding it beyond their reach.

The girls laughed, and were endeavouring to
regain it, when he slipped a ring from his finger,
and set it rolling on the floor, saying, " The hair
is mine—the ring belongs to whoever gets it."
The ring, obedient to the impulse he gave it, rolled
out of the room; the children eagerly followed,
he shut the door after them, and repeated, kissing
the lock of hair—" It is mine—is it not ?"

" Oh, no—no, Jasper—give it to me," cried Bessie, excessively confused.

" You will not give it to me !—well—' a fair ex-
change is no robbery,' " and taking the scissors
from Bessie's workbox, he cut off one of his own
luxuriant dark locks, and offered it to her. She
shook her head.

" That is unkind—most unfriendly, Bessie"—
he paused a moment, and then, still holding both
locks, he extended the ends to Bessie, and asked
her if she could tie a true love-knot. Bessie's

heart was throbbing; she was frightened at her own emotion; she was afraid of betraying it; and she tied the knot as the natural thing for her to do.

"There is but one altar for such a sacrifice as this," said Meredith, and he was putting it into his bosom, when Bessie snatched it from him, burst into tears, and left the room.

After this, there was a change in Bessie's manners—her spirits became unequal, she was nervous and restless—Meredith, in the presence of observers, was measured and cautious to the last degree in his attentions to her—when however they were alone together, though not a sentence might be uttered that a lawyer could have tortured into a special plea, yet his words were fraught with looks and tones that carried them to poor Bessie's heart with a power that cannot be imagined by those

"Who have ceased to hear such, or ne'er heard."

It was about this period that Meredith wrote the following reply to a letter from his mother.

"You say, my dear madam, that you have heard 'certain reports about me, which you are not willing to believe, and yet cannot utterly discredit.' You say, also, 'that though you should revolt with horror from sanctioning your son in those *liaisons* that are advised by Lord Chesterfield, and others of your friends, yet you see no harm in' lover-like attentions 'to young persons in inferior sta-

tions; they serve' you add, ' to keep alive and cul-
tivate that delicate finesse so essential to the suc
cess of a man of the world, and, provided they
have no immoral purpose, are quite innocent,' as the
object of them must know there is an ' impassable
gulf between her and her superiors in rank, and
is therefore responsible for her mistakes.' I have
been thus particular in echoing your words, that I
may assure you my conduct is in conformity to
their letter and spirit. Tranquillize yourself, my
dear madam. There is nothing, in any little fooleries I may be indulging in, to disquiet you for a
moment. The person in question is a divine little
creature—quite a prodigy for this part of the
world, where she lives in a seclusion almost equal to
that of Prospero's isle; so that your humble servant,
being scarce more than the ' third man that e'er
she saw,' it would not be to marvel at ' if he
should be the first that e'er she loved'—and if I am,
it is my *destiny*—my conscience is quite easy—
1 never have *committed* myself, nor ever shall:
time and absence will soon dissipate her illusions
She is an unaspiring little person, quite aware of
the gulf, as you call it, between us. She believes
that even if I were lover and hero enough to play
the Leander and swim it, my destiny is fixed on
the other side. I have no distrust of myself, and I
beg you will have none; I am saved from all responsibility as to involving the happiness of this
lily of the valley, by her very clear-sighted mother,

and her sage of a brother, her natural guar
dians.

"It is yet problematical whether, as you suppose, a certain lady's fortune will be made by the
apostacy of her disinherited brother. If the rebels
win the day, the property of the tories will be con-
fiscated, or transferred to the rebel heir. But all
that is in futuro—fortune is a fickle goddess; we
can only be sure of her present favours and deserve
the future by our devotion.

"With profound gratitude and affection,

"Yours, my dear mother,

"J. MEREDITH.

"P. S.—My warmest thanks for the inestimable
box, which escaped the sea and land harpies, and
came safe to hand. The Artois buckle is a *chef
d'œuvre*, worthy the inventive genius of the royal
\count whose taste rules the civilized world. The
scarlet frock-coat, with its unimitated, if not inimitable, capes, 'does credit (as friend Rivington would
say in one of his flashy advertisements) to the most
elegant operator of Leicester-fields.' I must reserve it till I go to New-York, where they always
take the lead in this sort of civilization—the boys
would mob me if I wore it in Boston. The um-
brella, a rare invention! is a curiosity here. I
understand they have been introduced into New-
York by the British officers. Novelty as it is, I
venture to spread it here, as its utility commends it
to these rationalists, who reason about an article

7*

of dress as they would concerning an article of
faith.

     " Once more, your devoted son,   M."

     Meredith's conscience was easy ! " He had not
committed himself !"—Ah, let man beware how he
wilfully or carelessly perverts and blinds God's
vicegerent, conscience.

     Meredith was suddenly recalled to New-York,
and Bessie Lee was left to ponder on the past, and
weave the future of shattered faith and blighted
hopes.   The scales fell too late from the eyes of
her mother and brother.   They reproached themselves, but never poor Bessie.   They hoped that
time, operating on her gentle, unresisting temper,
would restore her serenity.   She, like a stricken
deer, took refuge under the shadow of their love ,
she was too affectionate, too generous, to resign
herself to wretchedness without an effort.   She
wasted her strength in concealing the wound that
rankled at her heart.

CHAPTER V.

"I, considering how honour would become such a person, was
pleased to let him seek danger, where he was like to find fame."
SHAKSPEARE.

ANOTHER sorrow soon overtook poor Bessie; but
now she had a right to feel, and might express all
she felt, and look full in the face of her friends
for sympathy, for they shared the burden with her.

In the year 1778, letters were sent by General
Washington to the governors of the several states,
earnestly entreating them to re-enforce the army.
The urgency of this call was acknowledged by
every patriotic individual; and never did heart more
joyously leap than Eliot Lee's, when his mother
said to him—" My son, I have long had misgivings
about keeping you at home; but last night, after
reading the general's letter, I could not sleep; I
felt for him, for the country; my conscience told
me you ought to go, Eliot; even the images of the
children, for whose sake only I have thought it
right you should stay with us, rose up against me:
we should pay our portion for the privileges they
are to enjoy. I have made up my mind to it, and
on my knees I have given you to my country.
The widow's son," she continued, clearing her

voice, " is something more than the widow's mite, Eliot; but I have given you up, and now I have done with feelings—nothing is to be said or thought of but how we shall soonest and best get you ready."

Eliot was deeply affected by his mother's decision, voluntary and unasked; but he did not express his satisfaction, his delight, till he ascertained that she had well considered the amount of the sacrifice and was willing to meet it.   Then he confessed that nothing but a controlling sense of his filial duty had enabled him to endure loitering at the fireside, when his country needed the aid he withheld.

The decision made, no time was lost.   Letters were obtained from the best sources to General Washington, and in less than a week Eliot was ready for his departure.

It was a transparent morning, late in autumn, in bleak, wild, fitful, poetic November.   The vault of heaven was spotless; a purple light danced over the mountain summits; the mist was condensed in the hollows of the hills, and wound them round like drapery of silver tissue.   The smokes from the village chimneys ascended through the clear atmosphere in straight columns; the trees on the mountains, banded together, still preserved a portion of their summer wealth, though now faded to dun and dull orange, marked and set off by the surrounding evergreens.   Here and there a solitary elm stood bravely up against the sky, every limb, every stem defined; a naked form, showing the beautiful symmetry that had made its summer garments hang so gracefully. Fruits and flowers, even the hardy ones that venture on the frontiers of winter, had disappeared from the gardens; the seeds had dropped from their cups; the grass of the turf-borders was dank and matted down; all nature was stamped with the signet seal of autumn, *memory* and *hope*. Eliot had performed the last provident offices for his mother; every thing about her cheerful dwelling had the look of being kindly cared for. The strawberry-beds were covered, the raspberries neatly trimmed out, the earth well spaded and freshly turned; no gate was off its hinges, no fence down, no window unglazed, no crack unstopped.

A fine black saddle-horse, well equipped, was at the door. Little Fanny Lee stood by him, patting him, and laying her head, with its shining flaxen locks, to his side—" Rover," she said, with a trembling voice, " be a good Rover—won't you ? and when the naughty regulars come, canter off with Eliot as fast as you can."

" Hey ! that's fine !" retorted her brother, a year younger than herself. " No, no, Rover, canter up to them, and over them, and never dare to canter back here if you turn tail on them, Rover."

" Oh, Sam ! how awful; would you have Eliot killed ?"

" No, indeed, but I had rather he'd come deused near it than to have him a coward."

" Don't talk so loud, Sam—Bessie will hear you."

But the young belligerant was not to be silenced. He threw open the " dwelling-room" door, to appeal to Eliot himself. The half-uttered sentence died away on his lips. He entered the apartment, Fanny followed ; they gently closed the door, drew their footstools to Eliot's feet, and quietly sat down there. How instinctive is the sympathy of children ! how plain, and yet how delicate its manifestations !

Bessie was sitting beside her brother, her head on his shoulder, and crying as if her heart went out with every sob. The youngest boy, Hal, sat on Eliot's knee, with one arm around his neck, his cheek lying on Bessie's, dropping tear after tear, sighing, and half-wondering why it was so.

The good mother had arrived at that age when grief rather congeals the spirit than melts it. Her lips were compressed, her eyes tearless, and her movements tremulous. She was busying herself in the last offices, doing up parcels, taking last stitches, and performing those services that seem to have been assigned to women as safety-valves for their ever effervescing feelings.

A neat table was spread with ham, bread, sweet-meats, cakes, and every delicacy the house afforded —all were untasted. Not a word was heard except such broken sentences as "Come, Bessie, I will promise to be good if you will to be happy!"

"Eliot, how easy for you—how impossible for me!"

"Dear Bessie, do be firmer, for mother's sake. For ever! oh no, my dear sister, it will not be very long before I return to you; and while I am gone, you must be every thing to mother."

"I! I never was good for any thing, Eliot—and now—"

"Bessie, my dear child, hush—you have been —you always will be a blessing to me. Don't put any anxious thoughts into Eliot's mind—we shall do very well without him."

"Noble, disinterested mother!" trembled on Eliot's lips; but he suppressed words that might imply reproach to Bessie.

The sacred scene was now broken in upon by some well-meaning but untimely visiters. Eliot's approaching departure had created a sensation in Westbrook; the good people of that rustic place not having arrived at the refined stage in the prog-ress of society, when emotion and fellow-feeling are not expressed, or expressed only by certain conven-tional forms. First entered Master Hale, with Miss Sally Ryal. Master Hale "hoped it was no intru-sion;" and Miss Sally answered, "by no means; she had come to lend a helping hand, and not to intrude" —whereupon she bustled about, helped herself and her companion to chairs, and unsettled everybody else in the room. Mrs. Lee assumed a more tranquil mien; poor Bessie suppressed her sobs, and withdrew to a window, and Eliot tried to look composed and manly. The children, like springs relieved from a pressure, reverted to their natural state, dashed off their tears, and began whispering among themselves. Miss Sally produced from her workbag a comforter for Mr. Eliot, of her own knitting, which she "trusted would keep out the cold and rheumatism:" and she was kindly showing him how to adjust it, when she spied a chain of braided hair around his neck—" Ah, ha, Mr. Eliot, a love-token!" she exclaimed.

" Yes, it is," said little Fanny, who was watching her proceedings; " Bessie and I cut locks of hair from all the children's heads and mother's, and braided it for him; and I guess it will warm his bosom more than your comforter will, Miss Sally."

It was evident, from the look of ineffable tenderness Eliot turned on Fanny, that he " guessed" so too; but he nevertheless received the comforter graciously, hinting, that a lady who had been able to protect her own bosom from the most subtle enemy, must know how to defend another's from common assaults. Miss Sally hemmed, looked at Master Hale, muttered something of her not always having been invulnerable; and finally succeeded in recalling to Eliot's recollection a tradition of a love-passage between Miss Sally and the pedagogue.

A little girl now came trotting in, with " grandmother's love, and a vial of her *mixture* for Mr. Eliot—good against camp-distemper and the like."

Eliot received the *mixture* as if he had all grandmother's faith in it, slipped a bright shilling into the child's hand for a keepsake, kissed her rosy cheek, and set her down with the children.

Visiters now began to throng. One man in a green old age, who had lost a leg at Bunker's Hill, came hobbling in, and clapping Eliot on the shoulder, said, "this is you, my boy! This is what I wanted to see your father's son a-doing: I'd go too, if the rascals had left me both my legs. Cheer up, widow, and thank the Lord you've got such a son to offer up to your country—the richer the gift, the better the giver, you know; but I don't wonder you feel kind o' qualmish at the thoughts of losing the lad. Come, Master Hale, can't you say something? A little bit of Greek, or Latin, or 'most any thing, to keep up their *sperits* at the last gasp, as it were."

"I was just going to observe, Major Avery, to Mrs. Lee, respecting our esteemed young friend, Mr. Eliot, that I, who have known him from the beginning, as it were, having taught him his alphabet, which may be said to be the first round of the ladder of learning (which he has mounted by my help), or rather (if you will allow me, ma'am, to mend my figure) the poles that support all the rounds; having had, as I observed, a primordial acquaintance with him, I can testify that he is worthy every honourable adjective in the language, and we have every reason to hope that his future tense will be as perfect as his past."

" Wheugh !" exclaimed the major, " a pretty long march you have had through that speech !"

The good schoolmaster, quite unruffled, proceeded to offer Eliot a time-worn Virgil ; and finished by expressing his hopes that " he would imitate Cæsar in maintaining his studies in the camp, and keep the scholar even-handed with the soldier."

Eliot charmed the old pedagogue, by assuring him that he should be more apt at imitating Cæsar's studies than his soldiership, and himself bestowed Virgil in his portmanteau.

A good lady now stepped forth, and seeming somewhat scandalized that, as she said, " no serious truth had been spoken at this peculiar season," she concluded a technical exhortation by giving Eliot a pair of stockings, into which she had wrought St. Paul's description of the gospel armour. " The Scripture," she feared, " did not often find its way to the camp ; and she thought a passage might be blessed, as a single kernel of wheat, even sowed among tares, sometimes produced its like."

Eliot thanked her, said " it was impossible to have too much of the best thing in the world ; but he hoped she would have less solicitude about him, when he assured her that his mother had found place for a pocket Bible in his portmanteau."

A meek-looking creature now stole up to Mrs. Lee, and putting a roll of closely-compressed lint into her hand, said, "tuck it in with his things, *Miss* Lee. Don't let it scare you—I trust he will dress other people's wounds, not his own, with it.—My! that will come natural to him. It's made from the shirt Mr. Eliot stripped from himself, and tore into bandages for my poor Sam, that time he was scalt. Mr. Eliot was a boy then, but he has the same heart now."

Mrs. Lee dropped a tear on the lint, as she stowed it away in the closely-packed portmanteau.

"There comes crazy Anny!" exclaimed the children; and a woman appeared at the door, scarcely past middle age, carrying in her hand a pole, on which she had tied thirteen strips of cloth of every colour, and stuck them over with white paper stars. Her face was pale and weatherworn, and her eye sunken, but brilliant with the wild flashing light that marks insanity. The moment her eye fell on Eliot, her imagination was excited —"Glory to the Lord!" she cried—"glory to the Lord! A leader hath come forth from among my people! Go on, Eliot Lee, and we will gird thee about with the prayers of the widow and the blessings of the childless! This is comfort! But you could not comfort me, Eliot Lee, though you spoke like an angel that time you was sent to me with the news the boys was shot. I remember you shed tears, and it seemed to me there was a hissing in here (she put her hand on her head) as they fell. My eyes were dry—I did not shed one tear, though the doctor bid me. I cried them all out when he (she advanced to Eliot, and lowered her voice), the grand officer in the reg'lars, you know, decoyed away my poor Susy, the prettiest and kindest creature that ever went into Westbrook meeting; fair as Bessie Lee, and far more plump and rosy—to be sure Susy was but a servant-girl, but—' she raised her voice to a shriek, " I shall never lay down my head in peace till they are all driven into the salt sea, where my Susy was buried."

" We'll drive them all there," said Eliot, soothingly, laying his hand on her arm—" every mother's son of them, Anny—now be quiet, and go home, Anny."

" Yes, sir—thank you, sir,—yes, sir !" said she, calmed and courtesying again and again—" oh, I forgot, Mr. Eliot !" she drew from her bosom an old rag, in which she had tied some kernels of butternuts—" give my duty to General Washington, and give him these butternut meats—it's all I have to send him—I did give him my best—they were nice boys, for all—wer'n't they, Bob and Pete ?" And whimpering and trailing her banner after her, the poor bereft creature left the house.

A loud official rap was heard at the door, and immediately recognised as the signal of the *min-*

ister's approach. We must claim indulgence while we linger for a moment with this reverend divine, for the race of which he was an honoured member is fast disappearing from our land. Peace be with them! Ill would they have brooked these days of unquestioned equality of rights, of anti-monopolies, of free publishing and freer thinking, of universal suffrage, of steam-engines, rail-roads, and spinning-jennies,—all indirect contrivances to raze those fortunate eminences, by mounting which little men became great, and lorded it over their fellows: but peace be with them! How should they have known (till it began to tremble under them) that the height on which they stood was an artificial, not a natural elevation. They preached equality in Heaven, but little thought it was the kingdom to come on earth. They were the electric chain, unconscious of the celestial fire they transmitted.

We would give them honour due; and to them belongs the honour of having been the zealous champions of their country's cause, and of having fought bravely with the weapons of the church militant.

Our good parson Wilson was an Apollo " in little;" being not more than five feet four in height, and perfectly well made,—a fact of which he betrayed the consciousness, by the exact adjustment of every article of his apparel, even to his long blue yarn stockings, drawn over the knee, and kept sleek by the well-turned leg, without the aid of garters. On entering Mrs. Lee's parlour, he gave his three-cornered hat, gold-headed cane, and buck-skin-gloves to little Fanny, who, with the rest of the children, had at his approach slunk into a cor-ner (they need not, for never was there a kinder heart than parson Wilson's, though somewhat in the position of vitality enclosed in a petrefaction), and then giving a general bow to the company, he went to the glass, took a comb from his waistcoat-pocket, and smoothed his hair to an equatorial line around his forehead ; he then crossed the room to Mrs. Lee with some commonplace consolation on his lips ; but the face of the mother spoke too elo-quently, and he was compelled to turn away, wipe his eyes, and clear his throat, before he could recover his official composure. "Mr. Eliot," he then began, "though a minister of the gospel of peace, I heartily approve your going forth in the present warfare, for surely it is lawful to defend that which is our own ; no man has a right to that for which he did not labour ; to cities which he built not ; to olive-yards and vineyards which he planted not."

"I don't know about olive-yards and vineyards," interposed the major, "never having seen such things ; but I'm thinking we can eat our corn and potatoes without their help that have neither planted nor gathered them."

The parson gave an acquiescent nod to the ma-jor's emendation of his text, and proceeded :—" I have wished, my young friend, to strengthen you in the righteous cause in which you are taking up arms ; and, to that end, besides the prayers which I shall daily offer for you and yours at the throne of divine grace, I have made up a book for you (here he tendered a package, large enough to fill half the portmanteau of our equestrian traveller), consisting of extracts selected from three thousand eight hundred and ninety-seven sermons, preached on the Sabbaths throughout my ministry of forty-eight years, besides occasional discourses for peace and war, thanksgivings and fasts, associations and funerals. As you will often be out of reach of preaching privileges, I have provided here a word in season for every occasion, which I trust you may find both teaching and refreshing after a weary day's service."

Eliot received the treasure with suitable expressions of gratitude. The good man continued : —" I could not, my friends, do this for another ; but you know that, speaking after the manner of men, we look upon this dear youth as the pride and glory of our society."

" And I'm thinking, reverend sir," said the major, with that tone of familiarity authorized by age (but stared at by the children), " I'm thinking you'll not be called on again for a like service ; for after Eliot Lee is gone, there's not another what you can raly call a *man* in the parish. To begin with yourself, reverend sir ; you've never been a fighting character, which I take to be, humanly speaking, a necessary part of a man; then there's myself, minus a leg; and Master Hale here, who —I respect you for all, Master Hale—never was born to be handy with a smarter weapon than a ferule; then comes blind Billy, and limping Harris, and, to bring up the rear, Deacon Allen and the doctor." Here the major chuckled: " They both say they would join the army if 'twas not as it is; but they have been dreadful near-sighted since the war broke out. That's all of 'mankind,' as you may say, that's left in the bounds of Westbrook. Oh, I forgot Kisel—poor Kisel! Truly, he seems to have been made up of leavings. Kisel would not make a bad soldier either, if it were one crack and done. He is brave at a go-off, but he can't bear the sight o' blood; and if he shoots as crooked as he talks, he'd be as like to shoot himself as anybody else. But sometimes the fellow's tongue does hit the mark in a kind of providential manner. By the Lor—Jiminy, I mean !—there he comes, on Granny Larkin's colt !"

The person in question now halted before Mrs. Lee's door, mounted on an unbroken, ragged, party-coloured animal, such as is called, in country phrase, " a wishing horse," evidently equipped for travelling. His bridle was compounded of alternate bits of rope and leather; a sheepskin served him for a saddle, behind which hung on either side a meal-bag, filled with all his worldly substance.

His own costume was in keeping; an over-gar-
ment, made of an old blanket, a sort of long
roundabout, was fastened at the waist with a
wampum belt, which, tied in many a fantasti-
cal knot, dangled below his knees; his under
garments were a pair of holyday leather breeches
and yarn stockings of deep red; a conical cap
composed of alternate bits of scarlet and blue cloth,
covered his head, and was drawn close over his
eyebrows.—Nature had reduced his brow to the
narrowest precincts; his face was concave; his
eyes sparkling, and in incessant motion; his nose
thin and sharp; a pale, clean-looking skin, and a
mouth with more of the characteristics of the brute
than the human animal, complete the portrait of
Kisel, who, leaping like a cat from his horse,
appeared at the door, screaming out, in a cracked
voice, " Ready, Misser Eliot ?"

While all were exchanging inquiring glances,
and the children whispering, "Hush, Kisel—don't
you see Dr. Wilson ?" Eliot, who comprehended
the strange apparition at a glance, came forward
and said—

" No, Kisel; I am not ready."

" Well, well—all same—Kisel can wait, and
Beauty too—hey !"

" No, no, Kisel," replied Eliot, kindly taking
the lad's hand, " you must not wait—you must give
this up, my good fellow."

" Give it up !—Diddle me if I do—no, I told

you that all the devils and angels to bargain should not stop me, no—you go, I go—that's it, hey !"

Here Major Avery, who sat near the door, his mouth wide open with amazement, burst into a hoarse laugh, at which Kisel, his eyes flashing fire, gave him a smart switch with his riding-whip (a willow wand) over the face. The good-humoured man, deeming the poor lad no subject for resentment, passed his hand over his face as if a moscheto had stung him, saying—"Well, now, Kisel, that was not fair, my boy ; I was only smiling that such a harlequin-looking thing as you should think of being waiter to Mr. Eliot. He might as well take a bat, or a woodpecker."

Eliot did not need his poor friend should be placed in this ludicrous aspect to strengthen the decision which he had already expressed to him ; and drawing him aside beyond the irritation of the major's gibes, he said—"It is impossible, Kisel— I cannot consent to your going with me."

"Can't, hey ! can't ! can't !"—and for a few moments the poor fellow hung his head, whimpering ; then suddenly elevating it, he cried, " Then I go 'out consent—I go, anyhow ;" and springing back to the door, he called out—" *Miss* Lee, hear me—Miss Bessie, you too, and you, parson Wilson, for I speak gospel. When I boy, all boys laugh at me, knock me here, kick there—who took my part ?—Misser Eliot, hey ! When they tied me to old Roan, Beauty's mother, head to tail, who licked the whole tote of 'em ?—Misser Eliot. I sick, nobody care I live or die—Misser Eliot stay by me all night. When everybody laugh at me, plague me, hate me, I wish me dead, Misser Eliot talk to me, make me feel good, .glad, make me warm here." He laid his hand on his bosom —" He gone, I can't live !—but I'll follow him—I'll be his dog, fetch, carry, lay down at his feet. S'pose he sick, Miss Lee ? everybody say I good in sickness—S'pose, Miss Bessie, he lie on the ground, bleeding, horses trampling, soldiers flying, hey !—I bind him up, bring water, carry him in my arms—if he die, I die too !"

The picture Kisel rudely sketched struck the imaginations of mother and daughter. They knew his devotion to Eliot, and that in emergencies he had gleams of shrewdness that seemed supernatural. They were too much absorbed in serious emotions to be susceptible of the ludicrous ; and both joined in earnestly entreating Eliot not to oppose Kisel's wishes. Dr. Wilson supported their intercession · by remarking, "that it seemed quite providential he should have been able to prepare for such an expedition." The major took off the edge of this argument by communicating what he had hastily ascertained, that Kisel had bartered away his patrimony for " Granny Larkin's" wishing horse, yclept Beauty ; but he added two suggestions that had much force with Eliot, particularly the last ; for if there was a virtue that had supremacy in his well-ordered character, it was humanity. " The lad, Mr. Lee," he said, " may be of use, after all. It takes a great many sorts of folks to make a world, and so to make up an army. There's a lack of hands in camp, and his may come in play. Kisel is keen at a sudden call—and besides," he added, in a lower voice to Eliot, " it's true what the *creatur* says, when you are gone he'll be good for nothing— like a vine when the tree it clung to is removed, withering on the ground. Say you'll take him, and we'll rig him out according to Gunter."

Thus beset, Eliot consented to what half an hour before had appeared to him absurd; and the major bestirring himself, from his own and Mrs. Lee's stores soon rectified Kisel's equipment in all important particulars, to suit either honourable character of volunteer soldier or volunteer attendant on Mr. Eliot Lee. This done, nothing remained but the customary devotional service, still performed by the village pastor on all extraordinary occasions. On this, Doctor Wilson's feelings overpowered his technicalities. His prayer, sublimed by the touching language of Scripture, melted the coldest heart, and raised the most dejected. After bestowing their farewell blessing the neighbours withdrew, all treasuring in their hearts some last word of kindness from Eliot Lee, long remembered, and often referred to.

The family were now left to a sacred service more informal, and far more intensely felt. Eliot, locking his mother and sister in his arms, and the little ones gathered around him, with manly faith commended them to God their Father; and receiving their last embraces, sprang on to his horse, conscious of nothing but confused sensations of grief, till having passed far beyond the bounds of Westbrook, he heard his companion lightly singing—" I cries for nobody, and nobody cries for Kisel !"

VOL. I.—5

CHAPTER VI.

"I do not, brother,
Infer, as if I thought my sister's state
Secure, without all doubt or controversy;
Yet, where an equal poise of hope and fear
Does arbitrate the event, my nature is,
That I incline to hope rather than fear."—MILTON.

Eliot Lee to his Mother.

"—— *Town,* 1778.

"I HAVE arrived thus far, my dear mother, on my journey; and, according to my promise, am beginning the correspondence which is to soften our separation.

"My spirits have been heavy. My anxious thoughts lingered with you, brooded over dear Bessie and the little troop, and dwelt on our home affairs.

"I feared Harris would neglect the thrashing, and the wheat might not turn out as well as we hoped; that the major might forget his promise about the husking bee; that the pumpkins might freeze in the loft (pray have them brought down, I forgot it!); that the cows might fail sooner than you expected; that the sheep might torment you.

In short, dear mother, the grief of parting seemed
to spread its shadows far and wide. If Master
Hale could have penetrated my mental processes,
e would have deemed his last admonition, to
deport myself in *thought*, word, and deed, like a
scholar, a soldier, and a gentleman, quite lost upon
me. I was an anxious wretch, and nothing else.
Poor Kisel did not serve as a tranquillizer. His
light wits were throwing off their fermentation, in
whistling, laughing, and soliloquizing: and this,
with *Beauty's* shambling gait, neither trot, canter,
nor pace, but something compounded of all, irritated my nerves. Never were horse and rider
better matched. Together, they make a fair cen-
taur; the animal not more than half a horse, and
Kisel not more than half a man; there is a
ludicrous correspondence between them; neither
vicious, but both unbreakable, and full of all manner of tricks.

"Our land at this moment teems with scenes
of moral and poetic interest. We made our first
stop at the little inn in R——. The landlord's
son was just setting off to join the quota to be sent
from that county. The father, a stout old man,
was trying to suppress his emotion by bustling
about, talking loud, whistling, hemming, and cough-
ing The mother, her tears dropping like rain,
was standing at the fire, feeling over and over again
the shirts she was airing for the knapsack. 'He's
our youngest,' whispered the old man to me, ' and

E 2

mammy is dreadful tender of him, poor boy!'
'Not mammy alone,' thought I, as the old man
turned away to brush off his starting tears. The
sisters were each putting some love-token, socks,
mittens, and nutcakes into the knapsack, which they
looked hardy enough to have shouldered, while one
poor girl sat with her face buried in her handkerchief, weeping most bitterly. The old man patted
her on the neck—' Come, Letty, cheer up !' said
he ; ' Jo may never have another chance to fight
for his country, and marrying can be done any day
in the year.' He turned to me with an explanatory
whisper ; ' 'Tis tough for all—Jo and Letty are
published, and we were to have the wedding thanks-
giving evening.'.

    " All this was rather too much for me to bear,
in addition to the load already pressing on my
heart; so without waiting for my horse to be fed,
I mounted him and proceeded.

    " My next stop was in H——. There the com-
pany had mustered on the green, in readiness to
begin their march. Some infirm old men, a few
young mothers, with babies in their arms, and all
the boys in the town, had gathered for the last farewell. The soldiers were resting on their muskets,
and the clergyman imploring the benediction of
Heaven on their heads. ' Can England,' thought
I, ' hope to subdue a country that sends forth its
defenders in such a spirit, with arms of such a

temper?' Oh, why does she not respect in her children the transmitted character of their fathers!

"I arrived at Mrs. Ashley's just as the family were sitting down to tea. She and the girls are in fine spirits, having recently received from the colonel accounts of some fortunate skirmishes with the British. The changed aspect of her once sumptuous tea-table at first shocked me; but my keen appetite (for the first time in my life, my dear mother, I had fasted all day) quite overcame my sensibilities; the honest pride with which my patriotic hostess told me she had converted all her table-cloths into shirts for her husband's men, and the complacency with which she commended her sage tea, magnified the virtues of her brown bread, and self-sweetened sweetmeats would have given a relish to coarser fare more coarsely served.

"I have been pondering on the character of our New-England people during my ride. The aspect of our society is quiet, and, to a cursory observer, it appears tame. We seem to have the plodding, safe, *self-preserving* virtues; to be industrious, frugal, provident, and cautious; but to want the enthusiasm that gives to life all its poetry and almost all its charms. But it is not so; there is a strong under-current. Let the individual or the people be roused by a motive that approves itself to the reasoning and religious mind, a fervid energy, an all-subduing enthusiasm bursts forth, not like an accidental and transient conflagration,

9*

but operating, like the elements, to great effects, and irresistibly. This enthusiasm, this central fire, is now at its height. It not only inflames the eloquence of the orator, kindles the heart of the soldier, the beacon-lights and strong defences of our land ; but it lights the temple of God, and burns on the family altar. The old man throws away his crutch ; the yeoman leaves the plough in tne half-turned furrow ; and the loving, quiet matron like you, my dear mother, lays aside her domestic anxieties, dispenses with her household comforts, and gives the God-speed to her sons to go forth and battle it for their country. ·The nature of the contest in which we are engaged illustrates my idea. Its sublimity is sometimes obscured by the extravagance of party zeal. We have not been goaded to resistance by oppression, nor fretted and chafed, with bits and collars, to madness ; but our sages, bold with the transmitted spirit of freedom, sown at broadcast by our Pilgrim fathers, have reflected on the past and calculated the future ; and coolly estimating the worth of independence and the right of self-government, are willing to hazard all in the hope of gaining all ; to sacrifice themselves for the prospective good of their children. This is the dignified resolve of thinking beings, not the angry impatience of overburdened animals.

" But good-night, dear mother. After this I shall have incidents, and not reflections merely, to send you. The pine-knot, by the light of which

I have written this, is just flickering its last flame. 'I cannot afford you a candle,' said my good hostess when she bade me good-night; 'we sold our tallow to purchase necessaries for the colonel's men—poor fellows, some of them are yet barefooted!'

" I shall enclose a line to Bessie—perhaps she will show it to you; but do not ask it of her. Tell dear Fan I shall remember her charge, and give the socks she knit to the first 'brave barefooted sol dier' I see. Sam must feed Steady for me; and dear little Hal must continue, as he has begun, to couple brother Eliot with the 'poor soldiers' in his prayers. Again farewell, dear mother. Your little Bible is before me; my eye rests on the few lines you traced on the title-page; and as I press my lips to them, they inspire holy resolutions. God grant I may not mistake their freshness for vigour. What I may be is uncertain; but I shall ever remain, as I am now, dearest mother,

" Your devoted son,

" ELIOT LEE."

Eliot found his letter to his sister a difficult task. He was to treat a malady, the existence of which the patient had never acknowledged to him. He wrote, effaced, and re-wrote, and finally sent the following :—

" My sweet sister Bessie, nothing has afflicted me so much in leaving home as parting from you.

I am inclined to believe there can be no stronger
nor tenderer affection than that of brother and
sister ; the sense of protection on one part, and
dependance on the other ; the sweet recollections
of childhood ; the unity of interest ; and the communion of memory and hope, blend their hearts
together into one existence. So it is with us—is
it not, my dear sister ? With me, certainly ; for
though, like most young men, I have had my
fancies, they have passed by like the summer
breeze, and left no trace of their passage. All the
love, liking (I cannot find a word to express the
essential volatility of the sentiment in my experience of it) that I have ever felt for all my
favourites, brown and fair, does not amount to one
thousandth part of the immutable affection that I
bear you, my dear sister. I speak only of my
own experience, Bessie, and, as I well know,
against the faith of the world. I should be told
that my fraternal love would pale in the fires of
another passion, as does a lamp at the shining of
the sun ; but I don't believe a word of it—do *you*,
Bessie ? I am not, my dear sister, playing the
inquisitor with you, but fearfully and awkwardly
enough approaching a subject on which I thought
it would be easier to write than to speak ; but I
find it cannot be easy to do that, in any mode,
which may pain you.

"I have neglected the duty I owed you; and
yet, perhaps, no vigilance could have prevented

the natural consequence of your intercourse with one of the most fascinating men in the world There, it is out!—and now I can write freely. I said I had neglected my duty; but I was not conscious of this till too late. The truth is, my mind has been so engrossed with political subjects, so harassed with importunate cravings and conflicting duties, that I was for a long time unobservant of what was passing under my eye. I awoke as from a dream, and found (or feared) that my sister's happiness was at stake; that she had given, and given to one unworthy, the irrequitable boon of her affections; irrequitable, but, thank Heaven, not irrecoverable. No, I do not believe one word of all the trumpery about incurable love. I will not adopt a faith, however old and prevailing, which calls in question our moral power to achieve any conquest over ourselves. For my own part, I do not think we have any power over our affections to give or withdraw them, or even to measure their amount. This may seem a startling assertion, and contradictory of what I have said above; but it is not. The sentiment I there alluded to is generated by accidental circumstances, is half illusion, unsustained by reason, unauthorized by realities—not the immortal love infused by Heaven and sustained by truth; but a disease very mortal and very curable, dear Bessie, believe me. Such a mind as yours, so pure, so elevated, has a self-rectifying power. You have felt the

E 3

influence of the delightful qualities which M——
undoubtedly possesses; and why should you not,
for who is more susceptible to grace and refine-
ment than yourself? Heaven has so arranged the
relations of affections and qualities, that, as I have
said above, we can neither give nor withhold our
love—the heart has no tenants at will. If M——
has assumed, or you have imputed to him qualities
which he does not possess, your affection will be
dissipated with the illusion. But if the spell still
remains unbroken, I entreat you, my dear sister,
not to waste your sensibility, the precious food
of life, the life of life, in moping melancholy.

> " 'Attach thee firmly (I quote from memory) to the virtu-
>   ous deeds
> And offices of love—to love itself,
> With all its vain and transient joys, sit loose.'

"I have long had a lurking distrust of M——. He
has acted too cautious a part in politics for a sound
heart. Let a man run the risk of hanging for it
either way; but if he have a spark of generosity, he
will be either a whole-souled whig or a loyal tory
in these times.

"I know what M—— has so often reiterated.
'He had a mother in England; all his friends were
on the royal side; and, on the other hand, his property was here, and might depend on the favour of
the rebels; and indeed, there was so much to be
said on both sides, that a man might well pause!'

There are moments in men's histories when none but cowards or knaves, or (worse than either) cold-blooded, selfish wretches, would *pause!*

"It is possible that I misjudge him; Heaven grant it! All that I *know* is, that he is in New-York no longer, *pausing*, but the aid of General Clinton. It is barely possible that he has written; letters are not transmitted with any security in these times; but why did he not speak before he went? why, up to the very hour of his departure (as my mother says, you know I was absent), did he continue a devotion which must end in suffering and disappointment to you? There is a vicious vanity and selfishness in this, most unmanly and detestable. Do not think, dearest Bessie, that I am anxious to prove him unworthy—Alas, alas! I was far too slow to believe him so; and I now only set before you these inevitable inferences from his conduct, in the hope that your illusion will sooner vanish, and you will the sooner recover your tranquillity.

"I am writing without a ray of light, except what comes from the embers on the hearth. Perhaps you will think I am in Egyptian mental darkness. No, Bessie, I must be clear-sighted when I have nothing in view but your honour and happiness. They shall ever be my care, even more than my own. But why do I separate that which is one and indivisible? Good-night, dear sister. Let me fancy you listening to me; your sweet eye fixed on me; no dejected nor averted look; your face beam-

ing, as I have often seen it, with the tenderness
so dangerous here, so safe in heaven; the hope so
often defeated here, there ever brightening, the
joy so transient here, there enduring!—Let me see
this blessed vision, and I shall sleep sweetly and
sweetly dream of home.

" Ever thine, Bessie,

" E. L "

Bessie read her brother's letter with mixed emotions. At first it called forth tenderness for him;
then she thought he judged Meredith precipitately,
harshly even; and after confirming herself in this
opinion, by thinking of him over and over again in
the false lights in which he had shown himself,
she said, " even Eliot allows that we can neither
give nor withhold our love ; then how is Jasper to
blame for not giving it to one so humble, so inferior
as I am? and how could I withhold mine ?" Poor
Bessie! it is a common trick of human nature to
snatch from an argument whatever coincides with
our own views, and leave the rest. " If," she continued in her reflections, " he had ever made any
declarations, or asked any confessions—but I gave
my whole heart unasked and silently." She could
have recalled passionate declarations in his eye,
prayers in his devotion ; but her love had the essential characteristics of true passion ; it was humble,
generous, and self-condemning.

CHAPTER VII.

' Si tout le monde vous ressembloit, un roman seroit bientôt
fini !"—MOLIERE.

NOVEMBER's leaden clouds and fitful gleams of
sunshine, coming like visitations of heaven-inspired
thoughts, and vanishing, alas ! like illusions, harmonized with the state of Bessie's mind. She was
much abroad, rambling alone over her favourite
haunts, and living over the dangerous past. This
was at least a present relief and solace; and her
mother, though she feared it might minister to the
morbid state of her child's feelings, had not the
resolution to interpose her authority to prevent it.
Bessie was one evening at twilight returning homeward by a road (if road that might be called which
was merely a horse-path) that communicated at the
distance of a mile and a half with the main road to
Boston. It led by the margin of a little brook,
through a pine wood that was just now powdered
over with a light snow. Meredith and Bessie had
always taken their way through this sequestered
wood in their walks and rides, going and returning;
not a step of it but was eloquent with some treasur-
ed word, some well-remembered emotion. Bessie
had seated herself on a fallen trunk, an accustomed
resting-place, and was looking at a bunch of ground
10

pine and wild periwinkles as if she were perusing
them; the sensations of happier hours had stolen
over her, the painful present and uncertain future
were forgotten, when she was roused from her
dreamy state by the trampling of an approaching
horse. Women, most women, are cowards on instinct. Bessie cast one glance backward, and saw
the horse was ridden by a person in a military dress.
A stranger in this private path was rather an alarm-
ing apparition, and she started homeward with hasty
steps. The rider mended his horse's pace, and
was soon even with her, and in another instant had
dismounted and exclaimed—"Bessie Lee!—It *is*
you, Bessie—I cannot be mistaken!"

Bessie smiled at this familiar salutation, and did
not refuse her hand to the stranger, who with eager
cordiality offered his; but not being in the least a
woman of the world, it was plain she explored his
face in vain for some recognisable feature.—"No,
you do not remember me—that is evident," he said,
with a tone of disappointment. "Is there not a
vestige, Bessie, of your old playmate, in the whis-
kered, weather-beaten personage before you?"

"Herbert Linwood!" she exclaimed, and a glow
of glad recognition mounted from her heart to her
cheek.

"Ah, thank you, Bessie, better late than never;
but it is sad to be forgotten. You are much less
changed than I, undoubtedly; but I should have
known you if nothing were unaltered save the

colour of your eye ; however, I have always worn
your likeness here," he gallantly added, putting his
hand to his heart, " and in truth, you are but the
opening bud expanded to the flower, while I have
undergone a change like the chestnut, from the
tassel to the bearded husk " Bessie soon began to
perceive familiar tones and expressions, and she
consoled Herbert with the assurance that it was
only her surprise, his growth, change of dress, &c.,
that prevented her from knowing him at once.
They soon passed to mutual inquiries, by which it
appeared that Herbert had come to Massachusetts
on military business. The visit to Westbrook was
a little episode of his own insertion. He was to
return in a few weeks to West Point, where he
was charmed to hear he should meet Eliot.

"I am cut off from my own family," he said,
" and really, I pine for a friend. I gather from
Belle's letters that my father is more and more es-
tranged from me. While he thought I was fighting on the losing side, and in peril of my head, his
generous spirit was placable ; but since the result
of our contest has become doubtful, even to him,
he has waxed hotter and hotter against me ; and if
we finally prevail, and prevail we must, he will
never forgive me."

"Oh, do not say so—he cannot be so unrelenting ; and if he were, Isabella can persuade him—
she can do any thing she pleases."

" Yes, a pretty potent person is that sister of

mine.   But when my father sets his foot down, the
devil—I beg your pardon Bessie, and Belle's too—
I mean his metal is of such a temper that an angel
could not bend him."

"Isabella is certainly the angel, not its oppo
site."

"Why yes, she is, God bless her! But yet,
Bessie, she is pretty well spiced with humanity.
If she were not, she would not be so attractive
to a certain friend of ours, who is merely human."

Bessie's heart beat quicker; she knew, or feared
she knew, what Herbert meant; and after a pause,
full of sensation to her, she ventured to ask " if he
heard often from New-York ?"

" Yes, we get rumours from there every day—
nothing very satisfactory.   Belle, in spite of her
toryism, is a loving sister, and writes me as often
as she can; but as the letters run the risk of being
read by friends and foes, they are about as domestic and private as if they were endited for Rivington's Gazette."

" Then," said Bessie, quite boldly, for she felt a
sensible relief, "you have no news to tell me ?"

" No—no, nothing official," he replied, with a
smile ; " Belle writes exultingly of Meredith having, since his return to New-York, come out on the
right side, as she calls it—and of my father's pleasure and pride in him, &c.   Of course she says not
a word of her own sentiments.   I hear from an
old friend of mine, who was brought in a prisoner

the other day, that Meredith has been devoted to
her ever since his return. They were always
lovers after an April-day fashion, you know, Bessie,
and I should not be surprised to hear of their engagement at any time—should you?"

Fortunately for poor Bessie, her hood sheltered
the rapid mutations of her cheek; resolution or
pride she had not, but a certain sense of maidenly
decorum came to her aid, and she faintly answered,
"No, I should not." If this were a slight departure from truth, every woman (every young one)
will forgive her, for it was a case of self-preservation. Linwood was so absorbed in the happiness
of being near her, of having her arm in his, that he
scarcely noticed how that arm trembled, and how
her voice faltered. He afterward recalled it.

Herbert's visit to the Lees was like a saint's
day to good Catholics after a long penance. He
had in his boyhood been a prime favourite with
Mrs. Lee—she was delighted to see him again, and
thought the man even more charming than the boy.
She made every effort to show off her hospitable
home to Linwood in its old aspect of abundance
and cheerfulness; and, in spite of war and actual
changes, she succeeded. She had the skilful housewife's gift "to make the worse appear the better,"—
far more difficult in housewifery than in metaphysics. Herbert enjoyed, to her kind heart's content,
the result of her efforts. The poor fellow's appetite had been so long mortified with the sorry fare

10*

of the American camp, that no Roman epicurean
ever relished the dainties of an emperor's table
(such as canaries' eyes and peacocks' brains) more
keenly than he did the plain but excellent provisions
at Lee farm; the incomparable bread and butter,
ham, apple-sauce, and cream, the nuts the children
cracked, and the sparkling cider they drew for him.
We are quite aware that a hero on a sentimental
visit should be indifferent to these gross matters,
but our friend Herbert was no hero, no romantic
abstraction, but a good, honest, natural fellow, compounded of body and spirit, each element bearing
its due proportion in the composition.

Bessie yielded to the influence of old associations,
and, as her mother thought, was more light-hearted,
more *herself*, than she had been for many a weary
month.   " After all," she said, anxiously revolving
the subject in her mind, "it may come out right
yet.   Bessie cannot help preferring Herbert Linwood, so good-humoured and open-hearted as he
is, to Meredith, with his studied elegance, his hollow phrases, and expressive looks. Herbert's heart
is in his hand; and hand and heart he'll not be too
proud to offer her; for he sees things in their true
lights, and not with the world's eye."

Mrs. Lee was delicate and prudent; but she
could not help intimating her own sentiments to
Bessie. From that moment a change came over
her. Her spirits vanished like the rosy hues from
the sunset clouds. Herbert wondered, but he had

no time to lose in speculation. He threw himself at Bessie's feet, and there poured out his tale of love and devotion. At first he received nothing in return but silence and tears ; and, when he became more importunate, broken protestations of her gratitude and ill desert ; which he misunderstood, and answered by declaring " she owed him no gratitude ; that he was but too bold to aspire to her, poor wretch of broken fortunes that he was ; but, please Heaven, he would mend them under her auspices."

She dared not put him off with pretences. She only wept, and said she had no heart to give ; and then left him, feeling much like some poor mariner, who, as he is joyously sailing into a long-desired port, is suddenly enveloped in impenetrable mist.

Herbert was not of a temper to remain tranquil in this position. He knew nothing of the " blessing promised to those that wait," for he had never waited for any thing; and he at once told his perplexities to Mrs. Lee, who, herself most grieved and mortified, communicated slight hints which, by furnishing a key to certain observations of his own, put him sufficiently in possession of the truth. Without again seeing Bessie, he left Westbrook with the common conviction of even common lovers in fresh disappointments, that there was no more happiness for him in this world.

Mrs. Lee uttered no word of expostulation or reproach to Bessie; but her sad looks, like the old mother's in the ballad, "gaed near to break her heart."

There are few greater trials to a tender-hearted, conscientious creature like Bessie Lee, than to defeat the hopes and disappoint the expectations of friends, by opposing those circumstances which, as it seems to them, will best promote our honour and happiness. "Eliot," said Bessie, in her secret meditations, "thinks I am weakly cherishing an unworthy passion—my mother believes that I have voluntarily thrown away my own advantage and happiness—thank Heaven, the wretchedness, as well as the fault, is all my own."

Many may condemn Bessie's unresisting weakness; but who will venture to graduate the scale of human virtue? to decide in a given case how much is bodily infirmity, and how much defect of resolution. Certain are we, that when fragility of constitution, tenderness of conscience, and susceptibility of heart, meet in one person, the sooner the trials of life are over the better.

CHAPTER VIII.

"A name which every wind to Heaven would bear,
    Which men to speak, and angels joy to hear."

ANOTHER letter from Eliot broke like a sunbeam through the monotonous clouds that hung
over the Lees.

"MY DEAREST MOTHER,—I arrived safely at
headquarters on the 22d. Colonel Ashley received me with open arms. He applauded my
resolution to join the army, and bestowed his curses
liberally (as is his wont on whatever displeases him)
on the young men who linger at home, while the
gallant spirits of France and Poland are crossing
the ocean to volunteer in our cause. He rubbed
his hands exultingly when I told him that it was
your self-originating decision that I should leave
you. 'The only son of your mother—that is, the
only one to speak of' (forgive him, Sam and Hal),
'and she a widow !' he exclaimed. 'Let them talk
about their Spartan mothers, half men and demi-
monsters; but look at our women-folks, as tender
and as timid of their broods as hens, and as bold
and self-sacrificing as martyrs! You come of a
good stock, my boy, and so I shall tell the gin'ral

He's old Virginia, my lad; and looks well to blood in man and horse.'

"The next morning he called, his kind heart raying out through his jolly face, to present me to General Washington. If ever I go into battle, which Heaven of its loving mercy grant, I pray my heart may not thump as it did when I approached the mean little habitation, now the residence of our noble leader. 'You tremble, Eliot,' said my colonel, as we reached the door-step. 'I don't wonder—I always feel my joints give a little when I go before him. I venerate him next to the Deity; but it is not easy to get used to him as you do to other men.'

"When we entered, the general was writing. If Sam wishes to know whether my courage returned when I was actually in his presence, tell him I then forgot myself—forgot I had an impression to make. The general requested us to be seated while he finished his despatches. The copies were before him, all in his own hand. 'Every *t* crossed, and every *i* dotted,' whispered the colonel, pointing to the papers. 'He's godlike in that; he finishes off little things as completely as great.' I could not but smile at the comparison, though it was both striking and just. When the general had finished, and had read the letters of introduction from Governor Hancock and Mr. Adams, which I presented, 'You see, sir,' said my kind patron 'that my young friend here is calculating to enter

the army; I'll answer for him, he'll prove good
and true; up to the mark, as his father Sam Lee
was before him. He, that is, Sam Lee, and I, *fit*
side by side in the French war; I was no flincher,
you know, sir, and he was as brave as Julius Cæsar,
Sam was; so I think my friend Eliot here has a
pretty considerable claim.'

"'But, my good sir,' said the general, 'you
know we are contending against hereditary claims.'

"'That's true, sir; and thank the Lord, he can
stand on his own ground; he shot one of the first
guns at Lexington, and got pretty well *peppered*
too, though he was a lad then, with a face as smooth
as the palm of my hand.'

"'Something too much of this,' thought I; and I
attempted to stop my trumpeter's mouth by saying
'I had no claims on the score of the affair at Lexington; that my being there was accidental, and
I fought on instinct.'

"'Ah, my boy,' said the colonel, determined to
tell his tale out, 'you may say that—there's no
courage like that that comes by *natur*, gin'ral; he
stood within two feet of me, as straight as a tombstone, when a spent ball bounding near him, he
caught it in his hands just as if he'd been playing wicket, and said, " you may throw down your
bat, my boys, I've caught you out!"—was not that
metal ?'

" General Washington's countenance relaxed as
the colonel proceeded (I ventured a side glance),

and at the conclusion he gave two or three em-
phatic and pleased nods; but his grave aspect
returned immediately, and he said, as I thought, in
a most frigid manner, 'the request, Mr. Lee, of my
friends of Massachusetts, that you may receive
a commission in the service, deserves attention ;
Colonel Ashley is a substantial voucher for your
personal merit. Are you aware, sir, that a post of
honour in our army involves arduous labour, hardships, and self-denial? Do you know the actual
condition of our officers—that their pay is in ar-
rears, and their private resources exhausted ? There
are among them men who have bravely served
their country from the beginning of this contest ;
gentlemen who have not a change of linen ; to
whom I have even been compelled to deny, because I had not the power to divert them from
their original destination, the coarse clothes provided for the soldiers. This is an affecting, but a
true view of our actual condition. Should the
Almighty prosper our cause, as, if we are true to
ourselves, he assuredly will, these matters will im-
prove ; but I have no lure to hold out to you, no
encouragement but the sense of performing your
duty to your country. Perhaps, Mr. Lee, you
would prefer to reflect further, before you assume
new obligations ?'

 " ' Not a moment, sir. I came here determined
to serve my country at any post you should assign
me. If a command is given me, I shall be grate-

ful for it : if not, I shall enter the ranks as a private soldier.'

" General Washington exchanged glances with the colonel, that implied approbation of my resolution, but not one syllable dropped of encouragement as to the commission; and it being evident that he had no leisure to protract our audience, we took our leave.

" I confess I came away rather crest-fallen. I am not such a puppy, my dear mother, as to suppose my single arm of much consequence to my country, but I felt an agreeable, perhaps an exaggerated consciousness, that I deserved—not applause, but some token of encouragement. However, the colonel said this was his way; ' he *never* disappoints an expectation, seldom authorizes one.'

" ' Is he cold-hearted ?' I asked.

" ' The Lord forgive you ! Eliot,' he replied. ' Cold-hearted !—No, his heat does not go off by flashes, but keeps the furnace hot out of which the pure gold comes. Lads never think there is any fire unless they see the sparks and hear the roar.'

" ' But, sir,' said I, ' I believe there is a very common impression that General Washington is of a reserved, cold temperament—'

" ' The devil take common impressions. They are made on sand, and are both false and fleeting. Wait, Eliot—you are true metal, and I will venture your impressions when you shall know our noble commander better. Cold, egad,' he half muttered to himself; 'where the deuse, then, has the heat come from that has cemented our army together, and kept their spirits up when their fingers and toes were freezing?'"

———

"Give me joy, my dear mother; a kiss, Bessie; a good hug, my dear little sisters; and a huzza, boys! General Washington has sent me a lieutenant's commission, and a particularly kind note with it. So, it appears, that while I was thinking him so lukewarm to my application, he lost no time in transmitting it to Congress, and enforcing it by his recommendation. Our camp is all bustle. Soldiers, just trained and fit for service, are departing, their term of enlistment having expired. The new quotas are coming in, raw, undisciplined troops. The general preserves a calm, unaltered mien; but his officers fret and fume in private, and say that nothing effective will ever be achieved while Congress permits these short enlistments."

———

Thanks to you, dear mother; my funds have enabled me to purchase a uniform. I have just tried it on. I wish you could all see me in it. 'Every woman is at heart a rake,' says Pope; that every man is at heart a coxcomb, is just about as true. My new dress will lose its holyday gloss before we meet again, but the freshness of my love for you will never be dimmed, my dear mother; for Bessie, and for all the little band, whose bright faces are even now before my swimming eyes.

" Yours devotedly,

" Eliot Lee.

" P. S.—My poor jack-o'-lantern, Kisel, is of course of no use to me, neither does he give me much trouble. He is a sort of mountebank among the soldiers, merry himself and making others merry. If he is a benefactor who makes two blades of grass grow where but one grew before, Kisel certainly is, while he produces smiles where rugged toil and want have stamped a scowl of discontent."

In this letter to his mother, Eliot enclosed one to Bessie; reiterating even more forcibly and tenderly what he had before said. It served no purpose but to aggravate her self-reproaches.

F 2

CHAPTER IX.

" Come not near our fairy queen."

BEFORE mid-winter, Linwood joined Eliot Lee
at West Point, and the young men renewed their
acquaintance on the footing of friends.   There was
just that degree of similarity and difference between them that inspires mutual confidence and be-
gets interest.   Herbert, with characteristic frankness, told the story of his love, disappointment and
all. Eliot felt a true sympathy for his friend, whose
deserts he thought would so well have harmonized
with Bessie's advantage and happiness; but this
feeling was subordinate to his keen anxiety for his
sister.   This anxiety was not appeased by intelligence from home.   Letters were rare blessings
in those days—scarcely to him blessings.   His
mother wrote about every thing but Bessie, and his
sister's letters were brief and vague, and most un-
satisfactory.   The winter, however, passed rapidly
away.   Though in winter quarters, he had incessant occupation; and the exciting novelty of military
life, with the deep interest of the times, to an ardent
and patriotic spirit, kept every feeling on the strain.

Eliot had that intimate acquaintance with nature
that makes one look upon and love all its aspects,

as upon the changing expressions of a friend's face; and as that most interests us in its soul-fraught seriousness, so he delighted even more in the wild gleams of beauty that are shot over the winter landscape, than in all its summer wealth. To eyes like his, faithful ministers to the soul, the scenery of West Point was a perpetual banquet.

Nature, in our spring-time, as we all know (especially in this blessed year of our Lord 1835), rises as slowly and reluctantly from her long winter's sleep as any other sluggard. On looking back to our hero's spring at West Point, we find she must have been at her work earlier than is her wont; for April was not far gone when Eliot, after looking in vain for Linwood to accompany him, sauntered into the woods, where the buds were swelling and the rills gushing. At first his pleasure was marred by his friend not being with him, and he now for the first time called to mind Linwood's frequent and unexplained absences for the last few days. Linwood was so essentially a social being, that Eliot's curiosity was naturally excited by this sudden manifestation of a love of solitude and secrecy.

He however pursued his way; and having reached the cascade which is now the resort of holyday visiters, he forgot his friend. The soil under his feet, released from the iron grasp of winter, was soft and spongy, and the tokens of spring were around him like the first mellow smile of dawn. The rills that spring together like laugh-

11*

ing children just out of school (we borrow the obvious simile from a poetic child), and at their junction form " the cascade," were then filled to the brim from their just unsealed fountains. Eliot followed the streamlet where it pursues its head-long course, dancing, singing, and shouting, as it flings itself over the rocks, as if it spurned their cold and stern companionship, and was impatiently running away from the leafless woods to a holyday in a summer region. He forced his way through the obstructions that impeded his descent, and was standing on a jutting point which the stream again divided, looking up at the snow-white and feathery water, as he caught a glimpse of it here and there through the intersecting branches of hemlocks, and wondering why it was that he instinctively infused his own nature into the outward world : why the rocks seemed to him to look sternly on the frolicking stream that capered over them, and the fresh white blossoms of the early flowering shrubs seemed to yearn with a kindred spirit towards it, when his speculations were broken by human voices mingling with the sound of the water-fall. He looked in the direction whence they came, and fancied he saw a white dress. It might be the cascade, for that at a little distance did not look unlike a white robe floating over the gray rocks, but it might be a fair lady's gown, and that was a sight rare enough to provoke the curiosity of a young knight-errant. So Eliot, quickening

his footsteps, reachéd the point where the streamlet
ceases its din, and steals loiteringly through the
deep narrow.glen, now called Washington's Valley. He had pressed on unwittingly, for he was
now within a few yards of two persons on whom
he would not voluntarily have intruded. One was
a lady (a lady certainly, for a well-practised ear
can graduate the degree of refinement by a single
tone of the voice), the other party to the *tête-à-tête*
was his truant friend Linwood. The lady was
seated with her back towards Eliot, in a grape-vine
that hung, a sylvan swing, from the trees; and
Linwood, his face also turned from Eliot, was
decking his companion's pretty hair with wood
anemones, and (ominous it was when Herbert Linwood made sentimental sallies) saying very soft
and pretty things of their starry eyes. Eliot was
making a quiet retreat, when, to his utter con-
sternation, a lady on his right, till then unseen
by him, addressed him, saying, " she believed she
had the pleasure of speaking to Lieutenant Lee."
Eliot bowed; whereupon she added, " that she was
sure, from Captain Linwood's description, that it
must be his friend. Captain Linwood is there
with my sister, you perceive," she continued; " and
as he is our friend, and you are his, you will do us
the favour to go home and take tea with us."

By this time the *tête-à-tête* party, though sufficiently absorbed in each other, was aroused, and
both turning their heads, perceived Eliot. The
lady said nothing; Linwood looked disconcerted,

and merely nodded without speaking to his friend.
The lady rose, and with a spirited step walked towards a farmhouse on the margin of the Hudson,
the only tenement of this secluded and most lovely
little glen.   Linwood followed her, and seemed earnestly addressing her in a low voice.   By this time
Eliot had sufficiently recovered his senses to remember that the farmhouse, which was visible
from West Point, had been pointed out to him as
the temporary residence of a Mr. Grenville Ruthven.
Mr. Ruthven was a native of Virginia, who some
years before had, in consequence of pecuniary mis-
fortunes, removed to New-York, where he had held
an office under the king till the commencement of
the war.   His only son was in the English navy, and
the father was suspected of being at heart a royalist.   His political partialities, however, were not so
strong but that they might be deferred to prudence :
so he took her counsel, and retired with his wife
and two daughters to this safe nook on the Hudson, till the troubles should be overpast.

Eliot could not be insensible to the friendly and
volunteered greeting of his pretty lady patroness,
and a social pleasure was never more inviting than
now when he was famishing for it; but it was so
manifest that his presence was any thing but desi-
rable to Linwood and his companion, that he was
making his acknowledgments and turning away,
when the young lady, declaring she would not take
" no" for an answer, called out, " Stop, Helen—
pray, stop—come back, Captain Linwood, and intro-

duce us regularly to your friend ; he is so ceremonious that he will not go on with an acquaintance that is not begun in due form."

Thus compelled, Miss Ruthven stopped and submitted gracefully to an introduction, which Linwood was in fact at the moment urging, and she peremptorily refusing.

" Now, here we are, just at our own door," said Miss Charlotte Ruthven to Eliot, "and you must positively come in and take tea with us." Eliot still hesitated.

" Why, in the name of wonder, should you not ?" said Linwood, who appeared just coming to himself.

" You must come with us," said Miss Ruthven, for the first time speaking, " and let me show your friend how very magnanimous I can be."

" Indeed, you must not refuse us," urged Miss Charlotte.

" I cannot," replied Eliot, gallantly, " though it is not very flattering to begin an acquaintance with testing the magnanimity of your sister."

Helen Ruthven bowed, smiled, and coloured; and at the first opportunity said to Linwood, " your friend is certainly the most civilized of all the eastern savages I have yet seen, and, as *your* friend, I will try to tolerate him." She soon, however, seemed to forget his presence, and to forget every thing else, in an absorbing and half-whispered conversation with Linwood, interrupted only by singing snatches of sentimental songs, accompanying herself on the piano, and giving them the expressive application that eloquent eyes can give. In the meanwhile Eliot was left to Miss Charlotte, a commonplace, frank, and good-humoured person, particularly well pleased at being relieved from the *rôle* she had lately played, a cipher in a trio.

Mr. and Mrs. Ruthven made their appearance with the tea-service. Mr. Ruthven, though verging towards sixty, was still in the unimpaired vigour of manhood, and was marked by the general characteristics, physical and moral, of a Virginian : the lofty stature, strong and well-built frame, the open brow, and expression of nobleness and kindness of disposition, and a certain something, not vanity, nor pride, nor in the least approaching to superciliousness, but a certain happy sense of the superiority, not of the individual, but of the great mass of which he is a component part.

His wife, unhappily, was not of this noble stock. She was of French descent, and a native of one of our cities. At sixteen, with but a modicum of beauty, and coquetry enough for half her sex, she succeeded, Mr. Ruthven being then a widower, in making him commit the folly of marrying her, after a six weeks' acquaintance. She was still in the prime of life, and as impatient as a caged bird of her country seclusion, or, as she called it, imprisonment, where her daughters were losing every opportunity of achieving what she considered the chief end of a woman's life.

Aware of her eldest daughter's propensity to convert acquaintances into lovers, and looking down upon all rebels as most unprofitable suiters, she had sedulously guarded against any intercourse with the officers at the Point.

Of late, she had begun to despair of a favourable change in their position; and Miss Ruthven having accidentally renewed an old acquaintance with Herbert Linwood, her mother encouraged his visits from that admirable policy of maternal manœuvrers, which wisely keeps a *pis-aller* in reserve. Helen Ruthven was one of those persons, most uncomfortable in domestic life, who profess always to require an object (which means something out of a woman's natural, safe, and quiet orbit) on which to exhaust their engrossing and exacting desires. Mr. Ruthven felt there was a very sudden change in his domestic atmosphere, and though it was as incomprehensible to him as a change in the weather, he enjoyed it without asking or caring for an explanation. Always hospitably inclined, he was charmed with Linwood's good-fellowship; and while he discussed a favourite dish, obtained with infinite trouble, or drained a bottle of Madeira with him, he was as unobservant of his wife's tactics and his daughters' coquetries as the eagle is of the *modus operandi* of the mole. And all the while, and in his presence, Helen was lavishing her flatteries with infinite finesse and grace. Her words, glances, tones of voice even, might have turned a steadier head than Linwood's. Her father, good,

confiding man, was not suspicious, but vexed when
she called his companion away, just, as he said,
" as they were beginning to enjoy themselves," to
scramble over frozen ground or look at a wintry
prospect! or to play over, for the fortieth time, a
trumpery song.   Helen, however, would throw her
arms around her father's neck, kiss him into good-
humour, and carry her point; that is, secure the un-
divided attentions of Herbert Linwood.   Matters
were at this point, after a fortnight's intercourse,
when Eliot entered upon the scene; and, though
his friend Miss Charlotte kept up an even flow of
talk, before the evening was over he had taken
some very accurate observations.

When they took their leave, and twice after they
had shut the outer door, Helen called Linwood
back for some last word that seemed to mean
nothing, and yet clearly meant that her heart went
with him : and then

> So fondly she bade him adieu,
> It seemed that she bade him return."

The young men had a long, dark, and at first
rather an unsocial walk.   Both were thinking of
the same subject, and both were embarrassed by it.
Linwood, after whipping his boots for ten minutes,
said, " Hang it, Eliot, we may as well speak out;
I suppose you think it deused queer that I said
nothing to you of my visits to the Ruthvens ?"

" Why, yes, Linwood—to speak out frankly,
I do."

"Well, it is, I confess it. At first my silence
was accidental—no, that is not plummet and line
truth; for from the first I had a sort of a fear—no,
not fear, but a sheepish feeling, that you might
think the pleasure I took in visiting the Ruthvens
quite inconsistent with the misery I had seemed to
feel, and, by Heavens, did feel, to my heart's core,
about that affair at Westbrook."

" No, Linwood—whatever else I may doubt, 1
never shall doubt your sincerity."

" But my constancy you do ?" Eliot made no
reply, and Linwood proceeded : " Upon my soul, I
have not the slightest idea of falling in love with
either of these girls, but I find it exceedingly pleasant to go there. To tell the truth, Eliot, I am
wretched without the society of womankind; Adam
was a good sensible fellow not to find even Paradise tolerable without them. I knew the Ruthvens in New-York: I believe they like me the
better, apostate as they consider me, for belonging
to a tory family; and looking upon me, as they must,
as a diseased branch from a sound root, they certainly are very kind to me, especially the old gentleman—a fine old fellow, is he not ?"

" Yes—I liked him particularly."

" And madame is piquant and agreeable, and
very polite to me; and the girls, of course, are
pleased to have their hermitage enlivened by an
old acquaintance."

Linwood's slender artifice in saying " the girls,"

12

when it was apparent that Miss Ruthven was the magnet, operated like the subtlety of a child, betraying what he would fain conceal. Without appearing to perceive the truth, Eliot said, "Miss Ruthven seems to restrict her hospitality to *old* acquaintance. It was manifest that she did not voluntarily extend it to me."

"No, she did not. Helen Ruthven's heart is in her hand, and she makes no secret of her antipathy to a rebel—*per se* a rebel; however, her likes and dislikes are both harmless—she is only the more attractive for them."

Herbert had not been the first to mention Helen Ruthven; he seemed now well enough pleased to dwell upon the subject. "How did you like her singing, Eliot?" he asked.

"Why, pretty well; she sings with expression."

"Does she not? infinite!—and then what an accompaniment are those brilliant eyes of hers."

"With their speechless messages, Linwood?" Linwood merely hemmed in reply, and Eliot added, "Do you like the expression of her mouth?"

"No, not entirely—there is a little spice of the devil about her mouth; but when you are well acquainted with her you don't perceive it."

"If you are undergoing a blinding process," thought Eliot. When the friends arrived at their quarters, and separated for the night, Linwood asked and Eliot gave a promise to repeat his visit the next evening to the glen.

CHAPTER X.

"He is a good man.
"Have you heard any imputation to the contrary?"

FROM this period Linwood was every day at the glen, and Eliot as often as his very strict performance of his duties permitted. He was charmed with the warm-hearted hospitality of Mr. Ruthven, and not quite insensible to the evident partiality of Miss Charlotte. She did not pass the vestibule of his heart to the holy of holies, but in the vestibule (of even the best of hearts) vanity is apt to lurk. If Eliot therefore was not insensible to the favour of Miss Charlotte, an every-day character, Linwood could not be expected to resist the dazzling influence of her potent sister. A more wary youth might have been scorched in the focus of her charms. Helen Ruthven was some three or four years older than Linwood,—a great advantage when the subject to be practised on combines simplicity and credulity with inexperience. Without being beautiful, by the help of grace and versatility, and artful adaptation of the aids and artifices of the toilet, Miss Ruthven produced the effect of beauty. Never was there a more skilful manager of the blandishments of her sex. She knew how to in-

tuse into a glance "thoughts that breathe,"—how
to play off those flatteries that create an atmosphere of perfume and beauty,—how to make her
presence felt as the soul of life, and life in her absence a dreary day of nothingness. She had little
true sensibility or generosity (they go together); but
selecting a single object on which to lavish her
feeling, like a shallow stream compressed into a
narrow channel, it made great show and noise.
Eliot stood on disenchanted ground; and, while
looking on the real shape, was compelled to see
his credulous and impulsive friend becoming from
day to day more and more inthralled by the false
semblance. " Is man's heart," he asked himself,
" a mere surface, over which one shadow chaseth
another?" No. But men's hearts have different
depths. In some, like Eliot Lee's (who was destined
to love once and for ever), love strikes a deep and
ineradicable root; interweaves itself with the very
fibres of life, and becomes a portion of the undying
soul.

In other circumstances Eliot would have obeyed
his impulses, and endeavoured to dissolve the spell
for his friend; but he was deterred by the consciousness of disappointment that his sister was so soon
superseded, and by his secret wish that Linwood
should remain free till a more auspicious day should
rectify all mischances. Happily, Providence sometimes interposes to do that for us which we neglect
to do for ourselves.

As has been said, Linwood devoted every leisure hour to Helen Ruthven. Sometimes accompanied by Charlotte and Eliot, but oftener without them, they visited the almost unattainable heights, the springs and waterfalls, in the neighbourhood of West Point, now so well known to summer travellers that we have no apology for lingering to describe them. They scaled the coal-black summits of the "Devil's Peak;" went as far heavenward as the highest height of the " Crow's Nest;" visited " Bull-Hill, Butter-Hill, and Break-neck,"—places that must have been named long before our day of classic, heathenish, picturesque, and most ambitious christening of this new world.

Helen Ruthven did not affect this scrambling "thorough bush, thorough brier," through streamlet, snow, and mud, from a pure love of nature. Oh, no, simple reader! but because at her home in the glen there was but one parlour—there, from morning till bedtime, sat her father—there, of course, must sit her mother ; and Miss Ruthven's charms, like those of other conjurers, depended for their success on being exercised within a magic circle, within which no observer might come. She seemed to live and breathe alone for Herbert Linwood. A hundred times he was on the point of offering the devotion of his life to her, when the image of his long-loved Bessie Lee rose before him, and, like the timely intervention of the divinities of the ancient creed, saved him from impending danger.

12*

This could not last much longer. On each successive occasion the image was less vivid, and must soon cease to be effective.

Spring was advancing, and active military operations were about to commence. A British sloop-of-war had come up the river, and lay at anchor in Haverstraw Bay. Simultaneously with the appearance of this vessel there was a manifest change in the spirits of the family at the glen—a fall in their mercury. Though they were still kind, their reception of our friends ceased to be cordial, and they were no longer urged, or even asked, to repeat their visits. Charlotte, who, like her father, was warm and true-hearted, ventured to intimate that this change of manner did not originate in any diminution of friendliness; but, save this, there was no approach to an explanation; and Eliot ceased to pay visits that, it was obvious, were no longer acceptable. The mystery, as he thought, was explained, when they incidentally learned that Captain Ruthven, the only son of their friend, was an officer on board the vessel anchored in Haverstraw Bay. This solution did not satisfy Linwood. "How, in Heaven's name," he asked, "should that affect their intercourse with us? It might, to be sure, agitate them; but, upon my word, I don't believe they even know it;" and, in the simplicity of his heart, he forthwith set off to give them information of the fact. Mr. Ruthven told him, frankly and at once, that he was already aware of it,—and

Helen scrawled on a music-book which lay before them, "Do you remember Hamlet? ' ten thousand brothers !' " What she exactly meant was not plain; but he guessed her intimation to be, that ten thousand brothers and their love were not to be weighed against him. Notwithstanding this kind intimation, he saw her thenceforth unfrequently. If he called, she was not at home; if she made an appointment with him, she sent him some plausible excuse for not keeping it; and if they met, she was silent and abstracted, and no longer kept up a show of the passion that a few weeks before had inspired her words, looks, and movements. Herbert was not destined to be one of love's few martyrs; and he was fast reverting to a sound state, only retarded by the mystery in which the affair was still involved. Since the beginning of his intercourse with the family, his Sunday evenings had been invariably spent at the glen; and now he received a note from Miss Ruthven (not, as had been her wont, crossed and double-crossed), containing two lines, saying her father was ill, and as she was obliged to attend him, she regretted to beg Mr. Linwood to omit his usual Sunday evening visit! Linwood had a lurking suspicion—he was just beginning to suspect—that this was a mere pretext; and he resolved to go to the glen, ostensibly to inquire after Mr. Ruthven, but really to satisfy his doubts. It was early in the evening when he reached there. The cheerful light that usually shot forth its welcome from the parlour window was gone—all was darkness. " I was a rascal to distrust her !" thought Linwood, and he hastened on, fearing good Mr. Ruthven was extremely ill. As he approached the house he perceived that, for the first time, the window-shutters were closed, and that a bright light gleamed through their crevices. He put his hand on the latch of the door to open it, as was his custom, without rapping; but no longer, as if instinct with the hospitality of the house, did it yield to his touch. It was bolted ! He hesitated for a moment whether to knock for admittance, and endeavour to satisfy his curiosity, or to return as wise as he came. His delicacy decided on the latter course ; and he was turning away, when a sudden gust of wind blew open one of the rickety blinds, and instinctively he looked through the window, and for a moment was riveted by the scene disclosed within. Mr. Ruthven sat at a table on which were bottles of wine, olives, oranges, and other most rare luxuries. Beside him sat a young man—his younger self. Linwood did not need a second glance to assure him this was Captain Ruthven. On a stool at her brother's feet sat Charlotte, her arm lovingly resting on his knee. Mrs. Ruthven was at the other extremity of the table, examining, with enraptured eye, caps, feathers, and flowers, which, as appeared from the boxes and cords beside her, had just been opened.

But the parties that fixed Linwood's attention were Helen Ruthven and a very handsome young man, who was leaning over her chair while she was playing on the piano, and bestowing on him those wondrous glances that Linwood had verily believed never met an eye but his ! What a sudden disenchantment was that ! Linwood's blood rushed to his head. He stood as if he were transfixed, till a sudden movement within recalling him to himself, he sprang from the steps and retraced his way up the hill-side :—the spell that had wellnigh bound him to Helen Ruthven was broken for ever. No man likes to be duped,—no man likes to feel how much his own vanity has had to do with preparing the trap that insnared him. Linwood, after revolving the past, after looking back upon the lures and deceptions that had been practised upon him, after comparing his passion for Helen Ruthven with his sentiments for Bessie Lee, came to the consoling conclusion that he had never loved Miss Ruthven. He was right—and that night, for the first time in many weeks, he fell asleep thinking of Bessie Lee.

On the following morning Linwood confided to Eliot the *denœument* of his little romance. Eliot was rejoiced that his friend's illusion should be dispelled in any mode. After some discussion of the matter, they came to the natural conclusion that a clandestine intercourse had been for some time maintained by the family at the glen with

the strangers on board the sloop-of-war, and tha'
there were reasons for shaking Linwood and Eliot
off more serious than Linwood's flirtation having
been superseded by a fresher and more exciting
one.

In the course of the morning Eliot, in returning
from a ride, at a sudden turn in the road came
upon General Washington and Mr. Ruthven, who
had just met. Eliot was making his passing
salutation when General Washington said, " Stop
a moment, Mr. Lee, we will ride in together."
While Eliot paused, he heard Mr. Ruthven say,
" You will not disappoint me, general,—Wednesday evening, and a quiet hour—not with hat and
whip in hand, but time enough to drink a fair
bottle of 'Helicon,' as poor Randolph used to
call it—there are but two left, and we shall ne'er
look upon its like again. Wednesday evening—
remember." General Washington assented, and
the parties were separating, when Mr. Ruthven,
in his cordial manner, stretched out his hand to
Eliot, saying, " My dear fellow, I should ask you
too ; but the general and I are old friends, and I
want a little talk with him, by ourselves, of old
times. Besides, no man, minus forty, must have a
drop of my 'Helicon;' but come down soon and
see the girls,—they are Helicon enough for you
young fellows, hey ?"

As Mr. Ruthven rode away, " There goes," said
General Washington, " as true-hearted a man as

ever breathed. We were born on neighbouring plantations. Our fathers and grandfathers were friends. Our hearts were cemented in our youth, or at least in my youth, for he is much my elder, but his is a heart always fusible. Poor man, he has had much ill-luck in life; but the worst, and the worst, let me tell you, my young friend, that can befall any man, was an ill-starred marriage. His wife is the daughter of a good-for-nothing Frenchman; bad blood, Mr. Lee. The children show the cross—I beg Miss Charlotte's pardon, she is a nice girl, fair Virginia stock; but Miss Helen is—very like her mother. The son I do not know; but his fighting against his country is *primâ facie* evidence against him."

The conversation then diverged to other topics. There was in Eliot that union of good sense, keen intelligence, manliness, and modesty, that excited Washington's esteem, and drew him out; and Eliot had the happiness, for a half hour, of hearing him whom of all men he most honoured, talk freely, and of assuring himself that this great man did not, as was sometimes said of him,

> " A wilful stillness entertain,
> With purpose to be dress'd in an opinion
> Of wisdom;"

but that his taciturnity was the result of profound thought, anxiously employed on the most serious subjects.

Late in the afternoon of the same day, Linwood

received a note from Helen Ruthven, enclosing one
to General Washington, of which, after entreating
him to deliver it immediately, she thus explained
the purport.   " It contains a simple request to your
mighty commander-in-chief, to permit me to visit
my brother on board his vessel. I know that
Washington's heart is as hard as Pharaoh's, and as
unrelenting as Brutus's ; still it is not, it cannot be
in man to refuse such a request to the daughter of
an old friend. Do, dear, kind Linwood, urge it for
me, and win the everlasting gratitude of your unworthy but always devoted friend, HELEN RUTH-
VEN."

" *Urge* it !" exclaimed Linwood, as he finished
the note, " urge General Washington ! I should as
soon think of urging the sun to go backward or
forward ; but I'll present it for you, my 'devoted
friend, Helen,' and in merely doing that my heart
will be in my mouth."

He obtained an audience. General Washington read the note, and turning to Linwood, asked
him if he knew its purport.

" Yes, sir," replied Linwood, " and I cannot,"
he ventured to add, " but hope you will find it
fitting to gratify a desire so natural."

" Perfectly natural ; Miss Ruthven tells me she
has not seen her brother for four years."   Linwood
felt his honest blood rush to his face at this flat
falsehood from his friend Helen. Washington
perceived the suffusion and misinterpreted it.

" You think it a hard case, Mr. Linwood ; it is so, but there are many hard cases in this unnatural war. It grieves me to refuse Helen Ruthven— the child of my good friend." He passed his eye again over the note, and there was an expression of displeasure and contempt in his curling lip as he read such expressions as the following : " I cannot be disappointed, for I am addressing one who unites all virtues, whose mercy even surpasses his justice."—" I write on my knees to him who is the minister of Providence, dispensing good and evil, light and blessing, with a word." General Washington threw down the note, saying, " Miss Ruthven should remember that flattery corrupts the giver as well as the receiver. I have no choice in this matter. We have an inflexible rule prohibiting all intercourse with the enemy."

He then wrote a concise reply, which Linwood sent to the lady in a blank envelope.

" Ah !" thought Helen Ruthven, as she opened it, " this would not have been blank three weeks ago, *mais n'importe*. Mr. Herbert Linwood, you may run free now ; I have nobler prey in my toils." She unsealed General Washington's note, and after glancing her eye over it, she tore it into fragments and dispersed it to the winds, exclaiming, " I'll risk my life to carry my point; and if I do, I'll humble you, and have a glorious revenge !"

She spent a sleepless night in contriving, revol- ving, and dismissing plans on which, as she fancied, the destiny of the nation hung, and, what was far more important in her eyes, Helen Ruthven's destiny. She at last adopted the boldest that had occurred, and which, from being the boldest, best suited her dauntless temper.

The next morning, Tuesday, with her mother's aid and applause, she effected her preparations ; and having fortunately learned, during her residence on the river, to row and manage a boat, she embarked alone in a little skiff, and stealing out of a nook near the glen, she rowed into the current and dropped down the river. She did not expect to escape obser-vation, for though the encampment did not command a view of the Hudson, there were sentinels posted at points that overlooked it, and batteries that com-manded its passage. But rightly calculating on the general humanity that governed our people, she had no apprehensions they would fire on a defence-less woman, and very little fear that they would think it worth while to pursue her, to prevent that which she dared to do before their eyes and in the face of day.

Her calculations proved just. The sentinels levelled their guns at her, in token not to proceed ; and she in return dropped her head, raised her hands deprecatingly, and passed on unmolested.

At a short distance below the Point there is a remarkable spot, scooped out by nature in the rocky bank, always beautiful, and now a conse-crated shrine—a " Mecca of the mind." On the memorable morning of Miss Ruthven's enterprise, the welcome beams of the spring sun, as he rose in the heavens, casting behind him a soft veil of light clouds, shone on the gray rocks, freshening herbage, and still disrobed trees of this lovely recess. From crevices in the perpendicular rocks that wall up the table-land above, hung a sylvan canopy; cedars, studded with their blue berries, wild raspberries, and wild rose-bushes; and each moist and sunny nook was gemmed with violets and wild geraniums. The harmonies of nature's orchestra were the only and the fitting sounds in this seclusion: the early wooing of the birds; the water from the fountains of the heights, that, filtering through the rocks, dropped from ledge to ledge with the regularity of a water-clock; the ripple of the waves as they broke on the rocky points of the shore, or softly kissed its pebbly margin; and the voice of the tiny stream, that, gliding down a dark, deep, and almost hidden channel in the rocks, disappeared, and welled up again in the centre of the turfy slope, stole over it, and trickled down the lower ledge of granite to the river. Tradition has named this little green shelf on the rocks " Kosciusko's Garden;" but as no traces have been discovered of any other than nature's plantings, it was probably merely his favourite retreat, and as such is a monument of his taste and love of nature.

The spring is now enclosed in a marble basin,

and inscribed with his name who then lay extended beside it : Kosciusko, the patriot of his own country, the friend of ours, the philanthropist of all, the enemy only of those aliens from the human family who are the tyrants of their kind. An unopen book lay beside him, while, gazing up through the willows that drooped over the fountain, he perused that surpassing book of nature, informed by the spirit and written by the finger of God—a Book of revelations of his wisdom, and power, and goodness.

Suddenly his musings were disturbed by approaching footsteps; and looking up, he saw Linwood and Eliot winding down the steep pathway between the piled rocks. He had scarcely exchanged salutations with them, when the little boat in which Helen Ruthven was embarked shot out from behind the dark ledge that bounded their upward view of the river. They sprang forward to the very edge of the sloping ground. Helen Ruthven would most gladly have escaped their observation, but that she perceived was impossible ; and making the very best of her dilemma, she tossed her head exultingly, and waved her handkerchief. The young men instinctively returned her greeting. "A gallant creature, by Heaven !" exclaimed the Pole ; " God speed you, my girl !" And when Linwood told him who she was, and her enterprise, so far as he thought fit to disclose it,

he reiterated, " Again then, I say, God speed her !
The sweetest affections of nature should be free
as this gushing rill, that the rocks and the earth can't
keep back ; I am glad when they throw off the
shackles imposed by the cruel but inevitable laws
of war." They continued to gaze after the boat
till it turned and disappeared with the river in its
winding passage through the mountains.

On Wednesday morning it appeared that the
sloop-of-war had changed her position, and approached as nearly to West Point as was possible
without coming within the range of its guns. " I
am convinced," said Linwood to Eliot, taking up
the thread of conversation where they had dropped
it the day before, " I am convinced there is a
plot brewing."

" I am apprehensive of it too. Our obvious
duty, Linwood, is to go to General Washington, and
tell him all we know of the Ruthvens."

" My service to you !—no, he is the wariest of
human beings, and has grounds enough for suspicion without our prompting. Can't he put this
and that together—the old man's pressing invitation, Helen's flight, and the movement of the
vessel ?"

" Ah, if his suspicions were excited, as ours are,
by previous circumstances, these would suffice ;
but he has entire confidence in his old friend ; he
is uninformed of the strong tory predilections of
the whole family ; and, though he does not like

Helen Ruthven, he has no conception of what we have tolerable proof, that she has the talents of a regular bred French intriguer. Besides, as the fact of your having seen those men at the glen proves the practicability of their visiting it again, the general should certainly be apprized of it."

"No, Eliot, I'll not consent to it—this is my game, and I must control it. It is a violation of the Arab bread-and-salt rule, to communicate that which was obtained by our friendly intimacy at the glen."

"I think you are wrong, Linwood; it is a case where an inferior obligation should yield to a superior one."

"I don't comprehend your metaphysical reasoning, Eliot; I govern myself by the obligations I feel."

"By the dictates of your conscience, my dear fellow? so do I; therefore I shall go immediately to the general, with or without you."

"Not with me—no, I'll not tell him what I know, that's flat; and as to being questioned and cross-questioned by him, heavens and earth! when he but bends his awful brow upon me, I feel as if my heart were turning inside out. No, I'll not go near him. Why can't we write an anonymous letter?"

"I do not like anonymous letters—my course appears plain to me, so good morning to you."

"One moment, Eliot—remember, not a word of what I saw through the window at the glen."

"Certainly not, if you insist." Eliot then went to the general's markee, and was told he would see him in two hours. Eliot returned at the precise moment, and was admitted. "You are punctual, Mr. Lee," said the commander, "and I thank you for it. A young man should be as exact in military life as the play requires the lover to be! 'he should not break a part of the thousandth part of a minute.' Your business, sir?"

Eliot was beginning to disclose it, when they were interrupted by a servant, who handed General Washington a note. A single involuntary glance at the superscription assured Eliot it was from Linwood. General Washington opened it, and looked first for the signature, as one naturally does at receiving a letter in an unknown hand. "Anonymous!" he said; and refolding without reading a word of it, he lighted it in a candle, still burning on the desk where he had been sealing letters, and suffered it to consume; saying, "This is the way I now serve all anonymous letters, Mr. Lee. Men in public life are liable to receive many such communications, and to have their minds disturbed, and sometimes poisoned, by them. They are the resort of the cowardly or the malignant. An honest man will sustain by his name what he thinks proper to communicate."

"There is no rule of universal application to the

versatile mind of man," thought Eliot, and his heart
burned to justify his friend; when the general reminding him they had no time to lose, he proceeded concisely to state his apprehensions and their
grounds. Washington listened to him without in-
terruption, but not without an appalling change of
countenance. "I have heard you through, Mr.
Lee," he said; "your apprehensions are perhaps
natural; at any rate, I thank you for frankly communicating them to me ; but, be assured, your suspicions have no foundation. Do you think such
vile treachery could be plotted by a Virginian, my
neighbour, my friend of thirty years, my father's
friend, when all the grievous trials of this war
have not produced a single traitor? No, no, Mr.
Lee, I would venture my life—my country, on the
cast of Ruthven's integrity. If I do not lightly
give my confidence, I do not lightly withdraw it;
and once withdrawn it is never restored."

Eliot left Washington's presence, half convinced himself that his suspicions were unfounded. It never occurred to Washington or to Eliot
that there might be a conspiracy without Mr.
Ruthven being a party to it, and the supposition
that he was so invalidated all the evidences of a
plot.

In the afternoon Kisel asked leave to avail himself of a permit which Eliot had obtained for him,
to go on the opposite side of the river to a little
brook, whence he had often brought a mess of

trout for the officers' table; for our friend Kisel was skilled in the craft of angling, and might have served Cruikshank for an illustration of Johnson's definition of the word, " a fishing-rod, with a bait at one end and a fool at the other;" but happily, as it proved, our fool had some " subtlety in his simplicity." Eliot gave him the permission, with directions to row up to the glen when he returned, and await him there.

Eliot determined to go to the glen, and station himself on the margin of the river, where, in case (a chance that seemed to him at least possible) of the approach of an enemy's boat, he should descry it in time to give Washington warning. He went in search of Linwood, to ask him to accompany him; but Linwood was nowhere to be found. He deliberated whether to communicate his apprehensions to some other officer. The confidence the general had manifested had nearly dissipated his apprehensions, and he feared to do what might appear like officiousness, or like a distrust of Washington's prudence; that virtue, which, to remain, as it then was, the bulwark of his country's safety, must continue unsuspected.

Eliot in his anxiety had reached the glen while it was yet daylight; and, careful to escape observation, he stole along the little strip of pebbly beach where a mimic bay sets in, and seated himself on a pile of rocks, the extreme point of a hill that descends abruptly to the Hudson. Here the river, hemmed in by the curvatures of the mountains, has the appearance of a lake ; for the passage is so narrow and winding through which it forces its way, that the eye scarcely detects it. Eliot for a while forgot the tediousness of his watch in looking around him. The mountains at the entrance of the Hudson into the highlands, which stand like giant sentinels jealously guarding the narrow portal, appeared, whence he saw them, like a magnificent framework to a beautiful picture. An April shower had just passed over, and the mist was rolling away like the soft folds of a curtain from the village of Newburgh, which looked like the abode of all " country contentments," as the setting sun shone cheerily on its gentle slopes and white houses, contrasting it with the stern features of the mountains. Far in the distance, the Catskills, belted by clouds, appeared as if their blue heads were suspended in the atmosphere and mingling with the sky, from which an eye familiar with their beautiful outline could alone distinguish them. But the foreground of his picture was most interesting to Eliot; and as his eye again fell on the little glen sleeping in the silvery arms of the rills between which it lies—" can this place," he thought, " so steeped in nature's loveliness, so enshrined in her temple, be the abode of treachery ! It has been of heartlessness, coquetry, duplicity—ah, there is no power in nature, in the outward world, to convert the bad—blessings it has; blessings manifold, for the good."

The spirit of man, alone in nature's solitudes, is an instrument which she manages at will; and Eliot, in his deepening seriousness and anxiety, felt himself answering to her changing aspect. The young foliage of the well-wooded little knoll that rises over the glen had looked fresh and feathery, and as bright as an infant awaking to happy conscious-ness; but as the sun withdrew its beams, it ap-peared as dreary as if it had parted from a smiling friend. And when the last gleams of day had stolen up the side of the Crow's Nest, shot over the summit of Break-neck, flushed the clouds and dis-appeared, and the wavy lines and natural terraces beyond Cold Spring, and the mass of rocks and pines of Constitution Island, were wrapped in sad-coloured uniform, Eliot shrunk from the influence of the general desolateness, and became impatient of his voluntary watch.

One after another the kindly-beaming home lights shot forth from hill and valley, and Eliot's eye catching that which flashed from Mr. Ruth-ven's window, he determined on a reconnoitre; and passing in front of the house he saw Washington and his host seated at a table, served with wine and nuts, but none of those tropical luxuries that had been manifestly brought to the glen by the stranger-guests from the sloop-of-war. Eliot's heart gladdened at seeing the friends en-

joying one of those smooth and delicious passages
that sometimes vary the ruggedest path of life.
That expression of repelling and immoveable grav-
ity, that look of tension (with him the bow was always strained) that characterized Washington's
face, had vanished like a cloud; and it now se-
renely reflected the social affections (bright and
gentle spirits !) that, for the time, mastered his per-
plexing cares. He was retracing the period of his
boyhood ; a period, however cloudy in its passage,
always bright when surveyed over the shoulder.
He recalled his first field-sports, in which Ruthven
had been his companion and teacher ; and they
laughingly reviewed many an accident by flood
and field. " No wonder," thought Eliot, as in passing he glanced at Ruthven's honest, jocund face ;
" no wonder Washington would not distrust him !"

Eliot returned to his post. The stars had come
out, and looked down coldly and dimly through a
hazy atmosphere. The night was becoming obscure. A mist was rising ; and shortly after a
heavy fog covered the surface of the river. Eliot
wondered that Kisel had not made his appearance ;
for, desultory as the fellow was, he was as true to
his master as the magnet to the pole. Darkness
is a wonderful magnifier of apprehended danger ;
and, as it deepened, Eliot felt as if enemies were
approaching from every quarter. Listening in-
tently, he heard a distant sound of oars. He was
all ear. " Thank Heaven !" he exclaimed, " it is

Kisel—a single pair of oars, and his plashy irregular din !" In a few moments he was discernible; and nearing the shore, he jumped upon the rock where Eliot stood, crying out exultingly, " I've dodged 'em, hey !"

" Softly, Kisel ; who have you dodged ?"

" Them red birds in their borrowed feathers Cheat me ? No. Can't I tell them that chops, and reaps, and mows, and thrashes, from them that only handles a sword or a gun, let 'em put on what ev'yday clothes they will ?"

" Tell me, Kisel, plainly and quickly, what you mean."

A command from Eliot, uttered in a tone of even slight displeasure, had a marvellous effect in steadying Kisel's wits ; and he answered with tolerable clearness and precision :—" I was cutting 'cross lots before sunset with a mess of trout, long as my arm—shiners ! when I stumbled on a bunch of fellows squatted 'mong high bushes. They held me by the leg, and said they'd come down with provisions for Square Ruthven's folks; and they had not got a pass, and so must wait for nightfall ; and they'd have me stay and guide 'em across, for they knew they might ground at low water if they did not get the right track. I mistrusted 'em. I knew by their tongues they came from below; and so I cried, and told 'em I should get a whipping if I didn't get home afore sundown; and one of 'em held a pistol to my head, loaded, primed, and

14

cocked, and told me he'd shoot my brains out if
I didn't do as he bid me. 'Lo'd o' massy!' says I,
'don't shoot—'twon't do any good, for I hant got no
brains, hey!'"

"Never mind what you said or they said; what
did you do?"

"I didn't do nothing. They held me fast till
night; and then they pushed their boat out of a
kind o' hiding-place, and come alongside mine,
and put me into it, and told me to pilot 'em. You
know that sandy strip a bit off t'other shore? I
knew my boat would swim over it like a cob,—and
I guessed they'd swamp, and they did; diddle me
if they didn't!"

"Are they there now?"

"There! not if they've the wit of sucking turkeys. The river there is not deep enough to drown
a dead dog, and they might jump in and pull the
boat out."

A slight westerly breeze was now rising,
which lifted and wafted the fog so that half the
width of the river was suddenly unveiled, and
Eliot descried a boat making towards the glen.
"By Heaven! there they are!" he exclaimed;
"follow me, Kisel;" and without entering the
house, he ran to the stable close by. Fortunately,
often having had occasion, during his visits at the
glen, to bestow his own horse, he was familiar
with the "whereabouts;" and in one instant General Washington's charger was bridled and at the

door, held by Kisel; while Eliot rushed into the house, and in ten words communicated the danger and the means of escape. General Washington said not a word till, as he sprang on the horse, Ruthven, on whose astounded mind the truth dawned, exclaimed, "I am innocent." He replied, "I believe you."

Washington immediately galloped up the steep imbowered road to the Point. Eliot hesitated for a moment, doubting whether to attempt a retreat or remain where he was, when Mr. Ruthven grasped his arm, exclaiming, "Stay, for God's sake, Mr. Lee; stay, and witness to my innocence." The imploring agony with which he spoke would have persuaded a more inflexible person than Eliot Lee. In truth, there was little use in attempting to fly, for the footsteps of the party were already heard approaching the house. They entered, five armed men, and were laying their hands on Eliot, when Mr. Ruthven's frantic gestures, and his shouts of "He's safe—he's safe—he's escaped ye!" revealed to them the truth; and they perceived what in their impetuosity they had over looked, that they held an unknown young man in their grasp instead of the priceless Washington! Deep were the oaths they swore as they dispersed to search the premises, all excepting one young man, whose arm Mr. Ruthven had grasped, and to whom he said, "Harry, you've ruined me—you've made me a traitor in the eyes of Washington—the basest traitor ! He said, God bless him ! that he believed me innocent; but he will not when he reflects that it was I who invited him—who pressed him to come here this evening—the conspiracy seems evident—undeniable ! Oh, Harry, Harry, you and your mad sister have ruined me !"

The young man seemed deeply affected by his father's emotion. He attempted to justify himself on the plea that he dared not set his filial feeling against the importance of ending the war by a single stroke; but this plea neither convinced nor consoled his father. Young Ruthven's associates soon returned, having abandoned their search, and announced the necessity of their immediate return to the boat. "You must go with us, sir," said Ruthven to his father ; " for, blameless as you are, you will be treated by the rebels as guilty of treason."

" By Heaven, Harry, I'll not go. I had rather die a thousand deaths—on the gallows, if I must— I'll not budge a foot."

" He must go—there is no alternative—you must aid me," said young Ruthven to his companions. They advanced to seize his father. " Off— off !" he cried, struggling against them. " I'll not go a living man."

Eliot interposed ; and addressing himself to young Ruthven, said, " Believe me, sir, you are mistaking your duty. Your father's good name must be dearer to you than his life : and his good name is blasted for ever if in these circumstances he leaves here. But his life is in no danger —none whatever—he is in the hands of his friend, and that friend the most generous, as well as just, of all human beings. You misunderstand the temper of General Washington, if you think he would believe your father guilty of the vilest treachery without damning proof." Young Ruthven was more than half convinced by Eliot, and his companions had by this time become impatient of delay. Their spirit had gone with the hope that inspired their enterprise, and they were now only anxious to secure a retreat to their vessel. They had some little debate among themselves whether they should make Eliot prisoner; but, on young Ruthven's suggestion that Lieutenant Lee's testimony might be important to his father, they consented to leave him—one of them expressing in a whisper the prevailing sentiment, "We should feel sheepish enough to gain but a paltry knight when we expected a checkmate by our move."

In a few moments more they were off; but not till young Ruthven had vainly tried to get a kind parting word from his father. "No, Harry," he said, " I'll not forgive you—I can't; you've put my honour in jeopardy—no, never ;" and as his son turned sorrowfully away, he added, " Never, Hal, till this cursed war is at an end."

Early next morning Eliot Lee requested an audience of Washington, and was immediately

14*

admitted, and most cordially received. "Thank God, my dear young friend," he said, "you are safe, and here. I sent repeatedly to your lodgings last night, and hearing nothing, I have been exceedingly anxious. Satisfy me on one point, and then tell me what happened after my forced retreat. I trust in Heaven this affair is not bruited."

Eliot assured him he had not spoken of it to a human being—not even to Linwood ; and that he had enjoined strict secrecy on Kisel, on whose obedience he could rely.

" Thank you—thank you, Mr. Lee," said Washington, with a warmth startling from him, "I should have expected this from you—the generous devotion of youth, and the coolness and prudence of ripe age—a rare union."

Such words from him who *never* flattered and rarely praised, might well, as they did, make the blood gush from the heart to the cheeks. " I am most grateful for this approbation, sir," said Eliot.

" Grateful ! Would to Heaven I had some return to make for the immense favour you have done me, beside words; but the importance of keeping the affair secret precludes all other return. I think it will not transpire from the enemy,—they are not like to publish a baffled enterprise. I am most particularly pleased that you went alone to the glen. In this instance I almost agree with Cardinal de Retz, who says, ' he held men in greater esteem for what they forbore to do than for what they did.' I now see where I erred yesterday. It did not occur to me that there could be a plot without my friend being accessory to it. I did not err in trusting him. This war has cost me dear; but, thank Heaven, it has not shaken, but fortified, my confidence in human virtue!" Washington then proceeded to inquire into the occurrences at the glen after he left there, and ended with giving Eliot a note to deliver to Mr. Ruthven, which proved a healing balm to the good man's wounds.

Our revolutionary contest, by placing men in new relations, often exhibited in new force and beauty the ties that bind together the human family. Sometimes, it is true, they were lightly snapped asunder, but oftener they manifested an all-resisting force, and a union that, as in some chymical combinations, no test could dissolve.

CHAPTER XI.

"Our will we can command. The effects of our actions we cannot foresee."—MONTAIGNE.

Herbert Linwood to his Sister.

"*July* 30*th*, 1779.

"DEAREST BELLE,—I write under the inspiration of the agreeable consciousness that my letter may pass under the sublime eye of your commander-in-chief, or be scanned and sifted by his underlings. I wish to Heaven that, without endangering your bright orbs, I could infuse some retributive virtue into my ink to strike them blind. But the deuse take them. I defy their oversight. I am not discreet enough to be trusted with military or political secrets, and therefore, like Hotspur's Kate, I can betray none. As to my own private affairs, though I do not flatter myself I have attained a moral eminence which I may challenge the world to survey, yet I'll expose nothing to you, dear Belle, whose opinion I care more for than that of king, lords, and commons, which the whole world may not know without your loving brother being dishonoured thereby: so, on in my usual ' streak o' lightning style,' with facts and feelings.

" You have before this seen the official account of our successful attack on Stony Point, and have doubtless been favoured with the additional light of Rivington's comments, your veritable editor. These thralls of party editors ! The light they emit is like that of conjurers, intended to produce false impressions.

" Do not imagine I am going to send you a regular report of the battle. With all due deference to your superior mental faculties, my dear, you are but a woman, and these concernments of 'vile guns' must for ever remain mysteries to you. But, Belle, I'll give you the romance of the affair—'thy vocation, Hal.'

" My friend Eliot Lee has a vein of quixotism, that reminds me of the inflammable gas I have seen issuing from a cool healthy spring. Doctor Kissam, you know, used to say every man had his insanity. Eliot's appears in his affection for a half-witted follower, one Kisel; the oddest fellow in this world. His life is a series of consecutive accidents, of good and bad *luck*.

" On the 10th he had been out on the other side of the river, *vagrantizing* in his usual fashion, and returning late to his little boat, and, as we suspect, having fallen asleep, he drifted ashore at Stony Point. There he came upon the fort, and a string of trout (which he is seldom without) serving him as a passport, he was admitted within the walls. His simplicity, unique and inimitable, shielded him from suspicion, and a certain inspiration which seems always to come direct from Heaven at the moment of his necessity, saved him from betraying the fact that he belonged to our army, and he was suffered to depart in peace. The observations he made (he is often acute) were of course communicated to his master, and by him made available to our enterprise. Eliot and myself were among the volunteers. He, profiting by Kisel's hints, guided us safely through some 'sloughs of despond.' With all his skill, we had a killing scramble over pathless mountains, and through treacherous swamps, under a burning sun, the mercury ranging somewhere between one and two hundred, so that my sal volatile blood seemed to have exhaled in vapour, and my poor body to be a burning coal, whose next state would be ashes.

"Our General Wayne (you will understand his temper from his *nom de guerre*, 'mad Anthony') had ordered us to advance with unloaded muskets and fixed bayonets. He was above all things anxious to avoid an accidental discharge, which might alarm the garrison. At eight in the evening we were within a mile and a half of the fort, and there the detachment halted; while Wayne, with Eliot and some other officers, went to reconnoitre. They had approached within gunshot of the works, when poor Kisel, who away from Eliot is like an unweaned child, and who had been all day wandering in search of him, suddenly emerged from the wood, and in a paroxysm of joy discharged his musket. Wayne sprang forward, and would have transfixed him with his bayonet, had not Eliot thrown himself before Kisel, and turned aside Wayne's arm : some angry words followed, but it ended in the general leaving Kisel to be managed by Eliot's discretion. The general's displeasure, however, against Eliot, did not subside at once.

" When the moment for attack came, I felt my-self shivering, not with fear, no, '*franchement*' (as our old teacher Dubois used to say on the few occasions when he meant to tell the truth), *franchement*, not with fear, but with the recollection of my father's last words to me. The uncertain chances of a fierce contest were before me, and my father's *curse* rung in my ears like the voices that turn-ed the poor wretches in the Arabian tale into stone. Once in the fight, it was forgotten ; all men are bulldogs then, and think of nothing past or to come.

" They opened a tremendous fire upon us ; it was the dead of night, Belle, and rather a solemn time, I assure you. Our commander was wounded by a musket ball: he fell, and instantly rising on one knee, he cried, ' Forward, my brave boys, for-ward.' The gallant shout gave us a new impulse ; and we rushed forward, while Eliot Lee, with that singular blending of cool courage and generosity which marks him, paused and assisted the general's aid in bearing him on, in compliance with the wish

he had expressed (believing himself mortally
wounded), that he might die in the fort. Thank
God, he survived ; and being as magnanimous as he
is brave, he reported to the commander-in-chief
Eliot's gallantry and good conduct throughout the
whole affair, and particularly dwelt on the aid he
had given him, after having received from him in-
jurious epithets. In consequence of all this, Eliot
is advanced to the rank of captain. Luck is a
lord, Belle; I would fain have distinguished myself,
but I merely, like the rest, performed my part
honourably, for which I received the thanks of
General Washington, and got my name blazoned
in the report to Congress.

"I hear that Helen Ruthven is dashing away in
New-York, not, as I expected, after her romantic
departure hence, as the honourable Mrs. O——.
Well! all kind vestals guard her! Heaven knows
she needs their vigilance. Rumour says, too, that
you are shortly to vow allegiance to my royalist
friend. God bless you! my dear sister. If it
were true (alas ! nothing is more false) that matches
are made in Heaven, I know *who* would be your
liege-lord. Another match there was, that in my
boyhood—my boyhood! my youth, my maturity,
I believed Heaven had surely made. It is a musty
proverb, that. Farewell, Belle ; kiss my dear mother for me, and tell her I would not have her, like
the old Scotch woman, pray for our side, 'right or
wrong,' but let her pray for the right side, and then

her poor son will be sure to prosper. Oh, would that I could, without violating my duty to my country, throw myself at my father's feet. His loyalty is not truer to King George, than mine to him.

"Dearest Belle, may Heaven reunite us all.

"Yours, H. LINWOOD.

"P. S.—Kind love, don't forge it, to Rose."

A day or two after Herbert's letter was despatched, Eliot received a summons from Washington; and on his appearing before him, the general said, "I have important business to be transacted in New-York, Captain Lee. I have despatches to transmit to Sir Henry Clinton. My agent must be intrusted with discretionary powers. An expedition to New-York, even with the protection of a flag of truce, is hazardous. The intervening country is infested with outlaws, who respect no civilized usages. My emissary must be both intrepid and prudent. I have therefore selected you. Will you accept the mission?"

"Most gratefully, sir—but—"

"But what? if you have scruples, name them."

"None in the world, sir; on my own account I should be most happy, but I should be still happier if the office might be assigned to Linwood. It would afford him the opportunity he pines for, of seeing his family."

"That is a reason, if there were no other, why Captain Linwood should not go. Some embarrassment might arise. Your friend has not the coolness essential in exigencies."

Eliot well knew that Washington was not a man with whom to bandy arguments, and he at once declared himself ready to discharge, to the best of his ability, whatever duty should be imposed on him; and it was settled that he should depart as soon as his instructions could be made out.

Eliot soon after met Linwood, and communicated his intended expedition. "You are always under a lucky star," said Linwood; "I would have given all I am worth for this appointment."

"And you certainly should have it if it were mine to bestow."

"I do not doubt it, not in the least; but is it not hard? Eliot, I am such a light-hearted wretch, for the most part, that you really have no conception how miserable my father's displeasure makes me. I don't understand how it is. The laws of Heaven are harmonious, and certainly my conscience acquits me, yet I suffer most cruelly for my breach of filial obedience. If I could but see my father, eye to ye, I am sure I could persuade him to recall that curse, that rings in my ears even now like a death-knell. Oh, one half hour in New-York would be my salvation! The sight of Belle and my mother would be heaven to me! Don't laugh at me, Eliot," he continued, wiping his eyes, "I am a calf when I think of them all."

"Laugh at you, Linwood! I could cry with

joy if I could give my place to you ; as it is, I must hasten my preparations. I have obtained leave to take Kisel with me."

"Kisel! heaven forefend, Eliot. Do you know what ridicule such a valet-de-place as Kisel will call down on your head from those lordly British officers ?"

"Yes, I have thought of that, and it would be sheer affectation to pretend to be indifferent to it; but I can bear it. Providence has cast Kisel upon my protection, and if I leave him he will be sure to run his witless head into some scrape that will give me ten times more trouble than his attendance."

"Well, as you please; you gentle people are always wilful." After a few moments' thoughtful silence, he added, "How long before you start, Eliot ?"

"The general said it might be two hours before my instructions and passports were made out."

"It will be dark then, and," added Linwood, after a keen survey of the heavens, "I think, very dark."

"Like enough; but that is not so very agreeable a prospect as one would infer from the tone of your voice."

"Pardon me, my dear fellow; it was New-York I was thinking of, and not any inconvenience you might encounter from the obscurity of the night Your passports are not made out ?"

"Not yet."

"Do me a favour, then—let Kisel ride my gray. I cannot endure the thought of the harlequin spectacle you'll furnish forth, riding down the Broadway with your squire mounted on Beauty; besides, the animal is not equal to the expedition."

"Thank you, Linwood. I accept your kindness as freely as you offer it. You have relieved me of my only serious embarrassment. Now get your letters ready; any thing unsealed (my orders are restricted to that) I will take charge of, and deliver at your father's door."

"My father's door!" exclaimed Linwood, snapping his fingers with a sort of wild exultation that made Eliot stare, "oh, what a host of images those words call up! but as to the letters, there is no pleasure in unsealed ones; I sent a bulletin of my health to Belle yesterday; I have an engagement that will occupy me till after your departure; so farewell, and good luck to you, Eliot." The friends shook hands and parted.

The twilight was fading into night when Eliot was ready for his departure. To his great vexation Kisel was missing; and he was told he had ridden forward, and had left word that he would await his master at a certain point about three miles on their way. The poor fellow's habits were so desultory that they never excited surprise, though they would have been intolerable to one less kind-tempered than Eliot Lee. He found him at the point named. He had reined his horse up against the fence, and was awaiting his master, as Eliot saw, for he could just descry the outline of his person lying back to back to the horse, his legs encircling the animal's neck.

"Sit up, Kisel," said his master, in an irritated tone; "remember you are riding a gentleman's horse that's not accustomed to such tricks. And now I tell you, once for all, that unless you behave yourself quietly and reasonably, I will send you adrift."

Kisel whistled. He always either replied by a whistle or tears to Eliot's reproof, and the whistle now, as usual, was followed by a fit of sulkiness. The night was misty and very dark. Kisel, in spite of sundry kind overtures from his master, remained doggedly silent, or only answered in a muttered monosyllable. Thus they travelled all night, merely stopping at the farmhouses to which they had been directed to refresh their horses. On these occasions Kisel was unusually zealous in performing the office of groom, and seemed to have made a most useful transfer of the nimbleness of his tongue to his hands.

The dawn found them within the enemy's lines, at twenty miles distance from the city of New-York, and in sight of a British post designated in their instructions where they were to stop, exhibit their flag of truce, show their passports, and obtain others to the city. "Now, Kisel," said Eliot, "you

15*

must have done with your fooleries; you will disgrace me if you do not behave like a man; pull up
your cap—do not bury your face so in the collar
of your coat—sit upright."

Kisel threw the reins upon his horse's neck,
affected to arrange his cap and coat, and in doing
so dropped his whip. This obliged him to dismount and go back a few yards, which he did as
if he had clogs at his heels. In the meantime
Eliot spurred on his horse, and rode up to the door
where the enemy's guard was stationed. His
passports were examined, and returned to him
countersigned. He passed on; and the guard was
giving a cursory glance at the attendant, when it
seemed to strike him there was some discrepance
between the description and the actual person.
" Stop, my man," said he, " let's have another
glance. ' Crooked, ill-made person;' yes, crooked
enough—' sandy hair;' yes, by Jove, sandy as a
Scotchman's—' gray eyes, small and sunken;'
gray to be sure, but neither small nor sunken."

" Well, now," said Kisel, with beseeching simplicity, and looking eagerly after Eliot, who was
watering his horse at a brook a few rods in advance of him; " well, now, I say, don't *hender*
me—smallness is according as people thinks. My
eye ant so big as an ox's, nor tant so small as a
mole's; and folks will dispute all the way 'twixt
the two: so what signifies keeping captain waiting?"

" Well, well, it must be right—go on. I don't

know, though," muttered the inquisitor, as Kisel rode off at a sharp trot—" d—n these Yankees, they'd cheat the devil. The passport said, ' a turn-up nose'—this fellow's is as straight as an arrow. Here, halloo, sirs,—back." But Kisel, instead of heeding the recall, though seconded by his master, galloped forward, making antic gestures, laughing and shouting ; and Eliot, bitterly repenting his in-discretion in bringing him, retraced his steps. He found the inspector's faculties all awakened by the suspicion that he had been outwitted. " My friend," said Eliot, reproducing his passports, " this detention is unnecessary and discourteous. You see I am, beyond a question, the person here de-scribed ; and I give you my honour that my com-panion is the attendant specified. He is a fellow of weak wits, as you may see by his absurd con duct, who can impose on no one, much less on a person of your keenness."

" That is to say, if he is he. But I suppose you know, sir, that a wolf can wear a sheep's clothing. There are so many rebels that have con-nexions in the city, outside friends to his majesty, that we are obliged to keep a sharp look-out."

" Certainly, my friend : all that you say is per-fectly reasonable, and I respect you for doing your duty. But you must be satisfied now, and will have the goodness to permit me to proceed."

The man was conciliated ; and after making an entry in his note-book, he again returned the passports. Eliot put spurs to his horse; and as the man gazed after him, he said, "A noble-looking youth. The Almighty has written his passport on that face; but that won't serve him now-a-days without endorsements. That other fellow I doubt. Well, I'll just forward these notes I have taken down to Colonel Robertson, and he'll be on the look-out."

In the meantime Eliot followed Kisel at full speed; but, after approaching him within a few yards, he perceived he did not gain an inch on him; and, apprehensive that such forced riding might injure Linwood's horse, or, at any rate, that the smoking sides of both the steeds would excite suspicion, he reined his in, and wondered what new demon had taken possession of Kisel; for, while he now rode at a moderate pace, he had the mortification of seeing that Kisel exactly, and with an accuracy he had never manifested in any other operation, measured his horse's speed by his master's, so as to preserve an undeviating distance from him. Thus they proceeded till they approached Kingsbridge, where a British picket was stationed. Here Kisel managed so as to come up with his horse abreast to Eliot's. The horse seemed to take alarm at the colours that were flying from the British flagstaff, and reared, whirled around, and curvetted, so as to require all his rider's adroitness to keep on his back. Meanwhile the passports were being examined, and they were suffered to proceed without a particular investigation.

They had passed the bridge, and beyond observation, when Eliot, who was still in advance of his attendant, turned suddenly round with the intention of trying the whole force of a moral battery ; but he was surprised by a *coup de main* that produced a sudden and not very agreeable shock to his ideas.

His follower's slouched and clownish attitude was gone ; and in its place an erect and cavalier bearing. His head was raised from the muffler that had half buried it—his cap pushed back, and from beneath shone the bright laughing eye of Herbert Linwood.

" Now, Eliot, my dear fellow," he said, stretching out his hand to him, " do not look so, as if you liked the knave less than the fool."

" If I do look so, Linwood, it is because fools are easier protected than knaves. It is impossible to foresee what may be the consequence of this rash business."

" Oh, hang the consequence. I wish you would get over that Yankee fashion of weighing every possible danger; you are such a cautious race."

" Granted, Linwood, we are ; and I think it will take all my caution to get us out of a scrape that your heroism has plunged us into."

The first shaft of Linwood's petulance had glanced off from the shield of his friend's good-temper, and he had not another. " I confess," he said, in an altered voice, " that the boldness is worse than questionable that involves others in our own danger. But consider my temptations, and then try, my dear fellow, to pardon my selfishness. I have lived three years in exile—I, who never before passed a night out of my father's house. I am suffering the wretchedness of his displeasure ; and am absolutely famishing for the faces and voices of home. I could live a week upon the ticking of the old hall-clock."

" But what satisfaction can you expect, Linwood ? You have always told me you believed your father's displeasure was invincible—"

" Oh, I don't know that. His bark is worse than his bite. I cannot calculate probabilities. One possibility outweighs a million of them. I shall at any rate see my sister—my peerless, glorious sister, and my mother. And, after all, what is the risk ? If you did not detect me, others will not, surely."

" You did not give me a chance."

" Nor will I them. The only catastrophe I fear is the possibility of General Washington finding me out. But it was deused crabbed of him not to give me the commission. He ought to know that a man can't live on self-sacrifice."

" General Washington requires no more than he performs."

" That is true enough ; but is it reasonable to

require of children to bear the burdens of men ?—
of common men to do the deeds of heroes ?"

"I believe there is no limit, but in our will, to
our moral power."

"Pshaw !—and I believe the moral power of
each individual can be measured as accurately as
his stature. But we are running our heads into
metaphysics, and shall get lost in a fog."

"A New-England fog, Linwood ?"

"They prevail there," he answered, with a quizzical smile. "But we are wandering from the
point. I really have taken all possible precautions
to keep my secret. I obtained leave for four days'
absence on the pretext that I was going up the
river on my private business. The only danger
arises from my having been compelled to make a
confidant of Kisel."

"That occurred to me. How in the name of
wonder did you manage him ?"

"Oh, I conjured in your name. I made him
believe that your safety depended on his implicitly
obeying my directions ; so I obtained his holyday
suit (which you must confess is a complete disguise),
and sent him on a fool's errand up the river."

The friends entered the city by passing the
pickets at the Bowery. They were admitted without scruple :—letting animals into a cage is a very
different affair from letting them out. At Linwood's suggestion they crossed into Queen-street.
That great mart, now stored with the products of

the commercial world, and supplying millions from
its packed warehouses, was then chiefly occupied
by the residences of the provincial gentry.   Linwood had resumed his mufflers and his clownish
air ; but the true man from the false exterior
growled forth many an anathema as he passed
house after house belonging to the whig absentees
—his former familiar haunts—now occupied, and, as
he thought, desecrated by British officers, or resi-
dent royalists whose loyalty was thus cheaply paid.

" Look not to the right nor left, I pray you, Linwood," said Eliot ; " you are now in danger of being recognised.   We are to stop at Mrs. Billings's,
in Broad-street."

" Just above my father's house," replied Linwood, in a sad tone.   They rode on briskly ; for
they perceived that Eliot's American uniform and
grotesque attendant attracted observation.   They
had entered Broad-street, and were near a large
double house, with the carving about the doors and
windows that distinguished the more ambitious
edifices of the provincialists.   Two horses, equipped for their riders, stood at the door, and a black
servant in faded livery beside them.   The door
opened ; and a gentleman of lofty stature, attended
by a young lady, came forth.   She patted the animal that awaited her, and sprang into the saddle.
" It must be Isabella Linwood !" thought Eliot,
turning his asking eye to his companion, who, he
now perceived, had reined in his horse towards the

flagging opposite that where the parties who had attracted his observation were. "He is right and careful for once," thought Eliot. That Eliot would have thought it both right and inevitable to have indulged himself in a nearer survey of the beautiful young lady, we do not doubt; but as he again turned, her horse suddenly reared his hind legs in the air. Her father screamed—there were several persons passing—no one dared approach the animal, who was whirling, floundering, and kicking furiously. Some, gazing at Miss Linwood, exclaimed, "She'll be dashed to pieces!"—and others, "Lord, how she sits!" She did sit bravely; her face colourless as marble, and her dark eyes flashing fire. Eliot and Linwood instinctively dismounted, and at the risk of their lives rushed to her rescue; and, at one breath's intermission of the kicking, stood on either side of the animal's head. She was an old acquaintance and favourite of Linwood, and with admirable presence of mind (inspiration he afterward called it) he addressed her in a loud tone, in his accustomed phrase, "Jennet—Jennet, softly—softly!" The animal was quieted; and, as Linwood afterward affirmed, spoke as plainly to him with her eye as ever human voice spoke. At any rate, she stood perfectly still while Eliot assisted the young lady to dismount. The people now gathered round; and at the first burst of inquiry and congratulation, Herbert disappeared. "Thank God, you are not hurt, Belle!"

16

exclaimed her father, whose voice, though choked with emotion, was heard above all others. " What in Heaven's name possessed Jennet ?—she never kicked before ; and how in the world did you quiet her, sir ?" turning to Eliot. "It was most courageously done !"

" Miraculously !" said Miss Linwood ; her face, as she turned it to Eliot, beaming with gratitude. There are voices that, at their first sound, seem to strike a new chord that ever after vibrates ; and this first word that Eliot heard pronounced by Isabella Linwood, often afterward rung in his ears like a remembered strain of sweet music. There were persons present, however, not occupied with such high emotions ; and while Eliot was putting in a disclaimer, and saying, if there were any merit attending arresting the horse, it was his servant's, diligent search was making into the cause of the animal's transgression, which soon appeared in the form of a thorn, that, being entangled in the saddle-cloth, had pierced her side.

The first flow of Mr. Linwood's gratitude seemed to have been suddenly checked. " Papa has seen the blue coat," thought Isabella ; "and the gushings of his heart are turned to icicles !" And infusing into her own manner the warmth lacking in his, she asked what name she should associate with her preservation.

" My name is Lee."

" A very short one. May we prefix Harry or

Charles ?" alluding to two distinguished commanders in the American army.

"Neither. Mine is a name unknown to fame. Eliot."

"Eliot Lee!—Herbert's friend!—Bessie's brother! Papa, you do not understand. Mr. Lee is the brother of your little pet, Bessie Lee, and," she added, " Herbert's best friend."

Her father coloured ; and civilly hoped Miss Bessie Lee was well.

"Well! that is nothing," exclaimed Miss Linwood. " We hope all the world is well ; but I must know where Bessie is—what she is doing— how she is looking, and a thousand million et ceteras. Papa, Mr. Lee must come home with us."

" Certainly, Isabella, if Mr. Lee chooses."

Thus bidden, Mr. Lee could only choose to refuse, which he did ; alleging that he had no time at his own disposal.

Isabella looked pained, and Mr. Linwood felt uncomfortable ; and making an effort at an *amende honorable*, he said, " Pray send your servant to me, sir ; I shall be happy to express my obligations to him."

" Heaven smiles on Herbert !" thought Eliot ; and he replied eagerly, " I will most certainly send him, sir, this evening, at eight o'clock." He then bowed to Mr. Linwood, took Isabella's hand, which she again graciously extended to him, and thanking her for her last kind words—" Best—best love to Bessie ; be sure you don't forget it," he mounted his horse and was off.

"Send him !" said Mr. Linwood, reiterating Eliot's last words. "I'll warrant him !—trust a Yankee for not letting slip a shilling."

"He is quite right, papa. If he cannot obtain the courtesy due to the gentleman in return for the service he has rendered, he is right to secure the reward of the menial. You were savage, sir— absolutely savage. Mr. Lee will think we are barbarians—heathens—any thing but Christians."

"And so am I, and so will I be to these fellows. This young man did only what any other young man would have done upon instinct; so don't pester me any more about him. You know, Belle, I have sworn no rebel shall enter my doors."

"And you know, sir, 'that I have—not sworn, oh, no ! but resolved, and my resolve is the feminine of my father's oath, that you shall hang me on a gallows high as Haman's, before I cease to plead that our doors may be opened to one rebel at least."

"Never, never !" replied her father, shutting his hall-door after him as he spoke, as if all the rebel world were on the other side of it.

CHAPTER XII.

" Oui, je suis sûr que vous m'aimez, mais je ne le suis pas que vous m'aimiez toujours."—MOLIERE.

,WHEN Eliot rejoined his friend at the appointed rendezvous, Mrs. Billings's, Herbert listened most eagerly to every particular of Eliot's meeting with his father and sister, and thanked him over and over again for so thoughtfully smoothing the way for his interview with them in the evening. " Oh, Eliot," he said, " may you never have such a hurricane in your bosom as I had when I stood by my father and Belle, and longed to throw myself at his feet, and take my sister into my arms. I believe I did kiss Jennet—what the deuse ailed the jade? she is the gentlest creature that ever stepped. Never doubt my self-control after this, Eliot!" Eliot's apprehensions were not so easily removed. He perceived that Herbert was in a frame of mind unsuited to the cautious part he was to act. His feelings had been excited by his rencounter with his father and sister, and though he had passed through that trial with surprising self-possession, it had quite unfitted him for encountering the " botheration" (so he called it) that awaited him at Mrs. Billings's.

16*

"We are in a beautiful predicament here," he said; "our landlady, who is one of your ''cute Yankees,' will not let us in till she has sent our names and a description of our persons to the Commandant Robertson's :—this, she says, being according to his order. Now this cannot be--I will not implicate you—thus far I have proceeded on my sole responsibility, and if any thing happens, I alone am liable for the consequences. Are your instructions to stop at this house positive ?"

"Yes; and if they were not, we might not be better able to evade this police regulation elsewhere. I will see my countrywoman—'hawks won't pick out hawks' e'en,' you know they say; perhaps one Yankee hawk may blind another."

A loud rap brought the hostess herself to the door, a sleek lady, who, Eliot thought, looked as if she might be *diplomatized*, though a Yankee, and entitled to the discretion of at least forty-five years.

"Mrs. Billings, I presume ?"

"The same, sir—will you walk in ?"

"Thank you, madam. Kisel, remain here while I speak with the lady:" Mrs. Billings looked at the master, then at the man, then hemmed, which being interpreted, meant, "I understand your mutual relations," and then conducted Eliot to her little parlour, furnished with all the display she could command, and the frugality to which she was enforced, a combination not uncommon in more recent times. A carpet covered the middle of the floor, and just reached to the stately chairs that stood like grenadiers around the room, guarding the uncovered boards, the test of the housewife's neatness. One corner was occupied by a high Chinese lackered clock; and another by a buffet filled with articles, like the poor vicar's, "wisely kept for show," because good for nothing else; and between them was the chest of drawers, that so mysteriously combined the uses which modern artisans have distributed over sideboards, wardrobes, &c. The snugness, order, and sufficiency of Mrs. Billings's household certainly did present a striking contrast to the nakedness and desolation of our soldier's quarters, and the pleased and admiring glances with which Eliot surveyed the apartment were quite unaffected.

"You are very pleasantly situated here, madam," he said.

"Why, yes; as comfortably as I could expect."

"You are from Rhode Island, I believe, Mrs. Billings?"

"I am happy to own I am, sir;" the expression of hostility with which the lady had begun the conference abated. It is agreeable to have such cardinal points in one's history as where one comes from known—an indirect flattery, quite unequivocal.

"I have been told, madam," continued Eliot, "that you were a sufferer in the royal cause before you left your native state?"

"Yes, sir, I may say that; but I have never regretted it."

"The lady's loyalty is more conspicuous than her conjugal devotion," thought Eliot, who remembered to have heard that, with some other property, she had lost her husband.

"No, madam," he replied, "one cannot regret sacrifices in a cause conscientiously espoused."

"Your sentiments meet my views, sir, exactly."

"But your sacrifices have been uncommon, Mrs Billings ; you have left a lovely part of our country to shut yourself up here."

"That's true, sir ; but you know one can do a great deal from a sense of duty. I am not a person that thinks of myself; I feel as if I ought to be useful while I am spared." Our self-sacrificing philanthropist was driving a business, the gains of which she had never dreamed of on her steril New-England farm.

"I am glad to perceive, Mrs. Billings, that your sacrifices are in some measure rewarded. You have, I believe, the best patronage in the city ?"

"Yes, sir ; I accommodate as many as I think it my duty to ; my lodgers are very genteel persons and good pay. Still, I must say, it is a pleasure to converse with one's own people. The British officers are not sociable except among themselves."

"I assure you our meeting is a mutual pleasure,

Mrs. Billings. May I hope for the accommodation of a room under your roof for a day or two?"

"I should be very happy to oblige you, sir. It appears to me to be a Christian duty to treat even our enemies kindly; but our officers—I mean no offence, sir—look down upon the rebels, and I could not find it suitable to do what they would not approve."

"As to that, Mrs. Billings, you know we are liable to optical illusions in measuring heights—that nearest seems most lofty." Eliot paused, for he felt he had struck too high a note for his auditor; and lowering his pitch, he added, "you are a New-England woman, Mrs. Billings, and know we are not troubled by inequalities that are imaginary."

"Very true, sir."

"If you find it convenient to oblige me, I shall not intrude on your lodgers, as I prefer taking my meals in my own room." This arrangement obviated all objection on the part of the lady, and the matter was settled after she had hinted that a private table demanded extra pay. Eliot perceived he was in that common case where a man must pay his *quid pro quo*, and acknowledge an irrequitable obligation into the bargain: he therefore submitted graciously, acceded to the lady's terms, and was profuse in thanks.

Looking over the mantel-piece, and seeming to see, for the first time, a framed advertisement suspended there, "I perceive, madam," he said, "that your lodgers are required to report themselves to the commandant; but as my errand is from General Washington to Sir Henry Clinton, I imagine this ceremony will be superfluous; somewhat like going to your servants for leave to stay in your house. After obtaining it from you, madam, the honoured commander-in-chief ?"

" That would be foolish."

" Then all is settled, Mrs. Billings.   As my man is a stranger in the city, you will allow one of your servants to take a note for me to Sir Henry Clinton ?"

" Certainly, sir."

Thus Eliot had secured an important point by adroitly and humanely addressing himself to the social sympathies of the good woman, who, though ycleped " a 'cute calculating Yankee," was just that complex being found all the world over, made up of conceit, self-esteem, and good feeling; with this difference, that, like most of her country people, she had been trained to the devotion of her faculties to the provident arts of *getting along*.

In conformity to the answer received to his note, Eliot was at Sir Henry Clinton's door precisely at half past one, and was shown into the library, there to await Sir Henry.

The house then occupied by the English commander-in-chief, and afterward consecrated by the occupancy of Washington, is still standing at the southwestern extremity of Broadway, having been respectfully permitted by its proprietors to retain its primitive form, and fortunately spared the profane touch of the demon of change (*soi-disant* improvement) presiding over the city corporation.

In the centre of the library, which Eliot found unoccupied, was a table covered with the freshest English journals and other late publications: among them, Johnson's political pamphlets, and a poetic emission of light from the star just then risen above the literary horizon—Hannah More. Eliot amused himself for a half hour with tossing these over, and then retired to an alcove formed by a temporary damask drapery, enclosing some bookcases, a sofa, and a window. This window commanded a view of the Battery, the Sound, indenting the romantic shores of Long Island, the generous Hudson, pouring into the bay its tributary waters, and both enfolding in their arms the infant city, ordained by nature to be the queen of our country. " Ah!" thought Eliot, as his eye passed exultingly over the beautiful scene, and rested on one of his majesty's ships that lay anchored in the bay, " How long are we to be shackled and sentinelled by a foreign power! how long before we may look out upon this avenue to the ocean as the entrance to our independent homes, and open or shut it, as pleases us, to the commerce and friendship of the world!"

His natural revery was broken by steps in the adjoining drawing-room—the communicating door

was open, and he heard a servant say, " Sir Henry
bids me tell you, sir, he shall be detained in the
council-room for half an hour, and begs you will
excuse the delay of dinner."

" Easier excused than endured !" said a voice,
as soon as the servant had closed the door, which
Eliot immediately recognised to be Mr. Linwood's.
" I'll take a stroll up the street, Belle—a half hour
is an eternity to sit waiting for dinner !"

" If Dante had found my father in his Inferno,"
thought Isabella, " he certainly would have found
him *waiting* for dinner !"

The young lady, left to herself, did what we believe all young ladies do in the like case—walked
up to the mirror, and there, while she was re-
adjusting a sprig of jessamine with a pearl arrow
that attached it to her hair, Eliot, from his fortunate position, contemplated at leisure her image.
The years that had glided away since we first introduced our heroine on her vist to Effie, had
advanced her to the ripe beauty of maturity. The
freshness, purity, and frankness of childhood remained ; but there was a superadded grace, an
expression of sentiment, of thought, feelings, hopes,
purposes, and responsibilities, that come not within
the ken of childhood. Form and colouring may
be described. Miss Linwood's hair was dark, and,
contrary to the fashion of the times (she was no
thrall of fashion), unpowdered, uncurled, and un-
frizzed, and so closely arranged in braids as to

define (that rare beauty) the Grecian outline of her head. Her complexion had the clearness and purity that indicates health and cheerfulness. " How soon," thought Eliot, as he caught a certain look of abstraction to which of late she was much addicted, " how soon she has ceased to gaze at her own image ; is it that she is musing, or have her eyes a sibylline gaze into futurity !" Those eyes were indeed the eloquent medium of a soul that aspired to Heaven ; but that was not, alas ! above the " carking cares" of earth.

We must paint truly, though we paint the lady of our love ; and therefore we must confess that our heroine was not among the few favoured mortals whose noses have escaped the general imperfection of that feature. Hers was slightly—the least in the world—but incontrovertibly of the shrewish order ; and her mouth could express pride and appalling disdain, but only did so when some unworthy subject made these merely human emotions triumph over the good-humour and sweet affections that played about this, their natural organ and interpreter.

Her person was rather above the ordinaiy height, and approaching nearer to *embonpoint* than is common in our *lean* climate ; but it had that grace and flexibility that make one forget critically to mark proportions and dimensions, and to conclude, from the effect produced, that they must be perfect. We said we could describe form and colour; but who shall describe that mysterious changing and all-powerful beauty of the soul, to which form and colour are but the obedient ministers ?—who, by giving the form and dimensions of the temple, can give an idea of the exquisite spirits that look from its portals ?

Eliot was not long in making up his mind to emerge from his hiding-place, and was rising, when he was checked by the opening of the library door, and the exclamation, in a voice that made his pulses throb—" Nymph, in thy orisons be all my sins remembered !"

" *All*, Jasper ?" replied Miss Linwood, starting from her meditations, and blushing as deeply as if she had betrayed them—" *all* thy sins ; I should be loath to charge my prayers with such a burden."

" Not one committed against you, Isabella," replied Meredith, in a tone that made it very awkward for Eliot to present himself.

" It would make no essential difference in my estimation of a fault whether it were committed against myself or another."

" Perhaps so !"

Miss Linwood took up one gazette, and Meredith another. Suddenly recollecting herself—" Oh, do you know," she said, "that Eliot Lee is in town ?"

" Now," thought Eliot, "is my time."

" God forbid !" exclaimed Meredith. Miss Linwood looked at him with an expression of question and astonishment, and he adroitly added, " Of course, if he is in town he is a prisoner, and I am truly sorry for it."

" Spare your regrets—he comes in the honourable capacity of an emissary from his general to ours."

" It is extraordinary that he has not apprized me of his arrival—you must be misinformed."

Isabella recounted the adventure of the morning, and concluded by saying, " He must have some reason for withholding himself—you were friends ?"

" Yes, college friends—boy friendship, which passes off with other morning mists—a friendship not originating in congeniality, but growing out of circumstances—a chance."

" Chance—friendship !" exclaimed Isabella, in a half suppressed tone, that was echoed from the depths of Eliot's heart. He held his breath as she continued—" I do not understand this—the instincts of childhood and youth are true and safe. I love every thing and everybody I loved when I was a child. I now dread the effect of adventitious circumstances—the flattering illusions of society—the frauds that are committed on the imagination by the seeming beautiful." Isabella was perhaps conscious that she was mentally giving a personal investment to these abstractions, for her voice faltered ; but she soon continued with more steadiness and emphasis, and a searching of the eye that affected Meredith like an overpowering light—" *chance* friendship ! This chance friendship may remind you of a chance love, growing out of *circumstances* too."

"No, no, Isabella, on my honour, no. In these serious matters I am a devout believer in the divinity that shapes our ends. The concerns of my heart never were, never could be at the mercy of the blind, blundering blockhead chance."

"Then, if it existed," continued Isabella, her eye still riveted to Meredith's face, where the pale olive had become livid—"if it had existed you would not—or rather, if you speak truly, you could not cast aside love for the sister as carelessly as you do friendship for the brother."

"If it existed!—my thanks to you for putting the question hypothetically ; you cannot for a moment believe that I ever offered serious homage to that pretty little piece of rurality, Bessie Lee ! Certainly, I found her an interesting exception to the prosaic world she lives in—a sunbeam breaking through those leaden New-England clouds —a wild rose-bud amid the corn and potatoes of her mother's garden-patch. She relieved the inexpressible dulness of my position and pursuits. It was like finding a pastoral in the leaves of a statute-book—Aminte in Blackstone."

Poor Eliot : his ears tingled, his brain was giddy.

"The case may have been reversed to Bessie," answered Isabella, "and you may have been the statute-book that gave laws to her submissive heart."

"*Ça peut-être !*" replied Meredith; but he immediately checked the coxcomb smile that curled his lips, for it was very plain that Miss Linwood would bear no levity on the subject of her friend; and he added, apparently anxiously recalling the past,—" No—it is impossible—she could not make so egregious a mistake—she is quite unpresuming —she must have understood me, Isabella." There was now emotion, serious emotion in his voice. " Bessie Lee was not a simpleton; she must have known what you also know"—he faltered. Eliot would have given worlds for a single glance at Isabella's face at this moment; but even if the screen between them had fallen he could not have seen it, for she had laid her hands on the table and buried her face in her palms. " I appeal," continued Meredith, " from this stage of our being, troubled and darkened with distrust, to our childhood—that you say is true and unerring:—then, Isabella, believe its testimony, and believe that, from the fountain which you then unsealed in my heart, there has ever since flowed a stream, never diverted, and always increasing, till I can no longer control it. Not one word, not one look, Isabella? Again I appeal to the past :—were you unconscious of the wild hopes you raised when you said, ' I love everybody that I loved in my childhood?' "

" Oh !" cried Isabella, raising her head, " I did not mean that—not that !"

The drawing-room door opened, and Helen Ruthven appeared, calling out, " Isabella Linwood—a *tête-à-tête*—ten thousand pardons—but, Isabella

17*

dear, as the charm is broken, do come here, and you
too, Mr. Meredith—here is the drollest looking fellow at Sir Henry's door.   He was walking straight
into the hall, when the sentinel pointed his bayonet
at him. ' Now don't,' said he, 'that's a plaguy sharp
thing, and you'll hurt me if you don't take care ; I
only want to speak a word to my *kappen*,' meaning
captain, you know.   Finding the sentinel would not
let him pass, he screamed out to me as I was coming up the stairs, ' Miss, just please give my duty
to Gin'ral Clinton, and ask him if he wont be so
accommodating as to let me speak to Kappen Lee.'
Was it not comical ?"

"What did you say to the poor fellow ?" asked
Isabella, who at once concluded he was the coad-
jutor in her preservation.

" Say, my dear child ! of course, nothing."

They were now all gazing at the personation of
Kisel, seated on the door-step, his head down, and
he apparently absorbed in catching flies. " I think
I know the poor fellow," said Meredith, who recognised some odd articles of Kisel's odd apparel—
" he is a half-idiot, who from his infancy attached
himself to Eliot Lee, and clung to him as you have
seen a snarl of drifted seaweed adhere to a rock.
I am amazed that a man of Lee's common sense
should have such an attendant."

"I honour him for it," said Isabella ; "honest,
heartfelt, constant affection, elevates the humblest
and the meanest. From all I have heard of Eliot
Lee," she continued, after a moment's pause, " it

is not his fault if his friends in all conditions of life do not cling to him."

Isabella's remark was commonplace enough, but the tremulous tone in which it was uttered struck Miss Ruthven. Judging, as most persons do, from her own consciousness, she thought there was but one key to a young lady's emotions ; and whispering to Isabella, she said, " Your blush is beautiful, but a tell-tale."

" False, of course, then," replied Isabella, nettled and embarrassed ; and suddenly recollecting she had an unperformed duty towards the uncouth lad at the door, she left the drawing-room (declining Meredith's attendance) to perform it.

" This Captain Lee," said Miss Ruthven to Meredith, " must be a gentleman I sometimes saw at West Point. Our Charlotte was half in love with him."

" Indeed !"

" 'Indeed,' yes ; but be pleased now, Mr. Meredith, to recall your absent thoughts, and attend to me, who am cast upon your tender mercies. I have a word to charm back the wanderers—Isabella Linwood!—Ah, I see you are here—now tell me honestly, do you not think that was a false sentiment of hers ? do you think one must of necessity be constant in friendship or love ? You are in the constant vein now, but hear me out. Suppose I am interested, in love if you please, with a particular individual—I see another who is to him Hyperion to a satyr, and by a fixed law of nature

one attraction must be overcome by the other.   It
is not a deliberate or a voluntary change—it certainly is not caprice : I am but the passive subject
of an irresistible power."

" The object still changing, the sympathy true,
said Meredith, with a satirical smile. ,

"That was meant," replied Miss Ruthven,
"for a piquant satire : it is a mere truism," and
fixing her lustrous eyes on Meredith, she continued : " The heart must have an object, but
we are at the mercy of chance; and should we
cling to that first thrown in our way when taste is
crude and judgment unripe, and cling to it after
another appears ten thousand times more worthy ?   Should we, when daylight comes, shut out
the blessed sun, and continue to grope by a rush-
light?   We cannot—it will penetrate the crevices and annihilate the stinted beam that we thought
enough for us in the luminary's absence.   Ah,
Mr. Meredith, there is much puling parrotry about
constancy, and first love, and all that—*I am sure
cf it*, am sure the object may change, and the
sympathy remain, in the truest, tenderest hearts.
That sympathy—a queer name, is it not?—is always alive and susceptible, a portion of the soul, a
part of life; a part! life itself."

There was a strange confusion of ideas in Meredith's mind as he listened to this rhapsody of Helen
Ruthven.   By degrees one came clearly out of
the mist: and " is the girl in love with me ?" was
his mental interrogatory.

CHAPTER XIII.

" Is't possible that but seeing you should love her !"

In the meantime Eliot had been released from his durance, where he had suffered, as mortals sometimes mysteriously do, what he seemed in no-wise to have deserved ; and passing unobserved into the entry, he had preceded Miss Linwood down the stairs, and was standing within the outer door in conversation with his attendant, so earnest that he did not perceive her approach till she said, " Am I intruding ?"

She was answered by Herbert's suddenly turning his face to her, and uttering " Isabella !"

In the suddenness of surprise and joy she forgot every thing but his presence ; and would have thrown her arms around him but for Eliot's intervention.

" Herbert !—Miss Linwood ! I entreat you to be cautious—your brother's safety is at stake—not a moment is to be lost—is concealment pos sible at your father's house ?"

" Possible !—certain. I will instantly go home."

" Stop—pray hush, Herbert. Was the reason of your coming down stairs known to any one, Miss Linwood ?"

I 3

" Only to Helen Ruthven and Mr. Meredith."

" Two foxes on the scent!—that's all," said Herbert.

" Oh, no, Herbert; they would be the last to betray; but they do not suspect you."

" Then all may be managed," said Eliot; " trust no one, Miss Linwood—you cannot serve your brother better than by appearing at Sir Henry's table, and letting it be known, incidentally, that you have seen my attendant."

" I understand you, and will do my best. Heaven help us!—avoid by all means seeing mamma, Herbert—she will not dare incur the responsibility of concealing your presence. Go in at the back gate—you can easily elude Jupe— trust all to Rose. God bless you, dear brother," she concluded; and in spite of the danger of observation, she gave him one hasty embrace, and returned to the drawing-room to enact a part—a difficult task to Isabella Linwood.

The few guests expected soon after arrived; and Mr. Linwood reappeared from his walk with the air of a person who has tidings to communicate. " Ah, Isabella," said he, " I have news for you."

" The rebels have been crucifying more tories, I suppose ?"

" Pshaw, Belle—you know I did not believe that any more than you did when Rivington first published it. I have heard news of your Yankee preservers."

"Only heard!—then I have the advantage of you, for I have seen them."

"Seen them! Lord bless me—where, child?"

"In the hall below. I seized the opportunity of relieving you from the interview appointed this evening."

"You astonish me! Well, after all, Robertson's suspicions may be groundless. He has just received advice to look out sharply for the attendant of Captain Lee, who is suspected not to be the person he passes for."

"And what if he is not, papa?"

"What if he is not!—a true girl-question! Why, he may be an officer, who, under the disguise of a servant, may be a very efficient emissary for Mr. Washington. He may have come to confer with 'some of our whited sepulchres'—pretended tories, but whigs to the back-bone—we have plenty such."

"It would be very dangerous," said a sapient young lady, "to let such a person go at large."

"But, papa," continued Isabella, without noticing the last interlocutor, "it seems to me very improbable that General Washington would be accessary to any such proceeding."

"Ah, he'll take care to guard appearances. He is as chary of his reputation as Cæsar was of his wife's—a crafty one is Mr. Washington. The passport seems to have contained a true description of the true servant of this Captain Lee.

Probably some young Curtius has assumed the responsibility of the imposition. His detection will reflect no dishonour on the great head of the chismatics—only expose the poor youth to danger."

"*Danger*, papa !" Isabella's tone indicated that the word fell on her ear associated with a life she loved.

"Yes, Miss Linwood; he may find a short and complete cure for whiggism ; for, I take it, that in that department of t'other world which these gentry go to, they will find rebellion pretty well under."

"Oh my ! how you hate the whigs, Mr. Linwood !" exclaimed the aforesaid young lady. "Supposing it were poor dear Herbert who had disguised himself just to take a peep at us all."

"Herbert !" echoed Mr. Linwood, his colour deepening and flushing his high forehead,—"Herbert !—he is joined to idols—I should let him alone."

"My ! Isabella, is it not quite shocking to hear your father speak in such a hard-hearted way of poor Herbert ?" whispered the young lady, who still cherished a boarding-school love for Herbert. "But, dear me ! who is that coming in with Sir Henry ?—He must be one of the young officers who arrived in the ship yesterday. 'Captain Lee, an American officer !' " reiterating Sir Henry's presentation of his guest. "My ! I ought to have known the uniform ; but I had no idea there was such an elegant young man in the American army —had you, Isabella ?"

Isabella was too much absorbed in her own observations to return any thing more than bows and nods to her voluble companion. She saw Meredith advance to Eliot with that engaging cordiality which he knew so well how to throw into his manner; and she perceived that Eliot met him with a freezing civility, that painfully re-excited the apprehensions she had long felt, that there was " something rotten in the state of Denmark." Sir Henry, after addressing each of his guests with that official and measured politeness that marks the great man's exact estimate of the value of each nod, smile, and word vouchsafed to his satellites, advanced to her, and said in an under tone, " My dear Miss Linwood, I have sacrificed my tastes at your shrine—invited a rebel to my table in consideration of the service he had the honour of rendering you, and my valued friend your father, this morning."

" If all I have heard of the gentleman be true," replied Isabella, " Sir Henry will find his society an indulgence rather than a sacrifice of taste."

" Perhaps so." Sir Henry shrugged his shoulders. " He seems a clever person ; but you know antipathies are stubborn ; and, *entre nous*, I have what may be termed a natural aversion to an American. I mean, of course, a rebel American."

England was so much the Jerusalem of the

18

loyal colonists, the holy city towards which they always worshipped, that Sir Henry, in uttering this sentiment, had no doubt of its calling forth a responsive "amen" from Miss Linwood's bosom. But her pride was touched. For the first time an American feeling shot athwart her mind, and, like a sunbeam falling on Memnon's statue, it elicited music to one ear at least. "Have a care, Sir Henry," she replied aloud; "such sentiments from our rulers engender rebellion, and almost make it virtue. I am beginning to think that if I had been a man, I should not have forgotten that I was an American." Her eye encountered Eliot Lee's; and his expressed a more animated delight than he would have ventured to imbody in words, or than she would have heard *spoken* with complacency.

Sir Henry turned on his heel, and Eliot occupied his position. Without adverting to what he had just overheard, or alluding to the discords of the country, he spoke to Miss Linwood of her brother, of course, as if he had left him in camp; from her brother they naturally passed to his sister. Both were topics that called forth their most eloquent feelings. The consciousness of a secret subject of common concern heightened their mutual interest, and in half an hour they had passed from the *terra incognita* of strangers to the agreeable footing of friends.

"I saw you bow to Miss Ruthven," said Isabella: "you knew her at West Point?"

" Slightly," replied Eliot, with a very expressive curl of his lip.

" Did not I hear my name ?" asked Miss Ru'h-ven, advancing, hanging on Meredith's arm, and seating herself in a vacant chair near Miss Lin-wood.

" You might, for we presumed to utter it," replied Isabella.

" Oh, I suppose Captain Lee has been telling you of my escape from that stronghold of the enemy—indeed, I could endure it no longer. You know, Captain Lee, there is no excitement there but the scenery ; and even if I were one of those favoured mortals who find ' tongues in trees, books in the running brooks, and sermons in stones,' I have no fancy for them. -I prefer the lords of the creation," fixing her eyes expressively on Meredith, " to creation itself."

" Pray tell me, Captain Lee," asked Isabella, " is your sister such a worshipper of nature as she used to be ? it seemed to be an innate love with her."

" Yes, it is ; and it should be so, if, as some poets imagine, there is a mysterious correspondence and affinity between the outward world and pure spirits."

" Dear Bessie ! I am so charmed to hear from her again. She has sent me but one letter in six months, and that a very, *very* sad one." Isabella's eye involuntarily turned towards Meredith, but there was no indication that the sounds that entered his ears touched a chord of feeling, or even of memory. It was worth remarking, that while subjects had been alluded to that must have had the most thrilling interest for both Miss Ruthven and Meredith, they neither betrayed by a glance of the eye, a variation of colour, or a faltering of voice, the slightest consciousness. Truly, " the children of this world are wiser in their generation than the children of light."

At the very moment Isabella was speaking so tenderly of her friend, Meredith interrupted her with, " I beg your pardon, Miss Linwood, but I have a controversy with Miss Ruthven which you must decide. I insist there is disloyalty in discarding the Queen Charlotte bonnet; a fright, I grant, very like the rustic little affair your sister Bessie used to wear, Lee; and absolute treason in substituting *la vendange*, a Bacchante concern, introduced by the Queen of France, the patroness of the rebel cause—pardon me, Captain Lee—your decision, Miss Linwood ; we wait your decision—"

Isabella carelessly replied, " I wear *la ven-dange ;*" but not thus carelessly did she dismiss the subject from her mind. " Meredith could not so lightly have alluded to Bessie, in speaking to her brother," thought she, while she weighed each word in a tremulous balance, " if he had ever trifled with the affections of that gentle creature. I have been unjust to him ! he is no heart-break-er after all." There is no happier moment in the history of the heart than when it is relieved of a distrust; and most deeply to be pitied is a young, enthusiastic, and noble-minded creature, who, with a standard of ideal perfection, has her affections fixed, and her confidence wavering.

Eliot perceived that Miss Linwood's mind was abstracted, and feeling his position to be an awkward one, he withdrew to a distant part of the room. Meredith, too, made his observations. He was acute enough to perceive that he had allayed Isabella's suspicions. He was satisfied with the present, and not fearful of the future.

"Pray tell me, Meredith, do you know that Captain Lee?" asked a Major St. Clair.

"Very well; we were at Harvard together!"

"Ah! scholar turned soldier. These poor fellows have no chance against the regular bred military. Homer and Virgil are not the masters to teach our art."

"Our army would halt for officers if they were," said Miss Linwood.

"St Clair," said Meredith, "is of the opinion of the old Romans. Plutarch, you know, says they esteemed Greek and scholar terms of reproach."

"You mistake me, Meredith; I meant no reproach to the learned Theban; upon my word, he strikes me as quite a soldier-like looking fellow—a

keen, quick eye—powerful muscles—good air-
very good air, has he not, Miss Linwood ?"

" Just now he appears to me to have very much
the air of a neglected guest.   Jasper, pray present
Major St. Clair to your sometime friend."

" Excuse me, Miss Linwood," replied the major,
" we have *roturiers* enough in our own household.
I am not ambitious of making the acquaintance of
those from the rebel camp."

" May I ask," resumed Isabella, " who our *roturiers* are ?"

" Oh, the merchants—men of business, and that
sort of people."

" Our city gentry ?"

Major St. Clair bowed assent.

Isabella bowed and smiled too, but not graciously ; her pride was offended.   A new light had
broken upon her, and she began to see old subjects
in a fresh aspect.   Strange as it may appear to those
who have grown up with the rectified notions of
the present day, she for the first time perceived
the folly of measuring American society by a
European standard—of casting it in an old and
worn mould—of permitting its vigorous youth to be
cramped and impaired by transmitted manacles and
shackles.   Her fine mind was like the perfectly
organized body, that wanted but to be touched by
fire from Heaven to use all its faculties freely and
independently.

It was obvious that Meredith avoided Eliot, but

this she now believed was owing to the atmosphere of the court drawing-room. Eliot was not so uncomfortable as she imagined. A common man in his position might not have risen above the vanities and littlenesses of self. He might have been fearful of offending against etiquette, the divinity of small polished gentlemen. He might, an irritable man would, have been annoyed by the awkward silence in which he was left, interrupted only by such formal courtesies as Sir Henry deemed befitting the bearing of the host to an inferior guest. But Eliot Lee cared for none of these things—other and higher matters engrossed him. He was meditating the chances of getting Herbert safe back to West Point, and the means of averting Washington's displeasure. He was eagerly watching Isabella Linwood's face, where it seemed to him her soul was mirrored, and inferring from its eloquent mutations her relations with Linwood; and he was contrasting Sir Henry's luxurious establishment, and the flippant buzz of city gossip he heard around him, with the severe voluntary privations and intense occupations of his own general and his companions in arms. His meditations were suddenly put to flight.

Isabella had been watching for an opportunity to speak privately to Eliot of her brother. Miss Ruthven and Meredith never quitted her side. Miss Ruthven seemed like an humble worshipper incensing two divinities, while, like the false priest, she was contriving to steal the gift from the altar; or rather, like an expert finesser, she seemed to leave the game to others while she held, or fancied she held, the controlling card in her own hand. " I must make a bold push," thought Isabella, " to escape from these people ;" and beckoning to Eliot, who immediately obeyed her summons, she said, " Permit me, Sir Henry, to show Captain Lee the fine picture of Lord Chatham in your breakfasting-room ?"

" Lord Chatham has been removed to give place to the Marquis of Shelburne," replied Sir Henry, with a sarcastic smile.

" Shall I show you the marquis, then ? The face of an enemy is not quite so agreeable as that of a friend, but I am sure Captain Lee will never shrink from either."

" This Captain Lee," whispered Helen Ruthven to Meredith, " has a surprising faculty in converting enemies into friends—have a care lest he make friends enemies."

Unfortunately, Isabella's tactics were baffled by a counter-movement. She was met at the door by the servant announcing dinner, and Eliot was obliged to resign her hand to Sir Henry, to fall behind the privileged guests entitled to precedence, and follow alone to the dining-room.

There were no indications on Sir Henry's table of the scarcity and dearness of provisions so bitterly complained of by the royalists who remained in the city. At whatever rate procured, Sir Henry's dinner was sumptuous. Eliot compared it with the coarse and scanty fare of the American officers, and he felt an honest pride in being one among those who contracted for a glorious future, by the sacrifice of all animal and present indulgence.

Dish after dish was removed and replaced, and the viands were discussed, and the generous wines poured out, as if to eat and to drink were the chief business and joy of life. " A very pretty course of fish for the season," said Major St. Clair, who sat near Eliot, passing his eye over the varieties on the table : " Pray, Captain Lee, have you a good fish-market at West Point ?"

" We are rather too far from the seaboard, sir, for such a luxury."

" Ah, yes—I forgot, pardon me ; but you must have fine trout in those mountain-streams—a pretty resource at a station is trout-fishing."

" Yes, to idlers who need resources ; but time, as the lady says in the play, ' time travels in divers paces with divers persons'—it never ' stays' with us."

" You've other fish to fry—he ! he !—very good —allow me to send you a bit of brandt, Captain Lee ; do the brandt get up as far as the Highlands ?"

" I have never seen them there."

" Indeed !—but you have abundance of other game—wild geese, turkeys, teal, woodcock, snipe, broad-bills ?"

"We have none of these delicacies, sir."

"God bless me!—how do you live?"

Eliot was pestered with this popinjay, and he answered, with a burst of pardonable pride, " I'll tell you how we live, sir"—the earnest tone of his voice attracted attention—"we live on salt beef, brown bread, and beans, when we can get them ; and when we cannot, some of us fast, and some share their horses' messes."

" Bless me—how annoying!"

"You may possibly have heard, sir," resumed Eliot, " of the water that was miraculously sweetened, and of certain bread that came down from Heaven; and we, who live on this nutriment that excites your pity, and feel from day to day our resolution growing bolder and our hopes brighter, we fancy a real presence in the brown bread, and an inspiration in the water that wells up through the green turf of our native land."

There is a chord in the breast of every man that vibrates to a burst of true feeling—this vibration was felt in the silence that followed. It was first broken by Isabella Linwood's delicious voice. She turned her eye, moistened with the emotion he had excited, towards Eliot ; and filling a glass from a goblet of water, she pushed the goblet towards him, saying, " Ladies may pledge in the pure element—*our* native land! Captain Lee."

Eliot filled a bumper, and never did man drink a more intoxicating draught. Sir Henry looked tremendously solemn, Helen Ruthven exchanged glances with Meredith, and Mr. Linwood muttered between his teeth, "nonsense—d—d nonsense, Belle!"

It must be confessed, that Miss Linwood violated the strict rules that governed her contemporaries. She was not a lady of saws and precedents. But if she sometimes too impulsively threw open the door of her heart, there was nothing there exposed that could stain her cheek with a blush. We would by no means recommend an imitation of her spontaneous actions. Those only can afford them to whom they are spontaneous.

After the momentary excitement had passed, Eliot felt that he had perhaps been a little too heroic for the occasion. Awkward as the descent is from an assumed elevation, he effected it with grace, by falling into conversation with the major on sporting and fishing; in which he showed a science that commanded more respect from that gentleman, than if he had manifested all the virtues of all the patriots that ever lived, fasted, starved, and died for their respective countries.

It was hard for Eliot to play citizen of the world, while he saw Meredith courted, admired, and apparently happy, mapping out, at his own will, a brilliant career, and thought of his sister wasting the incense of her affections; no more to Meredith than a last summer's flower. "He deserves not," he thought indignantly, as his eye fell on Isabella, "the heart of this glorious creature—no man deserves; I almost wonder that any man should dare aspire to it."

When a man begins to be humble in relation to a woman, he is not very far from love; and absurd as Eliot would have deemed it to fall in love at first sight, and utterly absurd for him, at any time, to fall in love with Miss Linwood, it was most fortunate for him that he was suddenly taken from her presence, by a request from Sir Henry (who had just had a note put into his hands) that he would accompany him to his council-chamber. When there, he informed Eliot, that suspicions having been excited in relation to his attendant, a quest for him had been made at Mrs. Billings's—but in vain. "Captain Lee must be aware," he said, "that the disappearance of the man was a confirmation of the suspicions!"

Eliot replied, that "he was not responsible for any suspicions that might be felt by the timid, or feigned by the ill-disposed."

"That may be, sir," replied Sir Henry; "but we must make you responsible for the reappearance of the man—your flag cannot exempt you from this!"

"As you please, sir," replied Eliot, quite undaunted; "you must decide how far the privilege of my flag extends. You, sir, can appreciate the importance of not violating, in the smallest degree, the few humanities of war."

Sir Henry pondered for a moment before he asked, " Is there any thing in the character of your attendant which might betray him into an indiscretion ?"

" I am an interested witness, Sir Henry; but if you do not choose to infer the character from the action, which certainly has been sufficiently indiscreet, give me leave to refer you to Mr. Meredith; he knew the poor lad in Massachusetts."

" But how can you identify him with this man ?"

" He saw this man to-day."

Meredith was summoned and questioned : "He had seen Captain Lee's servant on Sir Henry's door-step, and recognised him at the first glance— the dullest eye could mistake no other man for Kisel."

" Do me the favour, Mr. Meredith," said Eliot, " to tell Sir Henry Clinton whether you think my man would be liable to a panic ; for it appears that having overheard that he was under suspicion, he has fled."

" True to himself, Kisel ! He would most assuredly fly at the slightest alarm. He is one of those helpless animals whose only defence is the instinct of cowardice. I have seen him run from the barking of a family dog, and the mewing of a house cat ; and yet, for he is a curious compound, such is his extraordinary attachment to Captain Lee, that I believe he would stand at the cannon's mouth for him. Poor fellow ! his mind takes no

durable impression ; to attempt to make one is like
attempting to form an image in sand ; and yet, like
this same sand, which, from the smelting furnace,
appears in brilliant and defined forms, his thoughts,
kindled in the fire of his affections, assume an
expression and beauty that would astonish you ;
always in fragments, as if the mind had been shattered by some fatal jar."

Meredith spoke *con amore*. He was delighted
with the opportunity of doing Eliot a grace ; and
Eliot, in listening to the sketch of his simple friend,
had almost forgot the subterfuge that called it forth.
He was not, however, the less pleased at its success, when Sir Henry told him that his despatches
and passports should be furnished in the course of
the evening, and that no · impediment would be
thrown in the way of his departure.

The three gentlemen then parted, Meredith expressing such animated regret at their brief meet·
ing, that Eliot was on the point of reciprocating it,
when the thought of his sister sealed his lips and
clouded his brow. Meredith's conscience rightly
interpreted the sudden change of countenance ; but
his retained its cordial smile, and his hand abated
nothing of its parting pressure.

Again we must quote that most apposite sentence—"Truly, the children of this world are wiser
in their generation than the children of light."

CHAPTER XIV.

"Oh, my home,
Mine own dear home."

WHILE Eliot was enjoying the doubtful advantage of Sir Henry's hospitality, Herbert Linwood,
a fugitive in his native city, was seeking concealment in his father's house. His ardent temperament, which had plunged him into this perplexity,
did not qualify him to extricate himself from it.
So far from not giving to any "unproportioned
thought its act," thought and action were simul-
taneous with him. His whole career had shown
that discretion was no part of his valour. He
never foresaw danger till he was in to the very lips;
and, unfortunately, he manifested none of the facil-
ity at getting out that he did at getting in. In
short, he was one of those reckless, precipitate,
vivacious, kind, and whole-hearted young fellows,
who are very dear and very troublesome to their
friends.

After leaving Sir Henry Clinton's, he turned
into a lane leading from Broadway to Broad-street,
and affording a side-entrance to his father's premises. As he was about to turn into his father's

K 2

gateway, he saw a man enter the lane from Broad-
street, and for once cautious, he continued his
walk. He fancied the stranger eyed him suspi-
ciously. As he turned into Broad-street the man
also turned into Broadway, and Herbert eagerly
retraced his steps ; but as he entered his father's
gate he had the mortification to see the man re-
pass the upper corner of the street, and to believe
that he was observed by him. He was once more
on his father's premises. His heart throbbed. The
kitchen-door was half open, and through the aper-
ture he saw Rose, who he was sure would joyfully
admit him into the garrison if he could open a communication with her ; but there were obstacles in
the way. Jupiter, whom Isabella had warned him
not to trust, was, according to his custom of filling
up all the little interludes of life, eating at a side-
table. Beside him sat Mars on his hind-legs, patiently waiting the chance mouthfuls that Jupe
threw to him. Mars was an old house-dog, an
enfant gaté, petted by all the family, and pampered
by Jupe. An acquaintance of Jupiter's had dropped in for an afternoon's lounge ; and Rose, who
had a natural antipathy to loungers of every degree,
was driving round with a broom in her hand, giving
with this staff of office the most expressive inti-
mations that his presence was unwelcome.

We must be permitted to interrupt our narrative,
and recede some nine or ten years, to record the
most remarkable circumstance in Rose's life. She

was a slave, and most faithful and efficient. Slaves at that period were almost the only servants in the province of New-York; and Rose, in common with many others, filled the office of nurse. Gifts and favours of every description testified her owner's sense of her value. On one memorable New-year's day, when Isabella was a child of eight years, she presented Rose a changeable silk dress. It was a fine affair, and Rose was pleased and grateful.

"Now," said Isabella, "you are as grand and as happy as any lady in the land—are you not, Rose?"

"Happy!" echoed Rose, her countenance changing; "I may seem so; but since I came to a thinking age, I never have had one happy hour or minute, Miss Belle."

"Oh, Rose, Rose! why not, for pity's sake?"

"I am a *slave*."

"Pshaw, Rosy, dear! is that all?—I thought you was in earnest." She perceived Rose was indeed in earnest; and she added, in an expostulating tone, "Are not papa and mamma ever so kind to you? and do not Herbert and I love you next best to them?"

"Yes, and that lightens the yoke; but still it is a yoke, and it *galls*. I can be bought and sold like the cattle. I would die to-morrow to be free to-day. Oh, free breath is good—free breath is good!" She uttered this with closed teeth and tears rolling down her cheeks.

Tears on Rose's cheeks! Isabella could not resist them, and pouring down a shower from her own bright eyes, she exclaimed, "You shall be free, Rose," and flew to appeal to her father. Her father kissed her, called her "the best little girl in the world," and laughed at her suit.

"Rose is a fool," he said; "she had reason to complain when she lived with her old mistress, who used to cuff her; but now she *was* free in every thing but the name—far better off than nine tenths of the people in the world." This sophistry silenced, but did not satisfy Isabella. The spirit of truth and independence in her own mind responded to the cravings of Rose's, and the thrilling tone in which those words were spoken, "it is a yoke, and it galls," continued to ring in her ears.

Soon after, a prize was promised in Isabella's school for the best French scholar. She was sadly behind-hand in the studies that require patient application; and her father, who was proud of her talents, was often vexed that she did not demonstrate them to others. "Now, Belle," he said, "if you will but win this prize, I'll give you any thing you'll ask of me."

"Any thing, papa?"

"Yes—any thing."

"You promise for fair, sir?"

"You gipsy! yes."

"Then write it down, please; for I have heard

you say, papa, that no bargain is good in law that is not written down."

Mr. Linwood wrote, signed, and sealed a fair contract. Isabella set to work. The race was a hard one. Her competitors were older than herself, and farther advanced in the language ; but a mind like hers, with motive strong enough to call forth all its energy, was unconquerable. Every day and evening found her with increasing vigour at her tasks. Her mother remonstrated, Herbert teased and ridiculed, and Rose fretted. "What signified it," she asked, "for Miss Belle to waste her rosy cheeks and pretty flesh over books, when, without book-learning, she was ten times brighter than other girls ?" Still Isabella, hitherto a most desultory creature in her habits, and quitting her tasks at the slightest temptation, persevered like a Newton; and like all great spirits, she shaped destiny. The prize was hers.

" Now, Belle," said her father, elated with the compliments that poured in upon him, " I will fulfil my part of the contract honourably, as you have done yours. What shall it be, my child ?"

" Rose's freedom, papa."

" By Christopher Columbus (his favourite oath when he was pleased), you shall have it ; and in half an hour you shall give her, with your own hand, Belle, the deed of manumission."

" Could we but find the right sort of stimulus," he afterward said to his wife, " we might make

Belle a great scholar." But the "right sort of stimulus" was not easily found; and Isabella soon recovered her "rosy cheeks and pretty flesh." Her mind fortunately resembled those rich soils, where every chance sunbeam and passing shower brings forth some beautiful production. Her schoolmates studied, plodded, and wondered they did not know half as much, and were never half as agreeable, as Isabella Linwood. Human skill and labour can do much, but Heaven's gifts are inimitable.

Rose's outward condition was in no wise changed, but her mind was freed from galling shackles by the restoration of her natural rights, and she now enjoyed the voluntary service she rendered.

We return from our digression. Herbert perceived, from a glance at the dramatis personæ that occupied the scene, that it was no time for him to enter; and slouching his cap over his face, he seated himself on the door-step, and whittled a stick, listening, with what patience he could muster, to the colloquy within.

"'Pon my honour, Mr. Linwood" (the slaves were in the habit of addressing one another by the names or titles of their masters), "'pon my honour, Mr. Linwood, you were in a 'dicament this morning," said Jupiter's friend.

"Just 'scaped with my life, gin'ral."

"That's always safe," muttered Rose, "that no-body would cry for if it were lost."

"That's not the case with Mr. Linwood," resumed the general, "for Miss Phillis, in patic'lar, turned as white as any lily when he stood by that kicking horse."

" It was a 'markable 'liv'rance, and I'll tell you how it happened, only don't tell anybody but Miss Phillis, with my 'spects. Just as Jennet had stopped one bout of kicking, and was ready to begin again, I heard an apparition of a voice crying out 'softly, softly Jennet, softly,' and 'pon my honour she stood stock still, trembling like a leaf—do you surmise who it was ?"

" Miss Isabella, to be sure, you fool," said Rose.

" No such ting, Rose, I was as calm as—"

" A scared turkey, Jupe."

' I say I was as calm as them tongs, and there was nobody near the horse but that rebel officer when I heard the apparition. As true as you sit there, general, it was Mr. Herbert's voice that quieted Jennet. I'll lay the next news we hear will be his death—poor 'guided young man !"

" 'Tis a pity," replied the believing general, " to cut him off 'fore he's a shock of wheat ; but then the rebels must die first or last, as they desarve, for trying to drive off the reg'lars. Pretty times we should have in New-York if they were gone : no balls, no races, no t'eatres, no music; no cast-off rigimentals, for your lawyers and traders ant genteel that way, Mr. Linwood."

" Very true, gin'ral. Here's 'fusion to the rebels !" and he passed his cup of cider to his compatriot.

"Now out on you, you lazy, slavish loons," cried Rose ; " can't you see these men are raised up to fight for freedom for more than themselves ? If the chain is broken at one end, the links will fall apart sooner or later. When you see the sun on the mountain-top, you may be sure it will shine into the deepest valleys before long."

" I s'pose what you mean, Rose, is, that all men are going to be free. I heard Mr. Herbert say, when he *argied* with master, that ' all men were born free and equal;' he might as well say, all men were born white and tall; don't you say so, gin'ral."

" Be sure, Mr. Linwood, be sure. And I wonder what good their freedom would do 'em. Freedom ant horses and char'ots, tho' horses and char'ots is freedom. Don't you own that, Miss Rose ?"

" He's a dog that loves his collar," retorted Rose.

"Don't be 'fronted, Miss Rose. Tell me now, don't you r'ally think it's Cain-like and ongenteel for a son to fight 'gainst his begotten father, and so on ?"

" I would have every man fight on the Lord's side," replied Rose, "and that's every man for his own rights."

" La, Miss Rose, then what are them to do what has not got any ?" Rose apparently disdained a reply to this argument, and the general interposed.

" It may be well Mr. Herbert is gone, if he ant dead and gone; for by what folks say, if the war goes on, there won't be too much left for Miss Isabella."

" 'Folks say!' " growled Rose, " don't come here, Mart, with any lies but your own."

" Well, well, Miss Rose, I did not say noting. I know Miss Isabella is sure to have a grander fortin nor ever her father had, and that 'fore long too—Jem Meredith tells me all about it."

" That being the case, Rose," said Jupe, " hand us on a bit of butter. You are as close as if we were in a 'sieged city."

" Butter for you, you old cormorant! and butter a dollar a pound! No, no; up, Jupe—out, out, Mars—let me clear away."

Rose was absolute in her authority. Jupiter rose, and Mars crawled most unwillingly out at the door. When there, the drowsy, surfeited animal was suddenly electrified; he snuffed, wagged his tail, barked, and ran in and out again. " What does all this mean?" demanded Rose; and pushing the door wide open, she espied a figure quietly seated on the steps, repressing Mars, and whittling with apparent unconcern. Now Rose, in common with many energetic domestics, had the same sort of antipathy to beggars that she had to moths and vermin of every description, considering them all equally marauders on the domicil.

" What are you doing here, you lazy varmint!

pretty time of day for a great two-fisted fellow to
be lying over the door, littering the steps this
fashion.   Fawning on a beggar, Mars! shame on
you! clear out, sir!"—and she gave a stroke with
her broom, so equally shared by the man and dog,
that it was not easy to say for which it was de-
signed.   The dog yelped, the man sprang adroitly
on one side of the step, raised his cap, and looked
Rose in the face.

It was a Gorgon glance to Rose.   For an instant she was transfixed; and then recovering her
self-possession, she said, so as to appear to her
auditors within to be replying to a petition :—
" Hungry, are you ?—well, well, go to the wash-
house, and I'll bring you some victuals—the hungry must be fed."

" That's what master calls sound doctrine, Rose,"
said Jupiter; " I hope you won't forget it before my
supper-time."

" You, you hound, you never fast long enough
to be hungry ; but I'll remember you at supper-time
—I've some fresh pies in the pantry—if you'll
take the big kettle to be mended.   Now is a good
time—Mart will lend you a hand."

Both assented, and thus in a few moments were
disposed of; and Rose repaired to the wash-house
to embark her whole heart in Herbert's concerns,
provided her mind could be satisfied on some cardinal points.   After she had given vent to the first
burst of joy, something seemed to stick in Rose's

throat—she hemmed, coughed, placed and displaced the moveables about her, and then speaking out her upright soul, she said, " you ant a deserter ?"

" A deserter, Rose ! I'd not look you in the face if 1 were."

" Nor a spy, Mr. Herbert ?"

"Indeed, I am not, Rose."

" Then," she cried, striking the back of one hand into the palm of the other, " then we'll go through fire and water for you ; but Miss Belle and I could not raise our hands for spy or deserter, though he were bone of her bone."

These preliminaries settled, nothing was easier than for Rose to sympathize fully with the imprudent intensity of Herbert's longings to see his own family.. Nothing beyond present concealment was to be thought of till a council could be held with Isabella. Her injunction was obeyed, and Rose immediately conducted Herbert to his own apartment. On his way thither he caught through a glass door a glimpse of his mother, who was alone, employing some stolen moments in knitting for her son;—stolen we say, for well beloved as he was, she dared not even allude to him in his father's presence. Mrs. Linwood was thoroughly imbued with the conjugal orthodoxy, that

> "Man was made for God,
> Woman for God in him."

She firmly believed that the husband ruled by divine right. She loved her son; but love was not with her as with Isabella, like the cataract in its natural state, free and resistless; but like the cataract subdued by the art of man, controlled by his inventions, and subserving his convenience. Such characters, if not interesting, are safe, provided they fall into good hands. Such as she was, her son loved her tenderly, and found it hard to resist flying to her arms; and he would actually have done so when he saw her take up the measure-stocking lying in her lap and kiss it, and Rose said, "It is yours," but Rose held him back.

Every thing in his apartment had been preserved, with scrupulous care, just as he had left it, and all indicated that he was daily remembered. There was nothing of the vault-like atmosphere of a deserted room, no dust had accumulated on the furniture. His books, his writing-materials, his little toilet affairs, were as if he had left them an hour before. Herbert had never felt more tenderly than at this moment, surrounded by these mute witnesses of domestic love, the sacrifice he had made to his country. He was destined to feel it more painfully.

Rose reappeared with the best refreshments of her larder. " Times are changed, Mr. Herbert," she said, "since you used to butter your bread both sides, and when you dropped it on the carpet say, ' The butter side is up, Rosy.' If the war lasts much longer we shall have no buttered side to our bread."

"How so, Rose? I thought you lived on the fat of the land in the city. Heaven knows our portion is lean enough."

"Oh, Mr. Herbert, it takes a handful of money now to buy one day's fare ; and money is far from being plentiful with your father, though I'd pull out my tongue before I'd say so to any but your father's son. There's little coming in from the rents, when the empty houses of the rebels (as our people call them) are to be had for nothing, or next to nothing. They say the commandant does take the rent for some, and give it to the poor ; which is like trying to cheat the devil by giving a good name to a bad deed."

"But, Rose, my father has property out of the city."

"Yes, Mr. Herbert ; but the farms are on what's called the neutral ground; and the tenants write that what one side does not take, t'other does not leave ; and so between friends and foes it's all Miss Isabella and I can do to keep the wheels agoing. She has persuaded your father to dispose of all the servants but Jupe and me—plague and no profit were they always, as slaves always are. There's no telling the twists and turns that she and your mother makes that your father may see no difference on the table, where he'd feel it most. If he does, he's sure to curse the rebels ; and that's a dagger to them."

"Rose, does my father never speak of me ?"

" Never, Mr. Herbert, never."

" Nor my mother ?"

Rose shook her head. " Not in your father's hearing."

" And my sister—is she afraid to speak my name ?"

" She !—the Lord forgive you, Mr Herbert. When did she ever fear to do what was right ? There's not a day she does not talk of you, though your mother looks scared, and your father looks black ; but I mistrust he's pleased. I heard her read to him out of a newspaper one day how General Washington had sent your name in to Congress as one of them that had done their duty handsome at Stony Point or some of them places ; and she clapped her hands, and put her arms round his neck, and said, with that voice of hers that's sweeter than a flute, ' Are you not proud of him ?'"

" My noble sister !—what did he say, Rose ?"

" Never a word with his lips ; but he went out of the room as if he'd been shot, his face speaking plainer than words."

" Oh, he'll forgive me !—I'm sure he will !" exclaimed Herbert, his ardent feelings kindling at the first light.

" Don't be too *sartin*, Mr. Herbert—will and heart are at war ; and will has been master so long that I mistrust heart is weakest—if, indeed," she added, averting her eye, " you should join the Reformees—"

"Ay, then the fatted calf would be killed for
me ! No, Rose, I had rather die with my father's
curse upon me."

"And better—better !—far better, Mr. Herbert :
your father's curse, if you don't *desarve* it, won't
cut in ; but the curse of conscience is what can't
be borne. I must not stay here longer. If you
get tired sitting alone, you can sleep away the
time. The bed has fresh linen—I change it every
month, so it sha'n't get an old smell, and put them
in mind how long you've been gone."

"After all," thought Herbert, as the faithful
creature quitted the room, "I have never suffered
the worst of absence—the misery of being forgotten !" But every solacing reflection was soon lost
in the anxieties that beset him. A light-hearted,
thoughtless youth, is like the bark that dances over
the waves when skies are cloudless, breezes light
and tides favourable, but wants strength and bal-
last for difficult straits and tempestuous weather.
"I have swamped myself completely," thought
Herbert. "Eliot must inevitably leave me in the
city. It was selfish in me to expose him to censure—that never occurred to me. Instead of getting my father's forgiveness—a fond, foolish dream
—I stand a good chance, if Rose is right, of being
handed over to the tender mercies of Sir Henry
Clinton. And if I escape hanging here I am lost
with General Washington : imprudence and rash-
ness are sins of the first degree with him. Would
20*

to Heaven I could get out of this net as easily as I ran into it! I always put the cart before the horse—action before thought."

With such meditations the time passed heavily; and Herbert took refuge in Rose's advice, and hrew himself on the bed within the closely-drawn curtains.

We hope our sentimental readers will not aban-don him, when we confess that he soon fell into a profound sleep, from which he did not awaken for several hours. They must be agitating griefs that overcome the strong tendencies of a vigorous con-stitution to eating and sleeping. And besides, it must be remembered in Herbert's favour, that the preceding night had been one long fatiguing vigil. Kind nature, pardon us for apologizing for thy gracious ministry.

CHAPTER XV.

"L'habitude de vivre ensemble fit naître les plus doux sentı-
mens qui soient connus des hommes."—ROUSSEAU.

HERBERT's sleep was troubled with fragments
and startling combinations of his waking thoughts.
At one moment he was at Westbrook, making love
to Bessie, who seemed to be deaf to him, and in-
tently reading a letter in Jasper Meredith's hand ;
while Helen Ruthven stood behind her, beckoning
to Herbert with her most seductive smile, which
he fancied he was not to be deluded by. Suddenly the scene changed—he had a rope round his
neck, and was mounting a scaffold, surrounded
by a crowd, where he saw Washington, Eliot, his
father, mother, and Isabella—all unconcerned spectators. Then, as is often the case, a real sound
shaped the unreal vision. He witnessed his own
funeral obsequies, and heard his father reading the
burial service over him. By degrees, sleep loosen-
ed the chain that bound his fancy, and the actual
sounds became distinct. He awoke : a candle was
burning on the table, and he heard his father
in an adjoining apartment, to which it had always
been his habit to retire for his evening devo-
tions. He heard him repeat the formula pre

scribed by the church, and then his voice, tremulous with the feeling that gushed from his heart, broke forth in an extempore appeal to Him who holds all hearts in the hollow of his hand. He prayed him to visit with his grace his wandering son ; and to incline him to turn away from feeding on husks with swine, and bring him home to his father's house—to his duty—to his God. " If it please thee," he said, " humble thy servant in any other form—send poverty, sickness, desertion, but restore my only and well-beloved boy ; wipe out the stain of rebellion from my name. If this may not be, if still thy servant must go sorrowing for the departed glory of his house, keep him steadfast in duty, so that he swerve not, even for his son, his only son."

The prayer finished, his door was opened, and he saw his father enter without daring himself to move. Mr. Linwood looked at the candle, glanced his eye around the room, and then sat down at the table, saying, as if in explanation, " Belle has been here." He covered his face with both his hands, and murmured in a broken voice, " Oh, Herbert, was it to store up these bitter hours that I watched over your childhood—that I came every night here, when you were sleeping, to kiss you and pray over your pillow ?—what fools we are ! we knit the love of our children with our very heart-strings—we tend on them—we pamper them

—we blend our lives with theirs, and then we are deserted—forgotten !"

" Never, never for one moment !" cried Herbert, who with one spring was at his father's feet. Mr. Linwood started from him, and then, obeying the impulse of nature, he received his son's embrace, and they wept in one another's arms.

The door softly opened. Isabella appeared, and her face irradiating with most joyful surprise, she called, " Mamma, mamma; here, in Herbert's room !" In another instant, Herbert had folded his mother and sister to his bosom ; and Mr. Linwood was beginning to recover his self-possession, and to feel as if he had been betrayed into the surrender of a post. He walked up and down the room, then suddenly stopping and laying his hand on Herbert's shoulder, and surveying him from head to foot, " I know not, but I fear," he said, " what this disguise may mean—tell me, in one word, do you return penitent ?"

" I return grieving that I ever offended you, my dear father, and venturing life and honour to see you—to hear you say that you forgive me."

" Herbert, my son, you know," replied Mr. Linwood, his voice faltering with the tenderness against which he struggled, " that my door and my heart have always been open to you, provided—"

" Oh, no *provideds*, papa ! Herbert begs your forgiveness—this is enough."

" I wish, sir, you would think it was enough,"
sobbed Mrs. Linwood.

" You must think so, papa; it is the sin and
misery of these unhappy times that divides you.
Give to the winds your political differences, and
leave the war to the camp and the field. Herbert has always loved and honoured you."

Mr. Linwood felt as if they were dragging him
over a precipice, and he resisted with all his might.
" A pretty way he has taken to show it!" he said,
" let him declare he has abandoned the rebels and
traitors, and their cause, and I will believe it."

Herbert was silent.

" My dear father," said Isabella.

" Nay, Isabella, do not ' dear father' me. I
will not be coaxed out of my right reason. If you
can tell me that your brother abandons and abjures
the miscreants, speak—if not, be silent."

" If it were true that he did abandon them, he
would be no son of yours, no brother of mine. If
he were thus restored to us, who could restore him
to himself? where could he hide him from himself?
Your own soul would spurn a renegado!—think
better of him—think better of his friends—they
are not all miscreants. There are many noble,
highminded—"

" What? what, Isabella ?"

" As deluded as he is."

" A wisely-finished sentence, child. But you
need not undertake to teach me what they are.   1

know them—a set of paltry schismatics—pet
tifogging attorneys—schoolmasters—mechanics—
shop-keepers—bankrupts—outlaws—smugglers—
half-starved, half-bred, ragged sons of Belial; banded together, and led on by that quack Catiline, that
despot-in-chief, Washington. 'No son of mine if
he abjures them!' I swear to you, Herbert, that
on these terms alone will I ever again receive you
as my son." Again he paused, and after some reflection, added, "You have an alternative if you
do not choose to avail yourself of Sir Henry's
standing proclamation, and come in and receive
your pardon as a deserter—you may join the corps
of Reformees. This opportunity now lost, is lost
for ever. Is my forgiveness worth the price I have
fixed ? speak, Herbert."

" Have I not proved how inexpressibly dear it is
to me ?"

" No faltering, young man ! speak to the point."

" Oh, my dear, dear son," said his mother, "if
you but knew how much we have all suffered for
you, and how happy you can now make us, if you
only will, you would not hesitate, even if the rebel
cause were a good one : you are but as one man to
that, and to us you are all the world."

This *argumentum ad hominem* (the only argument of weak minds) clouded Herbert's perception. It was a moment of the most painful vacil-
lation ; the forgiveness of his father, the minister-
ing, indulgent love of his mother, the presence of

his sister, the soft endearments of home, and all its dear familiar objects, solicited him. He had once forsaken them, but then he was incited by the immeasurable expectation of unrebuked youth, thoughts of high emprise, romantic deeds, and strange incidents; but his experience, with few and slight exceptions, had been a tissue of dangers without the opportunity of brilliant exploits; of fatigue without reward; and of rough and scanty fare, which, however well it may tell in the past life of a hero, has no romantic charm in its actual details. He continued silent. His father perceived, or at least hoped, that he wavered.

" Speak," he said, in a voice of earnest entreaty, " speak, Herbert—my dear son, for God's sake, speak."

" It is right above all things to desire his forgiveness," thought Herbert, " and it is plain there is but one way of getting it. I am in a diabolical hobble—if I succeed in getting back to camp, what am I to expect? Imprudence is crime with our general; and after all, what good have I done the cause ?—and yet—"

" Herbert," exclaimed Isabella, and her voice thrilled through his soul, "is it possible you waver ?"

He started as if he were electrified : his eye met hers, and the evil spirits of doubt and irresolution were overcome.

"Heaven forgive me !" he said, "I waver no longer."

"Then, by all that is holy," exclaimed Mr. Linwood, flushed with disappointment and rage, " you shall reap as you sow; it shall never be said that I sheltered a rebel, though that rebel be my son." He rang the bell violently; "Justice shall have its course—why does not Jupe come!—you too to prove false, Isabella! I might have known it when I saw you drinking in the vapouring of that fellow Lee to-day;" again he rang the bell: "you may all desert me, but I'll be true so long as my pulse beats."

No one replied to him. Mrs. Linwood, sustained by Herbert's encircling arm, wept aloud. Isabella knew the tide of her father's passion would have its ebb as well as flow; she believed the servants were in bed, and that before he could obtain a messenger to communicate with the proper authority, which she perceived to be his present intention, his Brutus resolution would fail. She was however startled by hearing voices in the lower entry, and immediately Rose burst open the door, crying, "Fly, Mr. Herbert—they are after you!"

The words operated on Mr. Linwood like a gust of wind on a superincumbent cloud of smoke His angry emotions passed off, and nature flamed up bright and irresistible. Every thought, every feeling but for Herbert's escape and safety, vanished. "This way, my son," he cried; "through your mother's room—down the back stairs, and out the side gate.—God help you!" He closed the door after Herbert, locked it, and put the key in his pocket. Isabella advanced into the entry to meet her brother's pursuers, and procure a delay of a few moments on what pretext she could. She was met by two men and an officer, sent by Colonel Robertson, the commandant. "Your pardon, Miss Linwood," said the officer, pushing by her into the room where her father awaited him.

"How very rude!" exclaimed Mrs. Linwood, for once in her life speaking first and independently in her husband's presence; "how very rude, sir, to come up stairs into our bedrooms without permission." The officer smiled at this pretended deference to forms at the moment the poor mother was pale as death, and shivering with terror. "I beg your pardon, madam, and yours, Mr. Linwood —this is the last house in the city in which I should willingly have performed this duty; but you, sir, are aware, that in these times our very best and most honoured friends are sometimes involved with our foes."

"No apologies, sir, there's no use in them—you are in search of Mr. Herbert Linwood—proceed —my house is subject to your pleasure."

The officer was reiterating his apologies, when a cry from the side entrance to the yard announced that the fugitive was taken. Mr. Linwood sunk into his chair; but instantly rallying, he asked whither his son was to be conducted.

"I am sorry to say, sir, that I am directed to lodge him in the Provost."

"In Cunningham's hands!—the Lord have mercy on him, then!"

The officer assured him the young man should have whatever alleviation it was in his power to afford him, until Sir Henry's further pleasure should be known. He then withdrew, and left Mr. Linwood exhausted by a rapid succession of jarring emotions.

Isabella retired with her mother, and succeeded in lulling her into a tranquillity which she herself was far enough from attaining.

The person whom, as it may be remembered, Linwood met in passing down the lane to his father's house, was an emissary of Robertson, who had been sent on a scout for Captain Lee's attendant, and who immediately reported to the commandant his suspicions. He, anxious, if possible, not to offend the elder Linwood, had stationed men in the lane and in Broad-street, to watch for the young man's egress. They waited till ten in the evening, and then found it expedient to proceed to the direct measures which ended in Herbert's capture.

L 2

CHAPTER XVI.

"Great is thy power, and great thy fame
Far kenn'd and noted is thy name!
An' tho' yon lowin' heugh's thy hame,
          Thou travels far."

                                        BURNS.

ELIOT LEE returned to his lodgings from Sir
Henry's in no very comfortable frame of mind.   It
was his duty, and this duty, like others, had the in-
convenient property of inflexibility, to return to
West Point with the despatches without attempting to extricate his friend from the shoals and
quicksands amid which he had so rashly rushed.
He consoled himself, however, under this necessity, by the reflection that he could in no way so
efficiently serve Herbert as by being the first to
communicate his imprudence and its consequences
to General Washington.   His anxiety to serve him
was doubled by the consciousness that he should
thereby serve Isabella.   An acquaintance of a day
with a young lady ought not, perhaps, to have
given a stronger impulse to the fervours of friendship; yet the truest friend of three-and-twenty
will find some apology for Eliot in his own experience, or would have found it, if, like Eliot, he had
just seen the incarnation of his most poetic ima-
ginings.

While he awaited in his room the despatches, he tried to adjust the complicated impressions of the day. He reviewed the scene in the library, and his conclusions from it were the result of his observations, naturally tinged by the character of the observer. Is it not impossible for any *man* to understand perfectly the intricate machinery of a woman's heart, its hidden sources of hope and fear, trust and distrust; all its invisible springs and complex action? "If," he thought, "Miss Linwood knew Meredith as I know him; if she knew what she now fears, that he had fed his vanity, his idol, self, on the exhalations of homage, love, trust, and hope, from a pure heart that, like a flower, withered in giving out its sweets, she would not love him; not that it is a matter of volition to love or not to love,—but she could not. If Isabella Linwood, gifted as she is in mind and person, were less sought—if, like my poor little Bessie, she were in some obscure, shady place of life, her pre-eminence unacknowledged and unknown, like her she would be deserted for an enthroned sovereign. This she cannot know; and she is destined to be one of the ten thousand mismated men and women who have thrown away their happiness, and found it out too late. Find it out she must; for this detestable selfishness dulls a man's perception of the rights of others, of their deserts, their wants, and their infirmities, while it makes him keenly susceptible to whatever touches self. He resembles those insects who, instead of the social senses of

21*

hearing and seeing which connect one sentient existence with another, are furnished with feelers that make their own bodies the focus of all sensation.

Eliot was roused from his sententious revery by a whistle beneath his window. He looked out and saw by the moonlight a man squatted on the ground, and so shaded by the wooden entrance to the door as to be but dimly seen. Eliot, conjecturing who it might be, immediately descended the stairs and opened the outer door. The man leaped from the ground, seized both Eliot's hands, and cried out in a half articulate voice—" Could not Kisel find you? hey! when the dog can't find his master, nor the bean its pole, nor the flower the side the sun shines, then say Kisel can't find you, Misser Eliot—hey!"

" My poor fellow! How in the name of wondei did you get here alone?"

" Ah, Misser Eliot, always told you you did not know what a salvation it was to pass for a fool, and all the while be just as wise as other folks. I have my own light," he pointed upwards,—" there's one that guides the owl as well as the eagle, and the fool better than the wise man."

" But how came the enemy to let you pass?"

" Let me! what for should not they? what harm could such as I do them? I told them so, and they believed me—good, hey!"

" You cannot have walked all the way?"

" Walked!—when did wit walk? No, Misser

Eliot, not a step of it. Hooked a fishing canoe and poled 'long shore some,—jumped into a wagon with a blind nigger fiddler and his wife, and rode some,—then up behind a cowboy, and paid him in whistling some,—boarded market-carts some,—and musquashed some."

" And here you are, and now I must take care of you."

" Yes, Misser Eliot, depend on you now, pretty much like other folks—Kisel, hey ! depends on Providence when he can get nothing else to depend on."

" Thank Heaven," thought Eliot, " I have not to draw on my extempore sagacity. Now that I have the real Dromeo, I shall get on without let or hinderance." He re-entered the house, encountered his landlady, and, imboldened by the presence of Kisel, laughed at the unnecessary suspicion that had been excited, ordered his horses, and having received his despatches and his countersigned passports from Sir Henry, he determined to profit by the moonlight, and immediately set forth on his return.

As they passed Mr. Linwood's house Eliot paused for a moment, but there was no intimation from its silent walls ; and hoping and believing that his friend was safe within them, and breathing a prayer for the peerless creature who seemed to him, like a celestial spirit, to sanctify the dwelling that contained her, he spurred his horse as if he would have broken the chain that bound him to the spot—the chain already linking in with his existence, and destined never to be broken till that should be dissolved.

He proceeded some twenty or five-and-twenty miles without incident, when, as he passed a narrow road that intersected the highway, five horsemen turned from it into the main road. Kisel, with the instinct of cowardice, reined his horse close to his master. The men remained in the rear, talking together earnestly in low tones. Suddenly, two of them spurred their horses and came abreast of the forward party, the one beside Kisel, the other beside Eliot. There was at best, impertinence in the movement, and it annoyed Eliot. It might mean something worse than impertinence. He placed his hand on the loaded pistol in his holster, and calmly awaited further demonstrations from his new companions. A cursory glance assured him they were questionable characters. They wore cloth caps, resembling those used by our own winter travellers, drawn close over the eyes, and having a sort of curtain that hid the neck, ears, and chin. The mouth and nose were the only visible features; and though they were dimly seen by the starlight (the moon had set), they seemed to Eliot, with a little aid from imagination, to indicate brutal coarseness and vulgarity. They had on spencers of a dreadnaught material, girded around them with a leathern strap.—" Good evening," said the man at Eliot's side.

Captain Lee made no reply; but his squire, eager to accept a friendly overture, and always ready on the least hint to speak, replied, "Good evening to you, neighbour; which way are you riding?"

"After our horses' noses," replied the fellow, gruffly.

"Oh, that's the way we are travelling—so we may as well be friendly; for in these times there's many a bird on the wing at night beside owls and bats—hey?"

"Where are you from, fellow?" asked the first speaker.

"From below."

"Where are you going?"

"Above."

The man, not disposed to be silenced by Kisel's indefinite replies, repeated his first question to Eliot.

"The true answer is safest," thought Eliot, who was determined, if possible, to avoid a contest where the odds were five to one; and he briefly communicated his destination and errand.

"Despatches!" replied the man, echoing Eliot. "Is that all you have about you? I wish you well, then, to your journey's end—and that wish is worth something, I can tell you. Come, Pat, spur your horse—we've no time to be lagging here."

"I'm thinking, captain, we had better change horses with these gentlemen, and give them our spurs to boot;" and suiting the action to the word,

he seized Kisel's bridle and ordered him to dismount.   At the same instant his comrade-captain
made a lunge at Eliot, as if for a corresponding
seizure; but Eliot perceived the movement in time
to evade it.   He roused the metal of his horse
with a word—the fine animal sprang forward—
Eliot turned him short round, and presented his
pistol to Kisel's antagonist, who let fall the bridle
and turned to defend himself.

" Now spur your horse and fear nothing, Kisel,'
cried his master.

Not to fear was impossible to Kisel; but the first
injunction he obeyed, even to the rowels of his
spurs ; and he and his master soon distanced their
pursuers, who, now partly incited by revenge,
pursued the hopeless chase for two or three miles.

Soon after losing sight of these men, Eliot
reached Gurdon Coit's.   Coit was a farmer, who, on
the borders of the river and on the neutral ground,
kept a public house as supplemental to his farm,
which, in these troubled times, was roughly handled
by friends and foes.   Friends and foes we say : for
though Coit observed, as beseemed a man of his
present calling, a strict outward neutrality, in heart
he was on his country's side; as he often testified,
with considerable risk to himself, by affording facilities to secret emissaries to the city, and by receiving
into his house valuable supplies, that were run up
from the city (where Washington had many secret
trusty friends) for the use of the army at West
Point.

Eliot stopped at Coit's, and announced his intention, received by a hurra from Kisel, of remaining there till daylight. Coit was roused from a nap in his chair by the entrance of his new guests. In reply to Eliot's request for refreshment and lodging, he said, "You see, captain" (he recognised Eliot, who had been at his house on his way down), "my house is brimful. Cæsar, and Venus, and all the little niggers, sleep in the kitchen. My wife's sisters are here visiting, and they've got the best bedroom, and my wife and the gals the other; for you know we must give the best to the women, poor creturs—so a plank here in the bar-room is the best sleeping privilege I can give you, and the barn to your man."

"Oh, Misser Eliot, I've got a trembling in my limbs to-night," interposed Kisel; " don't send me away alone."

Eliot explained the cause of poor Kisel's trembling limbs; and it was agreed that he should share his master's *sleeping privilege*. In answer to Eliot's communication, Coit said, "As sure as a gun, you've met the skinners; and you're a lucky man to get out of their hands alive. They've been harrying up and down the country like so many wolves for the last three weeks, doing mischief wherever 'twas to be done;—nobody has escaped them but Madam Archer."

" Who is Madam Archer ?"

" I mistrust, captain, you a'n't much acquainted with the quality in York state, or you'd know

Madam Archer of Beech-Hill; the widow lády with the blind twins. I believe the Lord has set a defence about her habitation; for there she stays, with those helpless little people, and neither harm nor the fear of it come nigh her, though she has nothing of mankind under her roof except one old slave; and them that are brought up slaves, you know, have neither sense nor pluck for difficult times."

Kisel interrupted the landlord's harangue to hint to his master that his fright had brought on a great appetite; and Eliot, feeling the same effect, though not from precisely the same cause, requested his host to provide him some supper, while he and his man went to look after their horses; a duty that he gratefully performed, rejoicing in the rustic education that made it light to him to perform services for which he often saw the noble animals of his more daintily-bred brother officers suffering.

"Who are these, my bed-fellows?" he asked of Coit, a few moments after, as he sat discussing some fine bacon and brown bread, and handing slice after slice to Kisel, who, squatting on the hearth, received it like a petted dog from his hand. The subjects of his inquiry were two long fellows wrapped in blankets, and their heads on their knapsacks, stretched on the floor, and soundly sleeping.

"They are soldiers from above," replied Coit in a whisper, "who have come here to receive some tea and sugar, and such kind of fancy articles for the ladies at the Point."

"And who is this noisy person on the settle?"

"He does snore like all natur," replied Coit, laughing, and then continued in a lowered voice:—"I don't know who he is, though I can make a pretty good guess; and if I guess right, he a'nt a person I should like to interfere with, and it's plain he don't choose to make himself known. He has a rough tongue, that does not seem like your born quality—he does not handle his victuals like them —but he has that solid way with him that shows he was born to command the best of you in such times as these, when, as you may say, we value a garment according to its strength, and not for the trimmings. No offence, captain?"

"None in the world to me, my good friend; I am not myself one of those you call the born quality."

"A'n't? I declare! then you've beat me—I thought I could always tell 'em." Coit drew his chair near to Eliot, and added, in an earnest tone, "The time is coming, captain, and that's what the country is fighting for; for we can't say we are desperately worried with the English yoke; but the time is coming when one man that's no better than his neighbour won't wear stars on his coat, and another that's no worse a collar round his neck; when one won't be born with a silver spoon in his mouth, and another with a pewter spoon, but all will start fair, and the race will be to the best fellow."

"Hey! Misser Eliot," cried Kisel, in his wonted tone, when a ray of intelligence penetrated the mists that enveloped his brain.

22

His shrill voice awakened the sleeper on the
settle, who, lifting up his shaggy head, asked
what " all this cackling meant ?"   Then seeming
to recover his self-possession, he keenly surveyed
Eliot and his man, covered his face with his ban
dana handkerchief, and again composed himself
to sleep.

Eliot, after securing a " sleeping privilege" for
Kisel, received from our friend Coit the best unoccupied blanket and pillow the house afforded;
and giving his fellow-lodgers, in seamen's phrase,
the best berth the width of the room admitted, he
was soon lost in the deep refreshing sleep compounded of youth, health, and a good conscience.

Our host was left to his own musings, which, as
he fixed his eye on Eliot's fine face, marked with
nature's aristocracy, were somewhat in the following strain:—" ' Not of the born quality !'—hum—
well, he has that that is quality in the eye of God,
I guess.   How he looked after his dumb beast,
and this poor creater here, that seems not to have
the wit of a brute ; he's had the bringing up of a
gentleman, any how.   I see it in his bearing, his
speech, his voice.   Well, I guess my children will
live to see the day when the like of him will be
the only gentlemen in the land.   The Almighty
must furnish the material, but the forming, polish-
ing, and currency, must be the man's own doings ;
not his father's, or grandfather's, or the Lord knows
who."

While Coit pursues his meditations, destined

soon to be roughly broken, we offer our readers some extracts from a letter which fortunately has fallen into our hands, to authenticate our veritable history. It was written by Mrs. Archer, of Beech Hill, to her niece, Isabella Linwood.

" No, no, my dear Belle, I cannot remove to the city—it must not be; and I am sorry the question is again mooted. ' A woman, and naturally born to fears,' I may be; but because I have that in convenient inheritance, I see no reason why I should cherish and augment it. Your imagination, which is rather an active agent, has magnified the terrors of the times; and it seems just now to be unduly excited by the monstrous tales circulated in the city, of the atrocities the Yankees have committed on the tories. I see in Rivington's Gazette, which you wrapped around the sugarplums that you sent the children (thank you), various precious anecdotes of Yankee tigers and tory *lambs*, forsooth! that are just about as true as the tales of giants and ogres with which your childhood was edified. The Yankees are a civilized race, and never, God bless them! commit gratuitous cruelties. If they still ' see it to be duty' (to quote their own Puritan phrase), they will cling to this contest till they have driven the remnant of your Israel, Belle, every tory and Englishman, from the land; but they will commit no episodical murders: it is only the ignorant man that is unnecessarily cruel. They are an instructed, kind-hearted, Christian people; and of this there will be abundant proof while the present war is remembered. Remember, Belle, these people have unadulterated English blood in their veins, which to you should be a prevailing argument in their favour; and believe me, they have a fair portion of the spirit of their freedom-loving and all-daring ancestors. Our English mother, God bless her, too, should have known better than to trammel, scold, and try to whip her sons into obedience, when they had come to man's estate, and were fit to manage their own household. Thank Heaven, I have outlived the prejudices against the people of New-England which my father transmitted to his children. 'There they come,' he used to say, when he saw these busy people driving into the manor; 'every snow brings them, and, d—n them, every thaw too!'

"What a pander to ignorance and malignity is this same prejudice, Belle! How it disturbs the sweet accords of nature, sacrilegiously severs the bonds by which God has united man to man, and breaks the human family into parties and sects! How it clouds the intellect and infects the heart with its earthborn vapours; so that the Englishman counts it virtue to scorn the American, and the *true* American cherishes a hatred of the Englishman. Our generous friends in the south look with contempt on the provident, frugal sons of the Puritans; and they, blinded in their turn, can see nothing but the swollen pride of slave-owners and hard-heartedness of slave-drivers in their brethren of the south. Even you, dear Belle, have not escaped this *atmospheric* influence. After a gen- .eral denunciation of the rebels, as you term the country's troops, you say, in the letter now before me, ' of course, you have nothing to fear from the British regulars ;' and I reply, like the poor brute in the fable, ' Heaven save me from my friends !' The British soldiers are aliens to the soil ; they have neither ' built houses nor tilled lands' here ; and they cannot have the same kindly and home feel- ing that a native extends to the denizens of his own land. Besides, they are, for the most part, trained to the inhuman trade of war ; and though I have all due respect for English blood, and know many of their officers to be most amiable and accomplished men, I never see a detachment of their troops, with their colours flying (and such often pass within sight of us), without a sudden coldness creeping over me. Then there are the Jagers and other mercenaries that our friends have brought over to fight out this family quarrel—is this right, Belle ? You will suspect me of having turned whig—well, keep your suspicion to your- self. The truth is, that living isolated as I do, I have a fairer point of view than you, surrounded as you are by British officers and tories devoted to the royal cause, and to you, my beautiful niece, their elected sovereign.

"My only substantial fear, after all, is of the cowboys and skinners, more especially the last,

22*

who have done some desperate deeds in my neighbourhood. I have taken care to have it well
known that I have sent all my plate and valuables
to the city, and I hope and believe they will not
pay me a visit. Should they, however, a widow
and two blind children have little to dread from
creatures who are made in the image of God, de-
faced as that image may be. Defenceless crea-
tures have a fortress in every human heart. No, I
repeat it, I cannot go to the city. You say I am
afraid of the shackles of city life! I confess, that
with my taste for freedom, and my long indulgence
in it, they would be galling to me. I could, however, bear them without wincing to be near you,
but my children, Belle—my *blind* children! my
paramount duty is to them, and is prescribed and
absolute. In the city they are continually remind-
ed of their privation, and the kinder their friends
the more manifold are the evidences of it; there
they feel that they are merely objects of compassion, supernumeraries in the human family, who
can only receive, not give. Here they have
motives to exertions, dependants on their care.
Their fruits and flowers, doves, rabbits, chickens,
ducks, dogs, and kittens, live and thrive by them.
Nature is to them a perpetual study and delight.
I have just been walking with them over the hill
behind my house. You remember the hill is frin-
ged with beech-trees, and crowned by their superior
forest brethren, the old tory oak, the legitimate
sovereign by the grace of God; the courtier elm
(albeit American!), that bows its graceful limbs to

every breeze ; the republican maple, that resists all
hostility ; and the evergreen pine, a loyalist—is it,
Belle ? well, be it so ; it always wears the same
coat, but they say its heart is not the soundest !—
Pardon me, we fall so naturally into political allusions in these times.

" My children have learned so accurately to dis-
criminate sounds, that as we walked over the hill,
they made me observe the variations of sound
when the breezes whispered among the light beech-
leaves, when they stole through the dense masses
of the maple foliage, fluttered over the pendent
stems of the elm, rustled along the polished oak-
leaves, and passed in soft musical sighs, like the
lowest breath of the Æolian harp, over the bristled
pines. Do you remember the lively little stream
that dashes around the rear of this hill, and winding quietly through the meadow at its base, steals
into the Hudson ? They, in their rambles, unat-
tended and fearless, have worn a footpath along
the margin of this stream, and wherever there
is a mossy rock, or fallen trunk of a tree, they
may be seen tying up wild flowers, or the arm of
each around the other, singing hymns and songs.
I have seen men with hard features and rough
hands arrested by the sound of their voices, and
as they listened, the tears trickling down their
weather-beaten faces. Can I fear for them, Belle ?
They both delight in gardening ; they love none
but flowers of sweet odour ; no unperfumed flower,
however beautiful, is tolerated ; but the lawn, the
borders of the walks, all their shady haunts, are

enamelled with mignionette, violets, lilies of the valley, carnations, clove-pinks, and every sweet-breathed flower. The magnificent view of the Hudson from the piazza they cannot see; but they have wreathed the pillars with honeysuckles and sweet-briers, and there they sit and enjoy the south-west breezes, the chief luxury of our climate. Could I pen them up in a city, where they will never walk into the fresh air but to be a spectacle, and where they must be utterly deprived of the ministration of nature through which God communes with their spirits? I am sure you will acquiesce in my decision, my dear Isabella. You need not try to convince your father of my rationality; the reasonableness of any woman is a contradiction in terms to him. Whatever may happen, your mother will not reproach me: she will only say again what she has so often said before, 'that she expected it, poor sister Mary was always so odd.' This letter is all about myself. I have anxieties too about you, but for the present I keep them to myself. The bright empyrean of hope is for youth to soar in, and your element shall not be invaded by croakings from the bogs of experience.   "Truly yours,

"MARY ARCHER."

The same conveyance that transported this letter, so full of resolution and trust, to Isabella, carried her information of the events related in the next chapter.

CHAPTER XVII.

" We are men, my liege.
" Ay, in the catalogue ye go for men."

SURPRISE has sometimes been expressed by our English friends who have travelled among us, that the Americans should cherish such lively recollections of the war that achieved their independence, when their countrymen had almost forgotten that such a contest ever existed. They seem to have forgotten, too, that while their part was enacted by soldiers by profession and foreign mercenaries, our battle was fought by our fathers, sons, and brothers; that while the scene of action was three thousand miles from them, it was in our *home-lots* and at our firesides; and above all, that while they fought for the preservation of colonial possessions, at best a doubtful good, we were contending for national independence—for the right and power to make the last and best experiment of popular government.

Such circumstances as it falls to our lot now to relate, are not easily forgotten; and such, or similar, occurred in some of the happiest homes of our land.

Mrs. Archer was quietly sleeping with her children, when she was awakened by unusual sounds in the room below her; and immediately her maid, who slept in the adjoining apartment, rushed in, crying out " that the house was full of men—she heard them on the stairs, in the parlour, hall, everywhere !"

Mrs. Archer sprang from the bed, threw on her dressing-gown, bade the girl be quiet, and beware of frightening the children ; and then, as they, startled by the noise, raised their heads from their pillows, she told them, in a calm and decidedly cheerful voice, that there were men in the house who she believed had come to rob it, but that they would neither do harm to them nor to her. She then ordered her maid to light the candles on the dressing-table, and again reassuring her trembling children, who had meanwhile crept to her side, she awaited the fearful visiters, whose footsteps she heard on the staircase.

A fierce-looking wretch burst into the apartment. The spectacle of the mother and her children arrested him, and he involuntarily doffed his cap. It was a moment for a painter, if he could calmly have surveyed the scene. The maid had shrunk behind her mistress's chair, and kneeling there, had grasped her gown with both hands, as if there were safety in the touch. Poor little Lizzy's face was hidden in her mother's bosom, and her fair silken curls hung over her mother's dark dressing-gown. Ned, at the sound of the opening door, turned his sightless eyeballs towards the villain. There was something manly and defying in his air and erect attitude, something protecting in the ex-

pression of his arm as he laid it over his sister, while
the clinging of his other arm around his mother's
neck, indicated the defencelessness of childhood
and his utter helplessness. Mrs. Archer had
thrown aside her nightcap; her hair was twisted up
in a sort of Madona style; but not of the tame
Madona cast was her fine, spirited countenance
which blended the majesty of the ideal Minervr
with the warmth and tenderness of the woman and
mother.

The marauder, on entering, paid her, as we say)
said, an instinctive homage; but immediately recovering his accustomed insolence, he replied to
her calm demand, of " what is your purpose ?"
" To get what we can, and keep what we get—my
name is Hewson, which, if you've heard it, will be
a warrant to you that I sha'n't do my work by
halves."

The name of the skinner was too notorious
not to have been heard by Mrs. Archer. Her
blood ran cold, but she replied, without faltering, " Proceed to your work ; the house is open to
you, not a lock in your way. Abby, give him
my purse off the dressing-table—there is all the
money I have by me—now leave my room, I pray
you."

" Softly, mistress—catch old birds with chaff.
First surrender your watch, plate, and jewels,
which I take to be in this very room that you are
so choice of."

" My watch, plate, and jewels, are in New-
York."

" The d—l they are !"   Then emptying out and
counting the gold and silver the purse contained,
" this will never do," he said—" this will not pay
the reckoning—live and let live—every one to his
trade."   He then proceeded, without further ceremony, to rip open beds and mattresses, emptied the
contents of every box, trunk, and drawer, explored
every corner and recess as adroitly as a trained dog
would unearth his game, and seized on such light
articles as attracted his eye, grumbling and swear-
ing all the time at being cheated and out-manœuvred
by a woman ; for in this light he seemed to view
the measures Mrs. Archer had taken to secure her
valuables.

In this humour he rejoined his comrades in the
dining-room ; who he found, with the exception of
a few dozen silver spoons and forks, had had an
equally bootless search, and were now regaling
themselves with cold meats, etc., from the pantry.

" Hey, boys—always after the provender before
you've done your work."

" There's no work to be done, captain—we can't
carry off chairs and tables—so what's the use of
bothering ? we've done our best, and nobody can
do better."

" Your best—maybe, Pat—but your and my
best are two.   We shall have whigs, tories, and reg-
'lars at our heels for this flash in the pan."   He
strided up and down the room, kicking out of his
way whatever obstacle was in it, and muttering to
himself a plan he was revolving : " Madam must
turn out the shiners," he concluded aloud.

" Ay, captain—but how's the bird that won't sing to be made to sing—she is a cunning old one, I'm thinking."

" Old !—Time has never made a track on her yet—cunning she may be, but I don't believe she lied to me—she seems high as the stars above that—but if she has not got the money, boys, she can get it—I'll make her, too—I'll wager your soul on that, Pat."

"Wager your own, honey, that's forfeit to the devil long ago."

A little more time was wasted in similar retorts, well shotted, in their own phrase, with oaths, and washed down with plentiful draughts of wine, when the captain returned to Mrs. Archer's apartment. "I say, mistress," he began, his flushed face and thickened voice indicating she had fresh cause for alarm, "I say we can't be choused— so if you want to save what's choicer than money," he shook his fist with a tiger-like expression at the children, "you must have two hundred guineas put under ground for me, on the north side of the big oak, at the bridge, and that before Saturday night; nobody to know it but you—no living soul but you and that gal there—no false play, remember. Come, strike while the iron's hot, or we'll say three hundred."

Mrs. Archer reflected for a moment. She would have given a bond for any sum by which she could relieve herself of the presence of the out-laws. They had already produced such an effect on little Lizzy, a timid, susceptible creature, that she expected every moment to see her falling into convulsions ; and with this dread each moment seemed an hour. She replied, that the money should, without fail, be placed in the appointed spot.

"That is not quite all, madam; I must have security. I know how the like of you look on promises made to the like of me. I got a rope as good as round my neck by trusting to them once, and no thanks to them that I slipped it. I'll clinch the nail this time—I'll have security."

"What security?" demanded Mrs. Archer, the colour for the first time forsaking her cheeks and lips ; for by the ruffian's glance, and a significant up and down motion of his head, she guessed his purpose.

"A pawn—I must have a pawn—one of them young ones. You need not screech and hold on so, you little fools. If you behave, I'll not hurt a hair of your head. The minute I handle the money you shall have 'em back ; but as sure as my name's Sam Hewson, I'll make 'em a dead carcass if you play me false."

"You shall not touch my children—any thing else—ask all—take all—any thing but my children."

"Take all !—ay, that we shall—all we can take ; and as to asking, we mean to make sure of what we ask—' a bird in the hand,' mistress."

"Oh, take my word, my oath—spare my children !"

"Words are breath, and oaths breath peppered. Your children are your life ; and, one of them in our hands, our secret is as safe with you as with us—we've no time to chaffer—make one of them ready."

"Oh, mother!—mother!" shrieked Lizzy, clinging round her mother's waist.

"Hush, Lizzy—I'll go," said Edward.

"Neither shall go, my children—they shall take my life first."

The outlaw had advanced with the intention of seizing one of them; but, awed by the resolution of the mother, or perhaps touched by the generosity of the boy, he paused and retreated, muttering to himself, "It's a rough job—Pat shall do it." He once more left the apartment and returned to his comrades.

A sudden thought occurred to Mrs. Archer; a faint hope dawned upon her. "Bring me the horn from the hall-table," she said to her servant. The girl attempted to obey, but her limbs sunk under her. Mrs. Archer disengaged herself from the children, ran down the stairs, returned with the horn, threw open her window, and blew three pealing blasts. The outlaws were engaged in packing their spoil.

"Ha!" exclaimed Hewson, "it rings well—again —again. Never mind; you'll wake nothing, mistress, but the dogs, cocks, and owls. Hear how they're at it!—'bow—wow—wow—the beggars are come to town,'—ha, ha—well done. But boys, I say, we'd best be off soon. Pat, you know" (he had already communicated his plan to Pat), "bring down one of them young ones."

Pat went—he lingered. "Come, boys, hurry," cried Hewson, who now began to apprehend the possibility of a response to Mrs. Archer's summons: "what the d—l ails that fellow?"—he went to the staircase and called. Pat appeared; but without the child, and looking as a wild beast might, subdued by a charm. "They're *blind*, captain—both *blind!*" he said. "I can't touch them —by all that's holy I can't—there's not strength in my arm to hold the sightless things—the one nor the t'other of 'em."

"Fool—baby!" retorted Hewson, "you know we don't mean to hurt 'em."

"Then do it yourself, captain—I can't, and there's an end on't."

Hewson hesitated. The image of the mother and her blind children daunted even his fierce spirit. An expedient occurred to him:—"A sure way," he thought, "of drowning feelings." In ransacking the pantry he had seen a flask of brandy, and then prudently concealed it from his men. He now brought it forth, and passed it round and round. It soon began its natural work: consumed in its infernal fires all intellectual power, natural affection, domestic and pitiful emotion; put out the light of Heaven, and roused the brute passions of the men.

Hewson saw the potion working; their "human countenances changed to brutish form." "It's a d—d shame,—ant it, boys," said he, "for this tory madam to balk us?—we shall have a hurra after us for this frolic, and nothing to show—we might as well have robbed a farmhouse, and who would have cared ?"

"We'll tache her better, captain," said Pat; "we'll make an example of her, as the judges say in Ireland when they hang the lads. I'll give her a blow over the head, if you say so, handy like— or wring the chickens' necks—it's asy done."

"Pshaw, Pat—it's only your asses of judges that think examples of any use. If we hook one of the chickens, you know, Pat, she'll be glad to buy it back with the yellow shiners, boy, that's lodged safe in York—fifty a piece—share and share alike—my turn is it ?—here's to you, boys— a short life and a merry one. I've charged 'em up to the mark," thought he; and in raising the flask to his lips, it slipped through his hands and was broken to fragments. "Ah, my men! there's a sign for us—we may have a worse slip than that ''tween the cup and the lip :' so let's be off—come, Pat."

"Shall I fetch 'em both, captain ?"

"No, no—one is as good as a thousand. But stay, Pat. Drunk as they are," thought Hewson, "I'll not trust them in the sound of the mother's screeches. First, Pat, let's have all ready for a start—tie up your bags, boys, come."

The men's brains were so clouded, that it seemed to Hewson they were an eternity in loading their beasts with their booty. Delay after delay occurred; but finally all was ready, and he gave the signal to Pat.

Pat now obeyed to the letter. He mounted the stairs, sprang like a tiger on his prey, and returned with Lizzy, already an unconscious burden, in his arms. One piercing shriek Hewson heard proceeding from Mrs. Archer's apartment, but not another sound. It occurred to him that Pat might have committed the murder he volunteered; and exclaiming, " The blundering Irish rascal has kicked the pail over !" he once more ascended the stairs to assure himself of the cause of the omi nous silence. Edward was in the adjoining apartment when Lizzy was wrested from her mother's arms. He was recalled by Mrs. Archer's scream ; and when Hewson reached the apartment, he found Mrs. Archer lying senseless across the threshold of the door, and Edward groping around, and calling, " Mother !—Lizzy !—where are you ?—do speak, mother !"

A moment after, Mrs. Archer felt her boy's arms around her neck. She returned to a consciousness of her condition, and heard the trampling of the outlaws' horses as they receded from her dwelling.

CHAPTER XVIII.

——— " Good vent'rous youth,
I love thy courage yet, and bold emprise."

" CAPTAIN !—Captain Lee ! don't you hear that
norn ?" said Gurdon Coit, shaking our soundly-
sleeping friend Eliot.

" Yes, thank you, I hear it ;—it's daylight, is it ?"

" No, no ; but there's something to pay up at
Madam Archer's. Those devils you met on the
road, I doubt, are there—the lights have been
glancing about her rooms this hour, and now
they've blown the horn—there's mischief, depend
on't."

" Why in the name of Heaven did not you wake
me sooner ?" exclaimed Eliot. " Rouse up these
fellows—wake that snoring wretch on the settle,
and we'll to her aid instantly."

The offensive snoring ceased as Coit whispered, " No, don't wake him—edge-tools, you know "
He then proceeded to wake the men from West
Point, who were sleeping on the floor. Eliot, as
they lifted their heads, recognised them—the one a
common soldier, the other a certain Ensign Tooler
—a man who had the most disagreeable modifi-
cation of Yankee character; knowingness over-
laid with conceit, and all the self-preserving virtues
concentrated in selfishness, as bad liquor is distilled

from wholesome grain. "Tooler, is that you?" exclaimed Eliot—"and you, Mason? up instantly!" —and he explained the occasion for their prompt service.

"And who is this Madam Archer?" asked Tooler, composedly resting his elbow on the floor.

"She is a woman in need of our protection. This is enough for us to know," replied Eliot, discreetly evading more explicit information.

"She lives in the big house on the hill, don't she?"

"Yes, yes."

"Then I guess we may as well leave her to her luck, for she belongs to the tory side."

"Good Heavens, Tooler!—do you hesitate?—Mason, go with me if you have the soul of a man."

"Lie still, Mason, we're under orders,—Captain Lee must answer for himself. It's none of our business if he's a mind to go off fighting windmills; but duty is duty, and we'll keep to the straight and narrow path."

"Cowardly, canting wretch!" exclaimed Eliot.

"I'm no coward, Captain Eliot Lee, and if Coit will say that Madam Archer is on our side, and you'll undertake to answer to General Washington for all consequences, I'll not hinder Mason's joining you."

The terms were impracticable. There was no time to be lost: "You will go with me, Coit?" said Eliot.

"Why, Captain Lee, it's a venturesome business."

" Yes or no, Coit ! not an instant's delay."

" I'll go, Captain Lee,—I'm not a brute."

Mason did not quite relish the consciousness of acting like a brute, and he half rose, balancing in his mind the shame of remaining, against the risk of disobeying his ensign's orders. " Lie still, Mason," said Tooler; " mind me and you're safe— I'll take care of number one."

The person on the settle now sprang up and poured a torrent of vituperative oaths and invectives on Tooler. Tooler looked up with the abject expression of a barking cur when he hears his master's voice. "Why, gen'ral," said he, "if I had known—"

" Don't gen'ral me !—don't defile my name with your lips ! A pretty fellow you, to prate of duty and orders in the very face of the orders of the Almighty commander-in-chief, to remember the widows and fatherless in their affliction. I always mistrust your fellows that cant about duty. They'll surrender the post at the first go off, and then expect conscience to let them march out with the honours of war."

" I'm ready to go, sir,—ready and willing, if you say so."

" No, by George !—I'd rather fight single-handed with fifty skinners, than have one such cowardly devil as you at my side." All this was said while " the gen'ral" was putting on his coat and hat, and arming himself; " are we ready, Captain Lee ?" he concluded.

" Perfectly," replied Eliot, wondering who this

sturdy authoritative auxiliary might be, but not
venturing to ask, as he thought " the gen'ral" had
implied his wish to remain incognito, and really not
caring at this moment whose arm it was, provided
it was raised in Mrs. Archer's defence. After one
keen survey of " the gen'ral's" person, he concluded, " I never have seen him." He had not. Once
seen, that frank, fearless countenance was never to
be forgotten ; neither could one well forget the
broad, brawny, working-day frame that sustained
it, or the peculiar limp (caused by one leg being
shorter than the other), the only imperfection and
marring of the figure of our rustic Hercules.

In an instant they were mounted, and in five
minutes more, the distance not much exceeding
half a mile, they were entering Mrs. Archer's
hall. An ominous silence reigned there. The
house was filled with smoke, through which the
lighted candles, left by Hewson's crew, faintly
glimmered, and exposed the relics of their feast,
with other marks of their forray. A bright light
shone through the crevices of the pantry door ;
Coit opened it, and immediately the flames of a
fire which had been communicated (whether inten-
tionally, was never ascertained) to a chest of linen
burst forth. " Good Heaven ! where are the family !" exclaimed Eliot and his companion, in a breath.

" Follow me," cried Coit, leading the way to
Mrs. Archer's apartment, and shouting " fire !"
His screams were answered by the female servants, who now rushed from their mistress's apartment. " Where's your lady ?" demanded " the

general." They were too much bewildered to reply, and both he and Eliot followed Coit's lead, and all three paused at the threshold of Mrs. Archer's door, paralyzed by the spectacle of the mother, sitting perfectly motionless with her boy in her arms, and looking like a statue of despair. The general was the first to recover his voice. " Lord of Heaven, madam !" he exclaimed, " your house is on fire !"

She made no reply whatever. She seemed not even to hear him. " Where is the little girl ?" asked Coit.

Mrs. Archer's face slightly convulsed. Her boy sprang from her arms at the sound of a familiar voice,—" Oh, Mr. Coit," he cried, " they've taken off Lizzy !"

The crackling of the advancing flames, and the pouring in of volumes of smoke, prevented any farther explanation at the moment. The instinct of self-preservation, awakened in some degree, renerved Mrs. Archer; and half sustained by Eliot's arm, she and her boy were conducted to an office detached from the house, and so far removed from it as to be in no danger from the conflagration. In the meantime the general had ascertained from the servants all that could be learned of the direction the skinners had taken, and that they were not more than fifteen minutes in advance of them. He and Coit had remounted their horses, and he was hallooing to Eliot to join them :—" Come, young man," he cried, " let's do what's to be done at once, and cry afterward, if cry we must."

"Recover her !" said Mrs. Archer, repeating the last words of Eliot's attempt to revive her hopes— "her lifeless body you may—God grant it !"

She paused, and shuddered. She still felt the marble touch of Lizzy's cheek—still saw her head and limbs drop as the ruffian seized her.

Eliot understood her : "My dear madam," he said, "she has fainted from terror, nothing more ; she will be well again when she feels your arm around her—take courage, I beseech you."

It is not in the heart of woman to resist such inspiring sympathy as was expressed in Eliot's face and voice. If Mrs. Archer did not hope, there was something better than despair in the feeling of intense expectation that concentrated all sensation. She seemed unconscious of the flames that were devouring her house. She did not hear the boyish exclamations with which Edward, as he heard the falling rafters and tumbling chimneys, interspersed his sobs for poor Lizzy ; nor the clamorous cryings of the servants, which would break out afresh as they remembered some favourite article of property consuming in the flames.

A few yards from Mrs. Archer's house, a road diverged from that which our pursuers had taken. They halted for a moment, when Coit, who was familiar with the localities of the vicinity, advised to taking the upper road. "They both," he said, "came out in one at a distance of about three miles. They would thus avoid giving the forward party any warning of their approach, and their horses being the freshest and fleetest, they might possibly arrive at the junction of the roads first, and surprise the skinners from an ambush."

" Lucky for us that there is another road," replied the general, as, conforming to Coit's suggestion, they turned into it. "The rascals we're after are foxes, and would be sure to escape if they heard the hounds behind them."

" I should think, from my observation of their horses," replied Eliot, "they have small chance of escaping us in a long pursuit."

"There I think you mistake ; they get their jades for no *vartu* under heaven but running away, and I've heard of their distancing horses that looked equal to mine ; speed a'n't Charlie's forte, though," he added, in a half audible voice ; and patting his beast lovingly, "you've done a feat at it once, Charlie. They know all the holes and hiding-places in the country," he continued, " and I have heard of their disappearing as suddenly as if the ground had opened and swallowed them up —I wish it would—the *varmin !*"

" Had we not best try the mettle of our horses ?" asked Eliot, who felt as if his companions were taking the matter too coolly.

" If you please."

The general put up his Bucephalus to his utmost speed ; but in spite of the feat his master boasted, he seemed to have been selected for other virtues than fleetness, for both Eliot and Coit soon passed

him, and so far outrode him as not to be able
to discern the outline of the rider's figure when
they reached the junction of the roads where they
hoped to intercept the skinners. They had perceived the faintest streak of dawn, while they could
see the eastern horizon and the morning star trembling and glittering above it. Now they entered a
little wood of thick-set pines and hemlocks, and
the darkness of midnight seemed to thicken around
them.

"Hark!" cried Eliot, suddenly halting—"don't
you hear the trampling of horses?"

"Yes," replied Coit, "there is a bridge just
ahead; let us secure a position as near it as possible." They moved on, and after advancing a few
yards, again halted, still remaining under cover
of the wood. "We are within twenty feet of the
other road," resumed Coit; "it runs along just
parallel to where we stand, and a few feet below
us; there is a small stream of water on the other
side of the pines, which we pass over by the bridge
as we fall into the other road; the rub will be to
get on to the bridge before they see us—I wish
the general would come up!"

"We must not wait for him, Coit."

"Not wait for him!" replied Coit, whose valour
was at least tempered by discretion, "we are but
two to five, and they such devils!"

"We have Heaven on our side—we must not
wait a breath—we *must* intercept them; follow me
when I give the spurs to my horse."

"Oh, if he would but come up!" thought Coit;

" this young man is as brave as a lion, but the general *is* a lion !"

The skinners had now approached so near to our friends that they fancied they heard the hard breathing of their horses. They halted at the brook, and Eliot distinctly heard Hewson say to Pat, " Don't she come to yet ?"

" I can't just say—once or twice she opened her sightless eyes like, and she gasped, but she's corpse-cold ; and captain, I say, I don't like the feel of her ; I am afeard I shall drop her, there's such a wonderful weight in her little body."

" You cowardly fool !"

" By the soul of my mother, it's true—try once the lift of her !"

" Pshaw ! I've twice her weight in this bundle before me. Hold up her head while I dash some water in her face ; they say the breath will go entirely if you let it stop too long." Hewson then dismounted, took from his pocket a small silver cup he had abstracted from Mrs. Archer's pantry, and was stooping to fill it, when he was arrested by the appearance of his pursuers.

" Now is our time !" cried Eliot, urging his horse down the descent that led to the bridge. There the animal instinctively stopped. The bridge was old, the rotten planks had given way, and as destruction, not reparation, was the natural work of those troubled times, the bridge had been suffered to remain impassable. Eliot looked up and down the stream ; it was fordable, but the banks, though not high, were precipitous and ragged. Eliot measured the gap in the bridge accurately with his eye : "My horse can leap it," was his conclusion, and he gave him voice, whip, and spur. The animal, as if he felt the inspiration of his master's purpose, made a generous effort and passed the vacant space. Eliot did not look back to see if he were followed. He did not heed Coit's exclamation, "you're lost!" nor did he hear the general, who, on arriving at the bridge, cried, "God help you, my boy!—I can't—my beast can't do it with my weight on him—follow me, Coit," and he turned to retrace his steps to a point where, as he had marked in stopping to water his horse, the stream was passable.

Eliot was conscious of but one thought, one hope, one purpose—to rescue the prey from the villains. He had an indistinct impression that their numbers were not complete. He aimed his pistol at Patrick's head—the bullet sped—not a sound escaped the poor wretch. He raised himself upright in his stirrups, and fell over the side of the horse, dragging the child with him.

At this moment two horsemen passed between Eliot and Pat, and one of them, dropping his bridle and stretching out his arms, screamed, "Misser Eliot—oh, Misser Eliot!"

It was poor Kisel, but vain was his appeal. One of the men smartly lashed Kisel's horse :—Linwood's spirited gray darted forward as if he had been starting on a race-course ; and Kisel was fain to cling to him by holding fast to his mane, so strong is instinct, though if he had deliberately chosen between death and separation from his master, he certainly would have chosen the former.

Meanwhile Hewson, springing forward like a cat, and disengaging the child from Pat's death-grasp, cried, "Fire on him, boys!—beat him down." and re-mounted his horse, intending to pass Eliot, aware that his policy was to get off before the attacking party should, as he anticipated, be re-enforced. Eliot, however, prevented this movement by placing himself before him, drawing his sword, and putting Hewson on the defence.

Hewson felt himself shackled by the child, and he was casting her off, when, changing his purpose, he placed her as a shield before his person, and again ordered his men to fire. They had been ridding themselves of the spoils that encumbered them, and now obeyed. Both missed their mark.

"D—n your luck, boys!" cried Hewson, who was turning his horse to the right and left to avoid a side stroke from Eliot, "out with your knives—cut him down!"

To defend himself and prevent Hewson from passing him, was now all that Eliot attempted; but this he did with coolness and consummate adroitness, till his horse received a wound in his throat that was aimed at his master, and fell dead under him.

"That's it, boys!" screamed Hewson, "finish him and follow me." But before the words had well passed his lips, a bullet fired from behind penetrated his spine. "I am a dead man!" he groaned.

24*

His men saw him reeling ; they saw Eliot's
auxiliaries close upon them ; and without waiting
to take advantage of his defenceless condition, they
fled and left their comrade-captain to his fate.

The general was instantly beside Eliot. Coit
received the child from the ruffian's relaxed hold.
" Oh, help me !" he supplicated ; " for the love of
God, help me !"

" Poor little one," said Coit, laying Lizzy's cheek
gently to his, " she's gone."

" Oh, I have not killed her ! I did not mean she
should be harmed—I swear I did not," continued
Hewson. "Oh, help me ! I'll give you gold, watch-
es, silver, and jewels—I'll give them all to you."

" You are wounded, my dear boy, you are
covered with blood," said the general to Eliot, as
he succeeded in disengaging him from the superincumbent burden of his horse.

" It's nothing, sir ; is the child living ?"

" Nothing ! bless your soul, the blood is dripping
down here like rain." While he was drawing off
Eliot's coat-sleeve, and stanching his wound, Hewson continued his abject cries.

" Oh, gentlemen," he said, " take pity on me ;
my life is going—I'll give you heaps of gold—it's
buried in—in—in—" His utterance failed him.

" Can nothing be done for the poor creature ?'
said Eliot, turning to Hewson, after having bent
over Lizzy, lifted her lifeless hand, and again
mournfully dropped it.

" We will see," replied the general, " though it
seems to me, my friend, you are in no case to look

after another; and this car'on is not worth looking after; but come, we'll strip him and examine
his wound—life is life—and he's asked for mercy,
what we must all ask for sooner or later. Ah,"
he continued, after looking at the wound, " he's
called to the general muster—poorly equipped to
answer the roll. But come, friends—there's no use
in staying here—there's no substitute in this warfare—every man must answer for himself."

" Oh !" groaned the dying wretch, " don't leave
me alone."

" 'Tis a solitary business to die alone," said
Coit, looking compassionately at Hewson as he
writhed on the turf.

" It is so, Coit; but he that has broken all bonds
in life can expect nothing better than to die like a
dog, and go to the devil at last. I must be back
at my post, you at yours, and our young friend
on his way to the camp, if he is able. General
Washington a'n't fond of his envoys' striking out
of the highway when they are out on duty. There's
no use—there's no use," he continued to Eliot, who
had kneeled beside the dying man, and was whispering such counsel as a compassionate being
would naturally administer to a man in his extremity.

" Repent !" cried Hewson, grasping Eliot's arm
as he was about to rise ; " repent !—what's that ?
Mercy, mercy—Oh, it's all dark ; I can't see you.
Don't hold that dead child so close to me !—
take it away ! Mercy, is there ?—speak louder—

I can't hear you—oh, I can't feel you !—Mercy ! mercy !"

"He's done—the poor cowardly rascal," said the general, who, inured to the spectacle of death, felt no emotion excited by the contortions of animal suffering, and who, deeming cowardice the proper concomitant of crime, heard without any painful compassion those cries of the wretched culprit, as he passed the threshold to eternal justice, which contracted Eliot's brow, and sent a shuddering through his frame.

"There's something to feel for," said the general, pointing to Eliot's prostrate horse ; "if ever I cried, I should cry to see a *spereted,* gentle beast like that cut off by such villanous hands."

"Poor Rover !" thought Eliot, as he loosed his girth, and removed the bits from his mouth, "how Sam and Hal will cry, poor fellows, when they hear of your fate. Ah, I could have wished you a longer life and a more glorious end; but you have done well your appointed tasks, and they are finished.—Would to God it were thus with that wretch, my fellow-creature !"

"You're finding this rather a tough job, I'm thinking," said the general, stooping to assist Eliot ; " our horses, especially in these times, are friends; and it's what Coit would call a solitary business to have to mount into that rogue's seat. But see how patiently the beast stands by his master, and how he looks at him ! Do you believe," he added, in a lowered voice, " that the souls of these noble *critters,* that have thought, affection, memory—all that we have, save speech, will perish ; and that low villain's live for ever ?—I don't."

Eliot only smiled in reply ; but he secretly wondered who this strange being should be, full of generous feeling and bold speculation, who had the air of accustomed authority, and the voice and accent indicating rustic education. It was evident he meant to maintain his incognito ; for when they arrived at a road which, diverging from that they were in, led more directly to Coit's (the same road that had proved fatal to poor Kisel), he said, "that he must take the shortest cut ; and that if Eliot felt equal to carrying the poor child the distance that remained he should be particularly glad, as Coit's attendance was important to him."

Eliot would far rather have been disabled than to have witnessed the mother's last faint hope extinguished ; but he was not, and he received the child from Coit, who had carried her as tenderly as if she had been still a conscious, feeling, and suffering being.

Coit charged Eliot with many respectful messages to Mrs. Archer, such as, that his house was at her disposal—he would prepare it for the funeral, or see that she and her family were safely conveyed to a British frigate which lay below, in case she preferred, as he supposed she would, laying her child in the family vault of Trinity Church. Eliot remembered the messages, but he delivered them as his discretion dictated.

As he approached Mrs. Archer's grounds, he

inferred from the diminished light that the flames
had nearly done their work ; and when he issued
from the thick wood that skirted her estate, he saw
in the smouldering ruins all that was left of her
hospitable and happy mansion. " Ah," thought he.
" a fit home for this lifeless little body !"

He turned towards the office where he had left
the mother. She was awaiting him at the door.
It seemed to her that she had lived a thousand
years in the hour of his absence. She asked no
questions—a single glance at the still, colourless
figure of her child had sufficed. She uttered no
sound, but stretching forth her arms, received her,
and sunk down on the doorstep, pressing her close
to her bosom.

Edward had sprung to the door at the first sound
of the horse's hoofs. He understood his mother's
silence. He heard the servants whispering, in
suppressed voices, " She's dead !" He placed his
hand on Lizzy's cheek : at first he recoiled at the
touch ; and then again drawing closer, he sat down
by his mother, and dropped his head on Lizzy's
bosom, crying out, " I wish I were dead too !"
His bursts of grief were frightful. The servants
endeavoured to sooth him—he did not hear them.
Her mother laid her face to his, and the touch of
her cheek, after a few moments, tranquillized him.
He became quiet ; then suddenly lifting his head,
he shrieked, " Her heart beats, mother ! her heart
beats !—Lay your hand there—do you not feel it ?
—It does, it does, mother ; I feel it, and hear it
too !"

Eliot had dismounted from his horse, and stood with folded arms, watching with the deep sympathy of his affectionate nature the progress of this family tragedy, while he awaited a moment when he might offer such services as Mrs. Archer needed. He thought it possible that the sharpened senses of the blind boy had detected a pulsation not perceptible to senses less acute. He inquired of the servants for salts, brandy, vinegar, any of the ordinary stimulants; nothing had been saved—nothing was left but the elements of fire and water. These suggested to his quick mind the only and very best expedient. In five minutes a warm bath was prepared, and the child immersed in it. Mrs. Archer was re-nerved when she saw others acting from a hope she scarcely dared admit. " Station yourself here, my dear madam," said Eliot; " there, put your arm in the place of mine—let your little boy go on the other side and take her hand—let her first conscious sensation be of the touch most familiar and dear to her—let the first sounds she hears be your voices—nothing must be strange to her. I do believe this is merely the overpowering effect of terror; I am sure she has suffered no violence. Put your hand again on her bosom, my dear little fellow—do you feel the beats now ?"

" Oh yes, sir! stronger and quicker than before."

" I believe you are right ; but be cautious, I entreat you—make no sudden outcry nor exclamation."

Mrs. Archer's face was as colourless as the child's over whom she was bending ; and her fixed eye glowed with such intensity, that Eliot thought it might have kindled life in the dead. Suddenly, he perceived the blood gush into her cheeks—he advanced one step nearer, and he saw that a faint suffusion, like the first almost imperceptible tinge of coming day, had overspread the child's face. It deepened around her lips—there was a slight distention of the nostrils—a tremulousness about the muscles of the mouth—a heaving of the bosom, and then a deep-drawn sigh. A moment passed, and a faint smile was perceptible on the quivering lip. " Lizzy !" said her mother.

" Dear Lizzy !" cried her brother.

" Mother !—Ned !" she faintly articulated.

" Thank God, she is safe !" exclaimed Eliot.

The energies of nature, once aroused, soon did their beneficent work; and the little girl, in the perfect consciousness of restored safety and happiness, clung to her mother and to Edward.

The tide of gratitude and happiness naturally flowed towards Eliot. Mrs. Archer turned to express something of all she felt, but he was already gone, after having directed one of the servants to say to her mistress that Coit would immediately be at her bidding.

It was not strange that the impression Eliot left on Mrs. Archer's mind was that of the most beautiful personation of celestial energy and mercy.

END OF VOL. I.

www.ingramcontent.com/pod-product-compliance
Lightning Source LLC
Chambersburg PA
CBHW030650020726
47493CB00006B/1954